Praise for *Feral Youth*

★ "A compelling examination of the teen psyche."
—**Booklist, starred review**

"From the first sentence ("I'm not a liar"), collection editor
Hutchinson grabs readers with a raw, spot-on monologue
that invites readers into heavy issues teens are struggling
to navigate, many with distant or absent parents. . . .
A compelling, uncomfortable narrative."
—*Kirkus Reviews*

Praise for *Violent Ends*

★ "An intriguing, powerful narrative . . . The storytelling
is wonderfully intense and distinctive on such a difficult,
tragic topic. Readers will be captivated."
—*VOYA*, **starred review**

"Provocatively and effectively illustrates the
multidimensionality of someone considered to be
a monster . . . Engaging and heart-wrenching."
—*Kirkus Reviews*

"A fresh and thought-provoking take on
a disturbing but relevant topic."
—*School Library Journal*

Praise for *The Apocalypse of Elena Mendoza*

★ "Surreal, brainy, and totally captivating."
—*Booklist*, starred review

Praise for *At the Edge of the Universe*

★ "An earthy, existential coming-of-age gem."
—*Kirkus Reviews*, starred review

Praise for *We Are the Ants*

★ "Hutchinson has crafted an unflinching portrait of the pain
and confusion of young love and loss, thoughtfully exploring
topics like dementia, abuse, sexuality, and suicide as they
entwine with the messy work of growing up."
—*Publishers Weekly*, starred review

★ "Bitterly funny, with a ray of hope amid bleakness."
—*Kirkus Reviews*, starred review

"A beautiful, masterfully told story by someone
who is at the top of his craft."
—*Lambda Literary*

★ "Shaun David Hutchinson's bracingly smart and unusual YA novel
blends existential despair with exploding planets."
—*Shelf Awareness*, starred review

Also by Shaun David Hutchinson

The Apocalypse of Elena Mendoza

At the Edge of the Universe

We Are the Ants

Violent Ends

The Five Stages of Andrew Brawley

fml

The Deathday Letter

Coming soon:
The Past and Other Things That Should Stay Buried

Shaun David Hutchinson • Suzanne Young
Marieke Nijkamp • Robin Talley • Stephanie Kuehn
E. C. Myers • Tim Floreen • Alaya Dawn Johnson
Justina Ireland • Brandy Colbert

FERAL YOUTH

SIMON PULSE

New York   London   Toronto   Sydney   New Delhi

SIMON PULSE

An imprint of Simon & Schuster Children's Publishing Division

1230 Avenue of the Americas, New York, New York 10020

First Simon Pulse paperback edition September 2018

Compilation and frame chapters copyright © 2017 by Shaun David Hutchinson

"The Butterfly Effect" and "The Chaos Effect" copyright © 2017 by Marieke Nijkamp,

"A Ruthless Dame" copyright © 2017 by Tim Floreen, "Look Down" copyright © 2017 by Robin Talley,

"Big Brother, Part 1" and "Big Brother, Part 2" copyright © 2017 by E. C. Myers, "The Subjunctive"

copyright © 2017 by Alaya Dawn Johnson, "A Cautionary Tale" copyright © 2017 by Stephanie Kuehn,

"Jackie's Story" copyright © 2017 by Justina Ireland, "Self-Portrait" copyright © 2017 by Brandy Colbert,

"A Violation of Rule 16" copyright © 2017 by Suzanne Young

Cover photograph copyright © 2017 by Christie Goodwin/Arcangel

Also available in a Simon Pulse hardcover edition.

All rights reserved, including the right of reproduction in whole or in part in any form.

SIMON PULSE and colophon are registered trademarks of Simon & Schuster, Inc.

For information about special discounts for bulk purchases, please contact Simon & Schuster

Special Sales at 1-866-506-1949 or business@simonandschuster.com.

The Simon & Schuster Speakers Bureau can bring authors to your live event.

For more information or to book an event contact the Simon & Schuster Speakers Bureau

at 1-866-248-3049 or visit our website at www.simonspeakers.com.

Cover designed by Jessica Handelman

Interior designed by Mike Rosamilia

The text of this book was set in Adobe Garamond Pro.

Manufactured in the United States of America

2 4 6 8 10 9 7 5 3 1

The Library of Congress has cataloged the hardcover edition as follows:

Names: Hutchinson, Shaun David, editor, author. |

Young, Suzanne, author. | Nijkamp, Marieke, author. | Talley, Robin, author. |

Kuehn, Stephanie, author. | Myers, E. C. (Eugene C.), 1978- author. | Floreen, Tim, author. |

Johnson, Alaya Dawn, 1982- author. | Ireland, Justina, author. | Colbert, Brandy, author.

Title: Feral youth / by Shaun David Hutchinson, Suzanne Young, Marieke Nijkamp, Robin Talley, Stephanie

Kuehn, E.C. Myers, Tim Floreen, Alaya Dawn Johnson, Justina Ireland, and Brandy Colbert.

Description: First Simon Pulse hardcover edition. | New York : Simon Pulse, 2017. |

Summary: Follows ten teens who are left alone in the wilderness amid a three-day survival test.

Identifiers: LCCN 2017010050 (print) | LCCN 2017037122 (eBook) | ISBN 9781481491136 (eBook) |

ISBN 9781481491112 (hardcover)

Subjects: | CYAC: Survival—Fiction. | Wilderness areas—Fiction.

Classification: LCC PZ5 (eBook) | LCC PZ5 .F38 2017 (print) |

DDC [Fic]—dc23 LC record available at https://lccn.loc.gov/2017010050

ISBN 9781481491129 (pbk)

FERaL
YOUTH

I'M NOT A LIAR. *You're* a liar. I'm just telling stories; that's all. And sometimes when you're telling a story, you can't let stupid shit like the truth get in the way.

Besides, what good is the truth for anyway? Folks get put in prison for shit they didn't do every single day, and telling the truth doesn't help them one bit. Ask any woman who's ever reported a sexual assault, and she'll tell you how much the truth is worth. Nothing. The truth isn't worth a damned thing. Only what people believe. And the funny thing is that most of the time, the story being told and how the person's telling it isn't as important as who's doing the telling. Ask any black person who's ever gone up against the police, and *they'll* tell you.

Nah. There's no such thing as an objective truth anymore. It's all about what you believe. Believe something hard enough and—to you at least—that's the truth forever and ever, and fuck anyone who tries to tell you otherwise.

Take these stories. I don't know if they're true or not, but I bet the ones doing the telling believe them. And that's kind of all that matters. Whether a story is true isn't important if you're hurting all the same because of it.

Regardless, I'm going to tell you the truth. Not my truth, not their truths. *The* truth. The truth about the three days we spent alone in the woods, trying to hike back to Zeppelin Bend. How one broke their leg, how others fought, how we all nearly died, and how we managed to get our shit together and make it back alive.

Believe it or don't. Makes no difference to me.

DAY 1

RECIPE FOR A CLUSTERFUCK: take ten teenagers the world believes are human garbage, toss in some hippy work-together-to-make-the-world-better bullshit, add a dash of insecurity and a dollop of fear, and then send the kids into the woods for three days and expect them not to kill and eat each other. Voilà! One glorious clusterfuck.

Zeppelin Bend isn't one of those summer camps where campers spend their time finger painting and canoeing and singing songs. It's the kind of place they send kids no one else wants and tell us it's our last chance to make a U-turn before we wind up in juvie until we're eighteen. Before Doug (which is the kind of name a parent gives their kid when they expect he's going to turn out to be a massive asshole) drove us into the woods blindfolded, kicked us out of the van, and told us we had three days to hike back to Zeppelin Bend on our own, we spent three weeks learning how to use a compass, find food that wouldn't kill us, start a fire without a lighter, and run from bears—since that's really all you *can* do if a bear comes your way. In short, we supposedly learned all the skills necessary for a bunch of delinquents like us to survive. Doug even told us we'd get a surprise if we made it back to the Bend by the end of the third day. I figured it was probably an ice cream party or some other stupid bullshit, but even that sounded good after weeks of plain oatmeal and whatever chunky meat was in the stews they served for dinner.

It was just after sunrise when Doug marooned us in the woods, and we spent the first hour arguing over who was going to be in charge. Every group needs a leader, and everyone thinks it should be them. Everyone but me, anyway. I hung in the background, waiting to see who was going to come out on top. No use picking sides if you're just going to pick the losing one. But eventually, we were going to have to choose someone, and I didn't think it mattered who because, like I said, we were a recipe for a clusterfuck, and even the best chefs break a few eggs.

I guess I should tell you what I know about the others. Most of it's shit I picked up around the Bend, so I can't vouch for the truth of it. That's why I like stories. They usually wind up revealing more about a person than what they'd tell you about themselves. It's not that they lie intentionally, but when people describe themselves they're really describing what they see in a mirror, and most mirrors are too distorted to show us the truth. If you listen hard enough, there's more truth in fiction than in all the other shit combined.

Jackie Armstrong was the first person I met after my uncle dropped me off at the Bend. She's kind of invisible in the way girls like her often are, and she was wearing a T-shirt with a logo from that werewolves in space TV show *Space Howl*. That was before we all got told we had to wear these shitty brown uniforms. It's easy to dismiss a girl like Jackie, but you're an idiot if you do.

Then there's Tino Estevez. We got a lot in common, mostly being we're both Mexican. Well, I'm mixed and he's not, but it's something. The kid's kind of quiet, but if you watch him real hard, you can see some anger bubbling there under the surface. Before we'd even been dumped in the woods, my money was on him clocking someone before we were done. He kind of thought he should be the leader, but he wasn't ready to fight for it hard enough.

Now, Jaila Davis is one badass motherfucker. She's like a foot shorter than anyone else, but she acts like she's a foot taller. I thought she was stuck-up when I first met her, but she's probably better equipped to spend three days in the woods than anyone else in our dysfunctional group. And I don't know how many languages she speaks, but she cusses in at least three.

David Kim Park was another one who thought he should be the leader, which was hilarious. The kid couldn't navigate his way out of a paper bag, and he's obsessed with sex. No lie. Anytime someone was like "Where's David?" chances are he was hiding somewhere beating off. It was so bad, Doug had to pull him aside and talk to him about it twice. Plus, David was convinced there was a Bigfoot or aliens or something in the woods.

The third of the *J* girls was Jenna Cantor. I basically pegged her as a rich white girl from day one, and she didn't do much to prove me wrong while we were at the Bend. She was kind of weird, too. Aside from being able to do calculations in her head I couldn't figure with a calculator, she was real quiet. But not like snobby quiet. More like she was living in a world the rest of us couldn't see.

Lucinda Banks wore her anger on her uniform. I tried to figure out why she'd been sent to the Bend, but she hardly ever talked except to complain about the shitty jumpsuits they made us wear. They weren't the worst things I'd ever owned, but Lucinda seemed to take having to wear one personally in a way I found particularly interesting.

Sunday Taylor was another one I thought I'd get along with, but she kept to herself and acted like she was the only good kid in a pack of misfits. Not like she was too good for us, but kind of like she was afraid if she got too close, the real Sunday would come out, and I'm pretty sure there's a hell-raiser somewhere inside that meek exterior.

The last two members of our homemade clusterfuck were Cody Hewitt and Georgia Valentine. I figured Georgia for another rich white girl, but she's the type who thinks she's progressive 'cause she likes that one Beyoncé song and has a gay best friend. She can be kind of type A, but she's always the first to take the jobs no one else wants to do and never talks shit about anyone.

Cody wasn't *Georgia's* gay best friend, but he was probably someone's. That boy knows more about old movies than anyone I ever met. Of all of us out there, he seemed to belong the least. I couldn't picture him doing anything worth getting sent to a shit hole camp for fuckups, but he was there, so he must've done something.

I don't want to say anything about me. I don't think the storyteller should get in the way of the stories, you know? But if you need a name, you can call me Gio.

* * *

Doug had taught us how to use a compass but hadn't actually given us one when he dropped us off. All we got were our packs, sleeping bags, empty canteens, little bottles of bleach to disinfect the water with, and the clothes on our backs. Jaila figured out which direction to hike to get back to the Bend, but it was David who suggested that we should find water first. He wasn't wrong. It didn't get too hot in Wyoming in the summer, but it was warm enough that we were sweating, and once David mentioned water, none of us could think of anything else.

I brought up the idea of telling stories, saying it might help keep our minds off being thirsty, which was mostly true. Tino said it was a stupid idea, and he wasn't interested in telling stories. The others didn't seem real thrilled either. Not until I mentioned I'd give a hundred bucks to the person who told the best story as judged by me. But then no one wanted to be first, so we kept walking, hoping Jaila actually knew what she was talking about when she said to find water we should look for animal tracks and head downhill.

I figured my story idea was dead since no one was willing to be the sacrificial lamb, and I was thinking I could start shit between Tino and Sunday to keep me entertained, when Jenna, who'd been so quiet I'd almost forgotten she was there, was like "I'll go first," which surprised the hell out of me.

"THE BUTTERFLY EFFECT"

by Marieke Nijkamp

I WONDER IF FLAMES are fractals, too. The fire is hardly symmetrical, of course, but I could stare at the individual flames forever. They burn bright yellow and orange and red before succumbing to thick black smoke. They dance across the smoldering hood of the car. Given time, I could find patterns in them.

Or perhaps I would just find chaos. But chaos is enough.

I wrap my arms around my chest when sirens tear through the night. A few feet away, Adam holds Mom's hand. Even though he stands her height these days, he looks young in his *Transformers* pajamas, frail in the fire's glow. On the other side of the street, Dad is talking to Grandpa. Trying to calm him down, most likely, but it doesn't seem to be working. He waves his hands and shouts something inaudible.

It's weird. I always envisioned car fires to be violent and explosive, but perhaps that's just Netflix and the movies. Grandpa's car burns hot enough to warm the neighborhood and bright enough to light up the dark. It's a steady roar.

I smile.

It's almost calming to listen to.

I can hear you think: What is the matter with you, Jenna? Are you a pyromaniac? Let me put the record straight: Pyromania is an impulse control disorder, and I can control my impulses quite well, thank you very much. I'm not doing this for attention or to relieve tension or because the fire gives me gratification. It gives me satisfaction, sure, but that's not quite the same thing. Car bad. Fire pretty.

No, it's chaos. Fractals.

Fractures.

And I am fractured, too.

Broken. I first noticed it in precalc, of all places. My favorite class, bar none. What can I tell you? I'm a card-carrying nerd. And with a name like mine, there is no escaping the pull of math. After all, as my esteemed not-ancestor Georg Cantor once said, "The essence of mathematics lies entirely in its freedom."

I wish I could tell him how much I long for that freedom, that entire essence.

Because it didn't start in precalc. Of course it didn't. It started long ago. But I always felt like I would mend the wounds and set the breaks and pretend like nothing was going on.

That day, today, for the first time, I can't anymore. I can't pretend class is normal and I'm normal. I've reached a breaking point. Perhaps I've already passed too many breaking points without noticing.

From the moment I settle into my spot in the back corner of the room, I try to focus on Mrs. Rodriguez's lesson, but nothing that she says reaches me. Something about solving more complex equations than we've done so far, but she may as well have been speaking German. I'm not used to this. I coast through other classes, sure. I have everything I need: solid test scores, college plans, a middle-class suburban white family with money.

But with precalc, I *want* to care.

I doodle around the edges of my notebook; endless—familiar—geometrical shapes. The repetition is some kind of comfortable at least.

"Jenna."

I blink and look next to me. Zoe is frowning at me, worry in her brown eyes. "Are you okay? I've whisper-called you five times at least."

I don't know what to say because just like with Mrs. Rodriguez's explanations, Zoe's words don't quite reach me. And after a moment, her frown grows deeper. *"Jenna,* are you *okay?* Do you want to go see the nurse?"

In front of us, Kamal turns and glances at me too.

I force myself to grimace. "Sorry; tired. Must've had bad dreams or something."

Though if I'm honest, I don't remember the last time I slept long enough to have dreams at all. Sleeping means letting my guard down, and I'm exhausted down to my bones.

"Sucks." Zoe reaches out to place a hand on my arm, and I flinch. I don't want to. It's *Zoe.* But I do.

"Just distract me, please? Maybe that'll help." Maybe Z. and I can still be normal even when everything else is shattering and slowly drifting out of reach.

"We'll go to the Coffee House after school. Get you a mocha with extra whip and an extra shot of espresso and one of those lava muffins. There's nothing extraordinary amounts of caffeine and sugar can't fix."

I roll my eyes, but my shoulders unclench a bit. Coffee with chocolate is Zoe's answer to everything. She doesn't need the caffeine; she has enough energy for the two of us—and most likely for half a dozen people more—even with swimming and volleyball. Her schedule is superhuman, and I don't know how she manages it all when I can barely keep my studies going.

But coffee with chocolate is comfort. And I give her a small nod.

Z. flicks a strand of light brown hair out of her face. "And in the interest of distraction . . ." She slides her notes over to my table. "Help me, please, oh math genius?"

I accept the piece of paper, but my stomach drops.

Math has always come naturally to me. I once told Dad it's my second language—the universal language. He would much rather I learn German, but I'm fluent in formulas, and I think in theorems. I sleep, dream, breathe math.

I stare at the equation. I recognize Z.'s handwriting—entirely consistent, all small round letters and numbers—but I have no idea what she just put in front of me.

Next to me, Z. does that puppy-eyes thing she's so good at. "I know you think cheating in math is a mortal sin, but I *really* don't know. And Coach told me to do something about my grades, or she won't include me in the starting lineup."

She graces me with a smile, and her smile always makes my lips twitch up in return. Today I feel this shatter too. It hurts. Her happiness makes my blood boil. It's not fair. I don't want to lose this too. I don't know what she's asking of me, I don't know how to give it to her, I don't know how I let it get this far, I don't know how to go on like nothing is wrong. This is the break.

I push the piece of paper back at her with too much force. It slides across her table and flutters to the floor.

"You should do your own work," I snap, loud enough for the entire class to hear.

Everyone—and everything—around me falls silent. At the front of the class, Mrs. Rodriguez pauses midlecture and turns around.

And Zoe's smile has melted off her face. She's grown deadly pale. "Jenna . . ."

I drop my books into my bag and get to my feet, knocking over my chair. I don't bother to pick it up. I don't bother to mend this. I can't.

"I'm done."

Mom always said my temper was flammable, easily combustible. I get that from her. As a kid it was triggered by the simplest things—not getting what I wanted, a broken toy, my brother. But I thought I had it under control. It's one more thing that's unraveling.

I avoid Zoe for the rest of the day. I leave school before homeroom and take a detour on my walk home.

Back when I was little, I used to take my anger out on a punching bag in the basement, but that's not an option. I don't want to go home. Out of all the places where I want to be and all the places where I want to go, I don't want to go home.

I walk north instead, to an old office building that's been empty for years. Zoe and I sneaked in dozens of times. It's safe enough, as long as you keep to yourself. It's an excellent place for sharing food or sharing secrets or for simply being alone. And alone is what I need right now.

I edge around the large fences that are set up haphazardly around the building. I don't think the owners or the city care anymore that people are coming here. There's no construction hazard, and at least the building is being put to *some* use. There are too many empty office buildings around here to begin with.

Slipping in through one of the broken windows, I make my way to the staircase on the ground floor and walk until I've reached the fourteenth floor. Being insensible is a blessing, sometimes. I don't care about the burning in my legs or the ache in my lungs—I'm not athletic like Zoe is. I don't care about Zoe—I only care about moving.

The door to the roof used to be locked, but someone broke the lock months ago, and the roof has turned into a popular nightspot. Now, midway through the afternoon, there's no one here but the wind and me. The wind howls and whips my long blond hair around my face. It's not particularly cold, but the chill gets into my bones regardless.

I sit down near the edge of the building and prop my elbows on my knees. I stare into the distance, focus on nothing in particular. The building isn't tall, but it's high enough to see the outline of the Twin Cities in the distance. It's high enough to turn the people down below into small figurines. And it's high enough to feel removed from the world.

I could stay up here forever and not come down. I could stay here, at least, until my parents listened to me. But they won't, and I won't. I'm a good girl who gets home on time for dinner because otherwise, what would the neighbors think.

I told you I first noticed the fractures that day. I first noticed the fire that day too. It was a discarded lighter, on the edge of the roof next to me. A cheap thing. Yellowed plastic. Covered in dust. A faded symbol of some sort.

I don't even know what drew me to pick it up, but I did. I do.

I roll the spark wheel carefully. It feels rusty, as if it hasn't been used for a while. Who knows when someone dropped it there? Judging by what else can be found on the corners of this roof—weed bags, condom wrappers—it's not like anyone actually comes and cleans here.

Turning the spark wheel doesn't do anything, not at first, and I'm tempted to just toss the thing. It's not like I ever used a lighter before. No one at home smokes, and Mom would kill me if I ever started. It may just be empty. But some stubbornness takes over, and I keep rolling the wheel, faster and faster, until it's almost a snap.

When the spark turns into a flame.

It's a tiny thing, blue with yellow edges. It doesn't look like it's particularly hot. But when I shield it with my hand, against the wind that dances around us, it gently sways along.

I stare at the flame until the palm of my hand turns red. I stare until the spark wheel becomes hot enough to burn my fingers.

And for the first time in a long time, I remember what it's like to hurt.

It was never meant to be like this. I was never meant to be here, on this rooftop, in this place, in this upside-down world. But the fire reminds me I can still feel, at least.

When I come home, Adam's in the kitchen, scarfing down a cup of yogurt. He rocks back and forth on the balls of his feet. "I'm going out to study with T. J. Mom and Dad are at the Williamsons' tonight for that neighborhood watch thing."

I grab an apple from the bowl on top of the bar and toss it up into the air before catching it. "'S fine. I'll eat leftovers again."

I don't mean for my words to sound bitter, but somehow they do.

Adam half turns to stare at me, his eyebrows arched in a perfect copy of Mom's. He inherited Dad's unruly hair and green eyes, but he has Mom's expressional eyebrows, and he has all her expressions down to a T. I don't look like either of them—apparently, I got my looks from Dad's younger sister. If you put my childhood photo next to Aunt Beate's, we could be twins. She lives halfway across the country, so we don't see her often, but our likeness always makes Dad smile when I bring it up.

I shrug and take a bite from the apple. "Or I may order a pizza."

Adam grins. To his twelve-year-old mind, ordering a pizza is the epitome of adulthood. We used to order massive pepperoni pizzas together, when Dad was working late and Mom was off at some PTA thing or other, but when you're twelve, hanging out with your friends—even when they live next door—is infinitely cooler than spending time at home with your nerdy older sister. I don't blame him.

He dumps his spoon in the dishwasher and grabs his bag. "Save me a slice, okay? Also"—he raises his voice—"Grandpa is home tonight, so you won't be alone."

"I am!" Grandpa's voice comes from the basement, where he's working on restoring and repainting his collection of old toy cars.

The chunk of apple sours in my mouth. Adam pulls the door shut, and the kitchen seems to close in on itself around me.

So I hide. In my own home. In my own room. I hide in daylight.

Zoe's texted me a few times, but I haven't opened any of them. I've tossed my phone onto my bed. I don't know what to tell her. *Come over. I'm sorry. Help me. Please don't leave me on my own.* But she would ask to understand, and that is a problem. She would ask me to share secrets I cannot, do not, ever think I can share.

After all, I tried to share them once and no one listened. I tried to share them twice and no one listened. I cannot do it a third time. Besides, I can't silence that small voice in the back of my mind that wonders: *Am I not to blame?* I didn't stop it. I let it get this far.

It's far easier to let myself go numb.

At the end of the day, all I have left is a house that doesn't feel like a home anymore either. A body that doesn't feel like my body anymore. A self that doesn't feel like myself anymore.

I am fractured.

I'm not a good person. I don't try hard enough. I get angry easily. I fight with my brother even when I don't want to and ignore my friends even when I shouldn't.

But I don't think I deserve this.

According to chaos theory, the present determines the future, but the approximate present does not approximately determine the future.

One small deviation can change the entire future. That's known as the butterfly effect. The idea that one flap of a butterfly's wings would be enough to alter the course of the weather forever. Or that traveling back in time and stepping on one butterfly can change the history of the human race.

The idea that one time, a girl was a solid B student who could take pride in her geeky accomplishments, who could laugh and feel her stomach flutter and her heart race, who mattered. Until all that changed and kept changing. Small causes have large effects.

It was raining outside. That was what I remember most clearly. It was the last week of freshman year, and it was hot and humid and raining. The type of rain that clings to you, all dust and warm water.

Zoe walked me home before she had to go to volleyball practice, and I was soaked through by the time I walked through the front door. I was itching to change into something dry and cool. But when I went to drop my backpack in the living room, I found Dad sitting on the couch.

I froze in the doorway, sure that something had happened. As a general manager at an insurance company, he worked long days, and we rarely saw him between dawn and dusk. He seemed out of place here. He'd left his jacket over the armrest, and he'd loosened his tie. His normally flawless hair was sticking up, as if he'd run his hand through it several times.

"Dad?"

I don't think he saw or heard me, at first. "Jenna?"

I let my soggy backpack slip off my shoulder and onto the hardwood floor. It immediately created a puddle of water around it. On any other day, Dad would not have let that go unmentioned—Mom hates the stains—but right there and then, he didn't even blink.

My heart leaped into my throat, and I tried desperately to find my voice. "Dad, what's wrong?"

"Jenna?" It took a long time for him to focus on me, longer to find the right words. But eventually they came. "Grandpa just called. We knew it might happen but . . . After everything he went through with the store, the bank is going to foreclose his home, too. He's lost everything. He's— Aunt Beate can't take him in, so he is going to come live with us for a while."

Grandpa arrived a week later, in his beat-up old car, with nothing but a large suitcase full of clothes, a baseball glove and baseball for Adam, a large photo album for Dad, and an old abacus from the store for me.

I liked him. He looked younger than I expected. He had an easy smile and a sharp sense of humor. He made Adam and me laugh throughout dinner.

That first weekend, he sat up with me and let me talk endlessly about math and chaos and fractals, everything that even Dad had grown tired of.

He took Adam to his games and took him out for milk shakes after while he told him stories about his endless road trips, first with Grandma, then alone. He loved his car as much as Mom hated the look of it.

The truth is, I didn't want him to come because although we live comfortably, our house isn't big enough to fit five. Some days it's barely big enough for four. And yet he fit in. Easily and without hesitation. He became a part of us.

* * *

I didn't have to murder a butterfly.

I didn't realize anything had changed until it was too late.

I slip into my bedroom and sag down against the door. I grab an old matchbox from my stack of collectibles, and I turn it around and around and around between my fingers.

I started collecting matchboxes when I was eight because matches are great for re-creating geometrical shapes. When my parents discovered what I was up to, they started bringing home matchboxes from every vintage store and every hotel where they could find them.

I switched to LEGOs, eventually, and virtual building materials. I discovered formulas and coding.

But I always kept the matches, and my parents kept up the tradition. They didn't know, but they gave me enough matches to burn down the world.

Still, I never lit matches before today, and doing so isn't as easy as I thought it would be.

The first match snaps and splinters.

The head of the second crumbles.

The third match lights up, and I'm so shocked I immediately drop it. It sears my jeans and extinguishes.

The fourth burns all the way down, scorching my fingertips.

I push the fifth against the tender skin of my forearm.

Then the sixth. And the seventh.

The flames are mesmerizing, and I can feel the pain.

I can *feel*.

I make my way through the entire matchbox, until the small

blotches on my arm itch and ache and my room smells of sulfur. Until the twilight outside gives way to night and the shadows creep in.

I tried to lock the door, but the shadows always creep in.

The world burns from the inside out. You don't see it until it's too late.

And then David goes, "Well, thank God someone here knows how to start a fire."

"Rude," Jackie said, and then everyone started going off on David while Jenna retreated into the background.

The water we found wasn't more than a slow stream, but we each filled our canteens and swished a couple of drops of bleach around in them so that we didn't wind up drinking the piss of whatever animals had used it as their toilet upstream. Already, little alliances were forming. We hadn't had much opportunity for that at the Bend. Dipshit Doug and his minions had worked us each day until the only thing we could think about at night was sleep. For a camp that had emphasized the value of teamwork, they hadn't actually let us become anything resembling a team. But now that we were out on our own, Cody and Georgia were starting to pair up, which made sense, and David had sort of inserted himself into their group. Jenna, Lucinda, and Tino hung around each other, though I wouldn't call them friends, while Jackie, Jaila, and Sunday seemed to have formed an uneasy alliance.

I danced from group to group with ease. That's always been one of my gifts. The ability to move around like a social chameleon. I fit in wherever the fuck I felt like being. And it's not that difficult, either. All you have to do is listen a hell of a lot more than you speak.

Before we'd even had a chance to rest, Tino started in on how we needed to move, figuring we could make the hike in two days instead of three and blow Doug's idiot mind. That kid was all bluster if you ask me.

"What's the point?" Cody asked. Even he looked surprised that he'd spoken up. He lowered his head sheepishly, like he was waiting for someone to tell him to shut his word hole.

"What do you mean?" Sunday asked.

Cody mumbled, "Forget it," and fell behind Georgia.

Jaila stepped up to finish Cody's thought, telling Tino that it was stupid to try to rush back to camp because we had nothing to gain by returning early, and if we weren't careful in the woods, someone might get hurt. It was clear to me, and probably to everyone else, that Jaila had the most experience and that we should listen to her, but Tino couldn't stand the idea that he wasn't in charge.

"I only have one inhaler," David said, holding the thing up into the air like he thought some of us didn't know what one was. "I don't think I can do much running."

"As much as I wouldn't mind abandoning the perv in the woods," Lucinda said, "Dipshit Doug would probably frown on it."

"Great," Tino said. "So we're stuck out here an extra day because David can't breathe. Just fucking great."

Lucinda clenched her fists. "That's not his fault. He can't breathe because he's got asthma, whereas you're just an asshole for no reason."

Jackie threw up her hands, grabbed her pack from where she'd dropped it, and started marching northeast, which I know because I asked. It was the direction Jaila had said camp was, and she was the only one even willing to make a guess, so it's what we went with.

The rest of us picked up and followed her—even Tino, though he grumbled about it for at least an hour.

"I'm hungry," Cody was saying to Georgia while we walked. "What're we going to do about food?"

Georgia shrugged.

"I'm not killing anything," Cody kept going.

Now that we had water, food was the next thing on all our minds. Some of them, like Cody and Georgia and Sunday, probably never worried about where their next meal was going to come from. They probably thought the food fairy delivered that shit to their fridges while they slept. But I figured even the rest of us had never hunted our own food. We couldn't have had at least one delinquent in our group who'd gone hunting or fishing?

As the day wore on, we started shedding layers. The ground was uneven, and our meandering route through the forest took us up some steep inclines that David struggled with. But he didn't complain. Much. Yeah, okay, he did some complaining, but he was only voicing the shit we were all thinking. About how this was fucking ridiculous. About how none of this was teaching us anything about being the "good citizens" Doug kept telling us we needed to be if we were going to stay out of juvie. All it had taught any of us so far was that we weren't cut out for living in the wilderness and that adults were a bunch of assholes who got off on torturing kids.

Jaila fell back to the middle, letting Tino take the lead for a while. It was a smart move on her part. He was walking in the direction she'd laid out, but he thought he was the one making the decisions, which kept him quiet. A good leader knows how to get people to do what she wants without them knowing they're doing it.

After we'd walked for about an hour, Cody jogged up to hike beside me. He asked if I really had a hundred dollars, keeping his voice low so that the others wouldn't hear.

"I do." I patted my pocket.

"Where'd you get it from?"

26

"Would you believe me if I said I stole it from Doug?"

Cody shook his head.

"Well, I did. I lifted it from his cabin the second night."

"That's a story I'd like to hear."

"I'm the judge of the competition," I said. "You all are the ones supposed to tell stories, not me."

Cody chewed on that for a moment. "I stole some money once. A lot more than a hundred bucks."

He'd said it loud enough that Lucinda had overheard. "I call bullshit," she said.

"It's not bullshit," he said. "Here, I'll prove it."

"A RUTHLESS DAME"

by Tim Floreen

TWO YEARS AGO this older couple moved into the house next door to mine. I heard they'd just bought the old three-screen movie theater downtown. I found that sort of interesting because I'm obsessed with movies. Not new ones, though, like the kind they show at that theater. I prefer those black-and-white ones with guys in neckties double-crossing each other over suitcases full of cash. "Film noir," they call movies like that. More than anything, I love the ladies from those movies, with their perfect hair cascading down over their shoulders in shiny waves, and their slinky dresses slit all the way up to the hip, and their cute little guns tucked under a garter. Just so I can stare at those actresses all the time, I printed a bunch of Hollywood glam shots off the Internet and taped them to the wall above my bed. My parents don't know what the hell to make of them. Probably they're just glad the pictures aren't of guys.

They haven't got a clue what gets me about those women. You know what it is? I mean, aside from the hair and the outfits and the way they look when they smoke. What I really love is that people always underestimate them. It happens over and over in those movies: the lady pulls out her cute little gun and aims it at the guy, and he doesn't think she'll pull the trigger. "You haven't got the *guts*." That's what he always says.

And then the lady does.

But anyway, like I was saying, that couple that moved in next door . . . It sort of interested me that they owned the movie theater, but apart from that, I didn't think much about them. Until Christmas break a year and a half ago, when their son came home from college for a visit.

I was standing in our driveway with my mom and dad and brother and sister at the time. We were about to get into the minivan to go to church. The guy pulled up in front of the Morettis' house in a loudly chugging, beat-up compact and got out. He had one of those scraggly billy-goat beards that makes a guy look like some kind of Middle Earth wannabe hipster. He stretched as if he'd been driving all night. His arms were still up in the air when he spotted us staring at him. Even Mom had paused in her ritual Sunday morning inspection of our faces and hair and outfits to check him out, because a new person in the neighborhood's always interesting.

The guy checked us out, too. His eyes moved from face to face and stopped on mine. I squirmed in my scratchy polyester-blend dress shirt and plaid necktie because I knew my church clothes only made me look dumpier than usual. But he gave a nod, and even though the others probably assumed he was nodding at all of us, for some reason, I got the feeling he meant the nod just for me.

I didn't see him again for a couple days, although I kept an eye out. Then one night after dinner, I ducked out to the backyard. It was cold as hell outside, but the rest of the family was in the living room playing Bible-opoly, and that always sends me running for the hills. I heard a noise and glanced over. There was the Morettis' son, standing on their back porch with a cigarette in his hand and one shoulder leaned up against the house, already watching me.

"You won't tell, will you?" he said, holding up his smoke. "The parents don't know I do this."

He didn't look all that worried, though. I wanted to come back with something clever, like the women in noir films always do, but I couldn't think of a thing to say.

He walked over to the waist-high chain-link fence separating our yards. For the first time I got a decent look at his face. He wasn't handsome, but gazing at him made my insides sort of flutter anyway. Maybe it was just because college-aged people automatically seem cooler, even if they have piece of junk cars and billy-goat beards. But I was pretty sure there was something else about him, something that had nothing to do with age, that overcame his lack of looks and excess of chin hair. He was like Humphrey Bogart. Bogie wasn't good-looking, but he had magnetism. This guy had magnetism too.

"I'm Mike."

"Cody," I managed.

He nodded, the cigarette wedged between his teeth, his eyes squinting as he grinned at me, like he was sizing me up. I sucked in my belly and shifted my weight onto one foot and rested my hand on my hip, hoping the pose would make me look svelte and alluring. He snatched his cigarette from his mouth and held it out to me, which struck me as odd, since I was fifteen and looked even younger, and he didn't even know me. Still, I wished again I had the confidence of a femme fatale. I'd grab the cigarette and take a drag and let the smoke leak slowly through my lips. Or maybe I'd blow it in a narrow stream over his shoulder or exhale it through my nostrils like a lady dragon. Those noir actresses knew a million different ways of exhaling cigarette smoke, and each one seemed to have a different meaning—like smoking was its own language.

I'd never smoked a cigarette in my life, though, so I shook my head. An awkward silence had started to set in, and I could see in another second he'd turn away and go back into the house, but by some miracle I finally thought of something to say.

"You're the Morettis' son?" Not exactly film noir–caliber dialogue, but at least I'd kept the conversation going.

"Yup. Home for break. I'm a sophomore down at the University of Atlanta. What about you? High school?"

"I'm a sophomore too. Hillville High."

He took another drag and nodded. "So what's there to do here in Hillville?"

I would've thought anyone on Earth could take one look at me and see I was the exact wrong person to ask a question like that, but I tried to play it off. "Not much," I said with a scoffing laugh, like I'd be out partying right that minute if only I lived in a cooler location. "Actually, I prefer to call this place Hellville. Hellville, West Virginia."

"Well, there must be a burger place at least. You like burgers?"

Wait a second, I thought. *What's happening right now? Is he asking me out?* I just nodded, since I'd once again lost the power of speech.

He stuck the cigarette between his teeth one more time so he

·

31

could pull out his phone. "What's your number? Maybe we can get a burger sometime."

I glanced over my shoulder, thinking maybe there was someone else behind me, someone thin and good-looking and probably female, because honestly, Mike seemed pretty straight to me.

"It's just that I don't know anyone in this town," he said. "And you seem cool."

I turned back around and looked up at him—he was a full head taller than me—and said, "Thanks. Sounds like fun."

Then something must've gotten into me, maybe the spirit of Barbara Stanwyck, because all of a sudden, without even planning to, I grabbed the cigarette right out of his mouth, put it between my lips, and took a puff.

I just about coughed my guts clear out of my body.

He didn't try anything the first time he took me to the Burger Barn. He was a gentleman. But he started texting me, and the texts got sexy way before he did in person. Maybe it was easier for him that way. I could tell he wasn't out of the closet and wanted to keep a low profile. (I got the impression the phone he'd programmed my number into wasn't his regular one. I noticed once during our meal he answered a call from his parents on a different phone.)

I didn't mind. Not only was I in the closet, I was also a total virgin who didn't even know for certain if I'd seen another homo in the flesh, aside from those two old guys at my mom's hair salon and this other boy at church I had strong suspicions about. And considering I was pudgy and girly and still let my mom pick out my clothes and home-cut my hair because I trusted her to know what a normal straight boy was supposed to look like way more than I trusted myself, meeting a guy who wanted to get friendly with me *that way* was literally the last thing I expected to happen.

But here it was happening. Over the course of the week between Christmas and New Year's, Mike sent a steady stream of texts. First: *u have a great sense of humor.*

Then: *u have a funny laugh.*

Then: *u have a cute nose.*

Then: *u have a hot ass.*

We only got to hang out one other time that week. That's another reason things didn't move faster when we were actually together. My parents were forcing me to do all these hellish Christmastime church activities (at least I'd finally outgrown the Nativity pageant), and I guess Mike's family kept him busy too. Plus, it was tricky figuring out excuses to sneak away and hang out with him. I knew I couldn't just tell my parents I had plans to randomly spend time with the way older son of our new neighbors. So both times we went out, I said I was going to have dinner at my friend Sarah's house. It scared the hell out of me, because I never lied to my parents, at least not about stuff like that. Not because I had some moral objection to it or thought God was going to strike me down or something. I'd just never had a reason before.

Mike took me to the Burger Barn again that second time, and still nothing funny happened. He never said a word about those sexy texts he'd sent me. When he dropped me off—a block away from our houses because he knew as well as I did we couldn't let our parents see us together—he touched my apparently cute nose with his index finger and gave me a wink, and that was the only moment that made the evening feel like sort of a date.

Then before I knew it, New Year's had passed, and it was just a day before he was supposed to go back to college, and I'd gone into a full-on panic. He texted, asking if I wanted to get together that night and go to his parents' movie theater after hours. He'd arranged something special, he said.

As I stared at my phone's screen, my chest started to heave. I thought I might faint, actually faint, the way nobody did in real life but my noir ladies did all the time. He had something special planned. What did that mean? Would we finally kiss tonight? Or would it be just like the other nights? I honestly didn't know which possibility scared me more.

He asked if I could sneak out of my house late. I knew that part I could manage. I had the only bedroom on the first floor, which meant I had zero privacy, but at least it made stealthy exits easy. Theoretically, at least. Of course I'd never actually tried. He told me to meet him on a corner a block away from our houses at midnight that night.

He drove me to the theater. It had already closed, but he pulled out a ring of keys and unlocked the back door. Inside, he went behind the snack counter and asked what I'd like. Probably blushing, I told him Milk Duds and a Cherry Coke. But I tried to say it the way a femme fatale would order a gin and tonic, with a toss of my head and a mysterious smile.

We went into one of the screening rooms, and he sat me down in the middle of the middle row.

"I'll be right back," he said with a wink.

I sat there alone in the big, dim screening room with its scratchy seats and hard armrests and sticky floor, my heart going *bang-bang-bang* in my chest. I popped a handful of Milk Duds and washed them down with a swallow of Cherry Coke. The room went dark. With a low mechanical hum, the old-fashioned red curtains at the front of the room slid apart to reveal the movie screen. On it the black-and-white Paramount logo appeared, and then the words "DOUBLE INDEMNITY."

I sucked in a breath.

Mike reappeared next to me. "Didn't you say you like this kind of movie? I found it in storage and thought of you."

I didn't know what to say. He grabbed my hand, and I felt shivers everywhere.

Then he pulled my hand over the armrest and put it in his lap.

Fade to black.

The next day he left. I watched from my bedroom window as he waved to his mom and dad, got in his piece of junk car, and chugged away. That night I told my family I didn't feel well. I went to my room and cried while I clutched my phone and stared at the screen. He'd said he'd text me.

Finally, he did. *I miss u.*

I cried even harder, tears of sadness and happiness mixed together. *I miss u 2!!!* I texted back.

how bout sending a pic?

I spent the next three hours working on it. I rehearsed my smokiest, sultriest femme fatale expression in the mirror on the back of my bedroom door, half closing my eyes and holding my head just so. I figured out camera angles and adjusted the lighting. I even tried dabbing Vaseline on my phone's little camera lens because I'd read somewhere that was what Hollywood photographers used to do to make their portraits of film stars look all blurry and beautiful. (It didn't work.) The picture I ended up with just made me look like I was really sleepy and had a stiff neck, but I knew I probably wouldn't do any better even if I tried for another three hours, so I sent it.

I clutched my phone again, wondering if all my effort had been worth it, wondering if he'd just find me hideous.

I didn't have to wait long. A response came less than a minute later. *I meant w/ no clothes on.* ;)

Outside my bedroom door, I could hear the rest of my family playing Christian charades. I knew other kids—far, far cooler kids—sexted each other, but it hadn't even crossed my mind that Mike might want something like that.

Another message showed up on my screen: *come on.*

Then: *I won't show it to anyone.*

Then: *I swear.*

Then: *I think ur gorgeous.*

Before I could lose my nerve, I adjusted the lights and figured out the camera angle again. I arranged my old Noah's ark–patterned sheets on my bed so they looked messy, to suggest . . . I don't know, that something interesting might have actually happened there. I pulled off all my clothes, fluffed my hair to make it look carelessly tousled, arranged myself on the bed, and snapped the picture.

In my very first shot, I had a more convincingly sultry expression than I'd had in my clothed pic after three hours of trying.

I sent it.

thx.

I waited for him to send another text, or maybe even a picture of his own, but I didn't hear from him again that night.

The next day I texted, *how's it going?*

good! classes starting might get busy.

yeah classes starting here too, I texted back.

I totally understood. I didn't expect him to keep sending me messages at the same rate he had over the break.

I waited a week. Then two. Nothing. I didn't allow myself to text him, though. I knew only losers let themselves seem too eager.

But after three weeks, I couldn't stand it anymore. *hi! how r u?*

Then: *u there?*

Then: *u okay?*

Then: *u mad at me?*

Then: *Mike? plz?*

He never did text me back. I went through the second semester of my sophomore year a zombie, barely paying attention in class, barely squeaking by with passing grades. I'd never felt so miserable. But how else had I expected things to end? I kept asking myself that. How could I reasonably expect *anyone* to fall in love with dumpy, pathetic me? Let alone a cool college boy? (Well, maybe not cool, but definitely magnetic.) All along, it had only been a matter of time before he came to his senses.

The day he'd left, I'd printed out a photo of him I'd found on Facebook and taped it on my wall, hidden underneath a shot of Lauren Bacall. At night I'd unstick the top of the Lauren Bacall picture and let it hang down, revealing the picture of Mike. I kept it there all semester and uncovered it every night and laid there in bed staring at it. Just to punish myself, I guess.

Then one Sunday morning the whole family was out by the minivan again, Mom busy with her pre-church inspection, when the Morettis stepped outside on their way somewhere else. (They didn't go to our church.) They paused near their car to make small talk with Mom and Dad, asking if we had any summer plans. Mom gabbed for a bit about the monthlong family Bible camp we were going to in August.

"What about you?" she asked.

"Italy," Mrs. Moretti gushed. "We're spending the whole summer."

Mom and Dad gave vague nods, like they'd never heard of the place before.

"I have some family there," Mr. Moretti explained. "Mike's coming home to run the theater while we're gone."

The back of my neck prickled under my poly-blend collar at the sound of his name. My mind started to race. The Morettis said good-bye and got into their car, and before Mom had even finished spit-smoothing my cowlicky hair, I had a plan. Because in spite of everything, part of me still hoped Mike hadn't just blown me off. He might've lost the phone he used to text me, and my number along with it. He might've gotten scared. Didn't I owe it to him, and to myself, to give him a chance?

The following Saturday afternoon I slipped out of the house and rang the Morettis' doorbell.

"I'm looking for a summer job," I blurted, my palms sweating, "and I love movies. Any chance you need someone to help out at the theater?"

That June I started behind the snack counter a week before Mike got home. It had taken some convincing to get Mom and Dad to agree. I'd had to promise only to work daytime shifts, when the matinees were playing, and never to sneak in and watch any of the R-rated movies.

So there I stood next to the popcorn popper in my paper hat and clip-on bow tie when Mike walked in. He still had the billy-goat beard, and he still had the inexplicable Humphrey Bogart magnetism. I felt it the second he walked in, even from all the way across the lobby. My heart started going faster.

Then it lurched to a stop. He had someone with him. A girl with a huge head of frizzy hair, like a mass of blond cotton candy. As I watched, he slung his arm over her shoulder.

Mr. and Mrs. Moretti followed them in. They'd all come so Mike's parents could show him the ropes. They stopped on the other side of the lobby, and Mr. Moretti started explaining how to work the cash register while Mike, only half listening, let his gaze wander.

His eyes landed on me. His face went pale. His arm sagged away from the girl.

Mrs. Moretti noticed him staring at me. "Mike, did you ever meet Cody? The neighbors' boy? He'll be working the snack counter this summer."

Mike's mouth opened but nothing come out. I could see him trying to figure out what he should say, what lie he should tell about us.

I was nervous too, but at least I'd expected this moment and rehearsed it in my head. I'd run through a million scenarios—although none where a girl with cotton-candy hair was standing next to him.

"I—I saw you a few times," I stammered. "I don't think we ever met, though."

Still he didn't utter a word. To fill the silence, I stepped out from behind the counter and held out my hand to the girl.

"I'm Cody."

"So nice to meet you!" she said, seizing my hand with both of hers and pumping it hard. "I'm Rochelle. I'll be working the ticket counter."

"She's my girlfriend," Mike finally said. His eyes had a steely set to them, and his beard seemed to bristle as he spoke. "She's spending the summer here."

"We're going to have so much fun!" Rochelle still hadn't released my hand. She gave it another excited shake and beamed at me, like she thought I was just adorable.

I mumbled something about needing to get back to work and scuttled behind the counter.

A couple hours later, after Mike's parents had gone home to pack, and the matinees were all underway, and Rochelle had left to have a look around downtown Hillville, Mike stalked back to the snack counter. "What the hell do you think you're doing?" he hissed between his teeth, slamming his palms on the glass.

I backed up against the popcorn popper. "I needed a summer job," I answered in a small voice.

"Here?"

"I wanted to see you." I could hear how pathetic the words sounded even as they fell out of my mouth. "I missed you."

"Not cool, Cody. My girlfriend's here. Things are different now. We need to forget Christmas break ever happened."

"I don't know if I can."

"Didn't you tell me yourself you can't have your parents finding out about you? You said you knew for a fact they'd kick you out if they knew you were gay. You said they pretty much told you so point-blank. Isn't that right?"

"Well, yeah." I felt dizzy. The smell of melted butter filled my nose and made me want to throw up. Behind me, the heat of the popper burned into my back. I could feel the thing shake with each tiny explosion of a popping kernel.

"So you have just as much to lose as I do," he said. "More probably. I mean, I'm not even gay, really. I just like messing around with guys sometimes. So let's just bury it, okay?"

My chin started to shake. "But I . . . I love you." The words landed in my ears with a pitiful thud.

Mike gave me a look of pure bafflement. "What are you *talking* about?" He glanced around, like he feared someone might see my little breakdown and draw conclusions. "Look, pull yourself together, okay? Let's talk later." He disappeared into the manager's office muttering, "Jesus, I *knew* I shouldn't have gotten involved with the neighbors' kid."

I tried to do what he said. As I stood there with my back still to the popper, though, I didn't get calmer. I got angrier. It seemed the mystery had been solved: Mike hadn't lost my number. He hadn't gotten scared. He'd just been an asshole. Behind me, the tiny explosions started coming faster. *Pop. Pop. Pop-pop-pop-pop-pop.*

I barreled through the office door, ready to let Mike have it, but I found the room empty. Behind the door to the manager's little private bathroom, I heard him moving around.

On the desk, though, lay Mike's phone. Not the one he used with his parents. The secret one he'd used with me. He wasn't texting me anymore. So who was he texting now? The screen still glowed. He must've set it down seconds ago without locking it.

Careful not to make a sound, I grabbed it. He had his photos app pulled up, and it only took me a couple taps to get to his most recent image. A selfie taken by some boy about my age, maybe even younger, naked, in a bedroom. I swiped through the previous photos and found more of the same. A parade of naked boys, all of them in sharp focus and bright color, unlike the Hollywood starlets that decorated my wall. Many were tubby like me. Maybe that was his type. Had he gotten together with all these guys in real life? Or just chatted with them online? Or gotten the photos off the Internet?

I swiped again, and my image appeared, right there among all the others.

"Cody?"

I jumped about a foot in the air. The voice calling my name hadn't come from the bathroom, though, but from the open office door. A kid I knew from church stood there. Ernest Kimball.

"I didn't know you worked here," he said.

A second ago I'd had my back to the door. Had Ernest spotted the image of me on the phone's screen? I didn't think so. I'd probably see it on his face right now if he had. I hoped Mike couldn't hear him talking from the bathroom.

"Hey, have you seen that movie *Samson* yet?" Ernest asked. "I've watched it three times now, and—"

Locking the phone and dropping it back on Mike's desk, I

hurried past Ernest, past the snack counter, past the popcorn popper still going *pop-pop-pop-pop-pop*.

A few minutes later I'd run out to the little parking lot behind the theater and pitched to my hands and knees on the rough asphalt. Whenever a lady in a noir movie had her heart broken, she'd throw herself diagonally across her bed, and the tears would slide down her cheeks like shiny pearls, and she'd still look gorgeous. In my case, I couldn't even bring myself to cry. I just wanted to puke.

I grabbed the paper hat off my head and crumpled it. Below me little shards of broken green and clear glass gleamed in the sunlight, like diamonds and emeralds. A little farther away, at the base of the theater's rear brick wall, among the weeds pushing up through cracks in the asphalt, lay a little pile of rusty, sharp-looking nails.

I grabbed a handful, hauled myself to my feet, and walked over to Mike's piece of junk car. Inside my body I imagined I could still feel little explosions going off, little hot kernels of rage bursting. *Pop-pop-pop-pop-pop*. I positioned a few of the nails under one of the tires. Then I went around to the other tires and did the same thing. I'd never tried this trick before, but my brother had gotten busted for it years ago. It was childish and stupid of me, and Mike would know exactly who'd done it and probably figure out a way to get back at me, but I didn't care.

I'd just finished when a shadow fell over me. I whirled around, sure it must be Mike.

Instead I found Ernest Kimball standing there, watching me, his hands on his hips. "What do you think you're doing?" he said, his gaze so sharp I swear I felt his eyes poke me in the chest.

"Um."

I'd known Ernest since kindergarten. We were friends back then, because we were both girly and liked to play with Barbies, although whereas I was chunky, he was so thin I bet his clothes weighed more than he did. When we got older and the fag comments started to come, we drifted apart. We never talked about it, but both of us must've realized we'd be safer if we kept our distance. Over time Ernest got more and more into church, just like I got more and more into noir. These days we went to different high schools, but I saw him at service every Sunday, sitting in the third row with his back very straight and a yellow notepad in his lap so he could take notes on the sermon.

Ernest had the same pad with him now. It stuck out of a canvas bag he had slung over his shoulder. I wondered if he took notes on *Samson*, too. You might've heard of that movie. It was really big last year with the Christian nutjob demographic. It tells the Samson and Delilah story, which makes it sort of like *Gladiator* for Bible-thumpers. I snuck in to watch it once during my first week at the theater, and I thought it sucked, but on the plus side, the guy who played Samson was hot as hell and spent half the film shirtless.

"Never mind," Ernest said. "I know what you were doing. Pulling a prank. Trying to ruin some poor person's day. Shame on you, Cody." He actually wagged his finger at me as he said it. "This isn't very Christian of you. I could report you, you know. It just so happens I'm on my way to the police station right now. As president of the Teen Council for Moral Decency, I have a meeting there every Tuesday afternoon to discuss worrying issues in our community. I bet if I mentioned this incident to Officer Crane, she'd have a few choice words for you. For your parents, too."

The mention of my parents jarred me into finding my voice again. "I wasn't just playing some random prank, Ernest. I'm having a really bad day, okay? Someone treated me like dirt, and I'm having a really bad day."

His expression softened. He turned his poky eyes on the car. "Who does this thing belong to?"

"A guy named Mike Moretti," I admitted.

"And what did he do to you?"

"I don't want to talk about it." With my free hand I tugged off the clip-on bow tie and undid the top button of my shirt. "He manages the movie theater," I added. "He's my boss." I hoped Ernest might assume I'd gotten mad at Mike for something work related.

It seemed like he did. "Have some self-respect, Cody," he said, but in a gentler tone. "Aren't you better than this? You need to follow a higher example."

That stopped me. I opened my fingers to reveal the leftover rusty nails nestled in my dirty palm. I glanced at the clip-on bow tie in my other hand and the crumpled paper hat lying on the ground where I'd dropped it. "You're right," I said. "I am. I do."

Ernest looked pleased. He didn't smile—I didn't think I'd ever seen him smile—but he gave an eager nod. "I understand you're mad, Cody, but you need to ask yourself what Jesus would do in this situation."

But Jesus wasn't the example I was thinking of. My head had filled with images of my film noir heroines. Rita Hayworth. Ann Savage. All of them. They wouldn't have done something so trashy and unimaginative and shortsighted as pop the tires of the guy who'd wronged them. They would've gotten back at him, but they would've thought about it first. They would've come up with a plan.

I needed to do the same thing. The only question was: Could I be ruthless? Did I have the *guts*?

I turned around and gathered up the nails from behind the tire next to me. "I'm sorry, Ernest. I was just being stupid."

"Not stupid." I could tell from the pink blush coloring his cheeks he hadn't expected his intervention to go this well. "Just human. We're all fallen creatures."

After we'd finished circling the car together and gathering up the rest of the nails, I said, "Can we keep this a secret, though? I just lost my head for a second. I don't usually do stuff like this, I swear."

Ernest bit his lip. "I suppose." He looked up from the nails in his hand, and his eyes poked me again, but more kindly this time. "Listen, if you ever need to talk about it—about why you were so angry, I mean—I just want you to know you can come to me." He gave my shoulder an awkward pat. "We can pray together."

"Thanks." I dropped the nails in the trash. "That's very nice of you. Maybe I will. But right now I'd better get back to work." I picked up my paper hat, smoothed it out, and stuck it back on my head. As I headed toward the movie theater's back exit, I could feel a little swing work itself into my hips, like the spirit of one of my heroines had once again slipped inside my body. I threw a glance over my shoulder and said, "You're a lifesaver, Ernie. I owe you one."

Two days later Mike's parents left for Italy. Mom watched from the living room window, shaking her head as they got into their taxi.

"Leaving your son and his girlfriend in your own house for a whole summer to do Lord knows what," she said. "It's something *I'd* never do, that's for sure."

I told her I was running out to the Sheetz a couple blocks away to get a snack. Once I got there, though, instead of going inside, I stopped at the old pay phone next to the door and slid a few coins in.

I dialed the police.

"Hello," I said, "I was just walking by 4537 Forest Street and saw someone suspicious entering the house. I really think you should send someone to check it out."

"Who is this?" the lady taking the information wanted to know. I wondered if by some coincidence she might be Officer Crane.

"I'm ever so sorry," I said with a breathy Rita Hayworth laugh, "but I don't want to get involved. I prefer to remain anonymous."

I hung up the phone and ran home in plenty of time to see, through my bedroom window, a police car pull up in front of the Morettis' house and a cop walk up to the front door.

At the theater the next day, during a lull when all three movies were running and Rochelle had run out to get a Burger Bucket at the Burger Barn, I sidled over to the manager's office door and stuck my head in. Mike and I hadn't talked over the past couple days. When he noticed me there, his face went dark. He pushed some papers around on his desk, like he actually had something important to be doing, and said, "What is it, Cody?"

"Sorry to bother you. I just wanted to say I hope things aren't going to be weird between us. I thought about it, and you're right. I was being silly. What happened between us last Christmas . . . It was just a casual thing, and I'm letting it go. I'm ready for us to have a purely professional relationship."

He squinted at me like he thought I was a lunatic. "Are you sure? Because it might be easier for both of us if you just stop working here. We can make up an excuse. No one would have to suspect a thing."

"No, Mike, please," I begged. "I need this job. My parents are so stingy with money, and this is the only way I can have some of my own. Plus, it gets me out of the house. I think I'm going to die if I have to spend another Saturday afternoon playing Christian Scrabble with them."

He blew out through his mouth and shook his head. It killed me to talk to him like that, like everything was just okay, and to beg him for my job, but I had to do it.

"Fine," he said. "Just keep your distance, all right?"

I nodded. "All right. I will. Thank you, Mike." I started to turn away. Then, exactly the way I'd rehearsed in front of the mirror in my bedroom, I stopped in his office doorway, like I'd just thought of something. "Hey, can I ask you a random question?"

He rolled his eyes. "Come on, man. Rochelle's going to be back any second."

"But we're just talking. She won't think that's weird. Anyway, the question's a quick one. Did the police come by your house yesterday?"

He tensed. All of a sudden his hands got antsy and started shuffling papers around again. "Why do you ask?"

"It's just that a cop rang our doorbell yesterday afternoon. He told my dad someone had called in saying there was a suspicious-looking

48

prowler in the neighborhood, and he asked if he could take a look around the house. So the guy came in and searched all over. He even went in my bedroom, which I thought was weird."

Mike gave a noncommittal shrug. "Okay."

"So after that," I said, "my dad was talking to Mr. O'Farrell on our other side, and he asked him if the cop had come to visit him too, and Mr. O'Farrell said he hadn't talked to any cop. That seemed odd, though, since the officer had said he was visiting all the houses in the area. My dad got suspicious, thinking maybe the guy had targeted us for some reason, so he went by a few other houses near us and asked the same question. The cop hadn't visited any of them either. And we just couldn't figure it out. Why would he only come to *our* house?"

Staring at a stack of papers gripped in his hands, Mike said in a low voice, "He came to my house too."

"Oh!" I opened my eyes wide in surprise. "So it *wasn't* just us. That makes me feel better." Once again I started to leave but then stopped. I grabbed the doorframe with one hand and peered back at him over my shoulder. "Although I still don't understand why he would visit your house and mine and no one else's."

Now I needed to talk to Ernest again. I knew I'd see him that Sunday at church, and sure enough, there he was in the third row, boring into Paster Pete with his eyes and scribbling away on his pad each time he heard something he thought was important. After the service everybody went downstairs for something called fellowship, which was basically a time for the congregation to mill around in the multipurpose room drinking bad coffee and eating stale pastries and gossiping. As soon as Mom and Dad and my brother and sister split off to yammer with their friends, I scanned the room until I spotted Ernest's round head of neatly combed hair. I closed in.

Ernest was deep in conversation with some old lady—it didn't seem like he had many friends his own age—but when I edged into his field of vision and gave a little wave, he made an excuse and came right over.

"Hello, Cody," he said, friendly but with a dash of sternness, like he wanted me to know he hadn't forgotten the circumstances of our last encounter.

"Sorry for bothering you, but you said if I ever needed to talk . . ."

His eye went big and hungry. "Of course! And I meant it!" He waved me over to a quiet corner, grabbing a couple pastries on the way. After motioning for me to sit down in a metal folding chair, he slid a Danish at me across the table and said, "Go ahead."

"You were wondering why I was so mad at Mike Moretti?"

He nodded.

"I think I'm ready to tell you. I think as president of the Teen Council on Moral Decency you should be aware."

"Cody, I promise, you'll feel so much better once you let it all out." His eyes drilled into me as he absently unwound his cinnamon roll.

I folded my hands on the table, leaving the Danish untouched. It would only get in the way of my delivery. "Well, I know you've been going to the theater a lot lately, so you've probably noticed that sign next to the popcorn that says 'Real Butter,' right?"

"Sure. I get a carton every time I go."

"And a small lemonade. I remember. But you see, Ernest, that sign, it's a lie. A dark, dirty lie."

His hand went to his mouth. The way he stared at me with his huge eyes, I felt like I was a movie screen. "What do you mean?" he asked.

"Last week I discovered the theater isn't using real butter at all, at least not anymore. It's using soybean oil with artificial butter flavoring."

"No!"

"Yes. Apparently, Mike switched from real butter to fake as soon as he took over, and he's pocketing the savings. When I found out I confronted him about it. I told him I couldn't in good conscience keep a secret like that. He flew into a rage and said he'd fire me if I told anyone. I didn't want to lose my job. It's the first I've ever had, and I don't want my parents to be disappointed in me. So when he said that, I just felt so powerless and angry. That's why I wanted to do something to hurt him."

Ernest grabbed the edge of the table with both hands. "Your parents won't be disappointed! Not if it's a matter of conscience! Not if you're standing up for your beliefs!"

"You're probably right. But after I got that talking-to from you the other day, I finally calmed down enough to really think, and I realized maybe I shouldn't be so mad at Mike. Maybe I should feel sorry for him instead. Maybe the Lord called me to this job for a purpose. So I talked to Mike some more, and he's not *really* a bad guy. Just misguided. Have you seen him at the theater? Do you know who I'm talking about?"

He gave a nod, and a flush of pink colored his cheeks. I suspected I wasn't the only one to notice Mike's Humphrey Bogart charm.

"I think somewhere deep down he wants to be redeemed," I said.

"But he needs someone better at redeeming than me. That's why I thought of you."

You should've seen it. I had him in the palm of my hand. He fanned out his fingers on his chest as if to say *Me?* He hadn't taken a bite of his cinnamon roll, but he'd fully unwound it. The thing lay there on his plate like a snake.

"I think you should go to his house," I said. "Talk to him. But don't let on that you know about the butter. If he finds out I told anyone about that, he'll skin me alive, and I bet he won't talk to you anymore either. Make it seem like you're just going around the neighborhood knocking on people's doors to spread the Good News and talk about the church."

"Yes." His eyes shifted away from me and narrowed as he thought about it. "That's probably the best approach."

"But at the same time, be persistent. I really think with a little push, he'll tell you everything."

I kept watch all that afternoon through my bedroom window. Sure enough, at two o'clock on the dot, Ernest came marching up the Morettis' front walk, his hair neatly combed, the excitement in his face visible even from that distance. I couldn't see him once he got to the front door, but I kept an eye on the clock on my nightstand, and he didn't reappear for a full five minutes, which meant at least Mike couldn't have sent him away right off the bat.

The next day at the theater, I slid over to Mike's office door again.

"What is it?" he said, giving me the same wary look he always did these days. I must've been making his life hell, showing up there every day with his girlfriend just a few feet away, but even though he was aware I had more to lose than he did if our little secret got out—which was true, by the way, because my parents really would kick me out—I guess he was just scared enough of me not to actually give me the boot.

"I know this is another really random question," I said, "but you didn't get a visit from a really enthusiastic Christian kid who wanted to convert you over the weekend, did you?"

He went stiff, just like he had when I'd asked him about the cop. "Why? Did you?"

"Yeah. I know him actually. Ernest Kimball. He goes to my church. He came by our house yesterday, and he specifically wanted to talk to me. I always thought he seemed a little odd, but yesterday he said something about the Lord telling him I needed help because I'd been victimized or something."

He screwed up his face. "Victimized? What the hell was he talking about?"

"That's just the thing. I don't know. It was a really weird conversation, and of course I didn't say a word about us, but . . ." I stood there wringing my hands.

"But what? What the hell are you talking about?"

"It just made me wonder. Like, if somehow he knows what we did."

His face scrunched up even more. "How? You think the Lord was really talking to him? I thought you didn't believe in that shit."

"I don't. But once he left yesterday, I watched him from my window, and I thought I saw him go over to your house. And after that weird police visit a few days ago, it made me wonder if they might be related. Mike, what if that cop was looking for something specific?"

His face hardened. In an equally hard voice, he said, "What do you think he would've been looking for, Cody?"

My hands continued to grab at each other. Ladies in noir movies did that all the time when they were anxious—or faking it. "Look, I should probably tell you something else. Last week after you got mad at me your first day here, I went to your office, but you were in the bathroom, and you'd left your phone on the desk—unlocked. So I went through it."

"What?" he snapped.

"I was upset. I wanted to see who you else you were texting with. I found all those pictures of boys on your phone. And right after I got to the picture of me, I noticed Ernest Kimball standing at the door behind me. I thought he might've seen what I was looking at."

It was almost the truth. That was the beauty of it. Maybe Mike even remembered hearing voices in the office that day while he was in the bathroom.

He smacked his hand down hard on the desk, making me jump. That I didn't fake. "Get to the point, Cody."

"So all those pictures of underage guys on your phone . . . Isn't that possession of child porn? Technically, I mean? And isn't that a felony?"

His eyes jumped to Rochelle behind the ticket counter, visible through his office door. He shot out of his desk chair, yanked me all the way into the office, and banged the door shut. "Is this some kind of threat?" he snarled. "Is that what this is? Are you trying to get back at me?"

He'd shoved me up against the big corkboard on his wall. Push-pins dug into my back in a dozen places. I shook my head. "It's not.

I swear. If the police find out what we did, it'll be the end for me."

"No, it won't. It'll be the end for *me*. I could go to prison if they catch me for something like that."

"Look, all I'm saying is this isn't a threat, okay? I'm scared too."

He let me go and turned away, still breathing hard as he raked his fingers through his hair.

I didn't say anything. I waited.

"That kid Ernest did come to see me," Mike said. "He said the Lord told him to come. He said we all have sins, and he had a feeling I was ready to confess mine."

I fluttered my hand to my throat. "Oh God."

"But what makes you think that has something to do with the cop?"

"Because Ernest's the president of the Teen Council on Moral Decency at our church. And I heard sometimes they work with the police, like when they think there's something seriously bad going on in the community."

Mike looked unsteady. His face had gone sweaty and greenish. "So you think he saw the pictures on my phone and told the police about them? And now they're investigating?"

I nodded. "And maybe he's doing his own investigation too. Maybe that's why he asked you to confess your sins and why he's always carrying around that pad and pen. He's taking *notes*."

Mike's office chair creaked as he dropped into it. He pitched forward and clutched his head in his hands. "This can't be happening."

"Don't freak out," I said, leaning in, rubbing his shoulder, speaking in a soothing voice. "When the cop came to search your house, did he see the phone?"

He shook his head. "I'm pretty sure I had it in my pocket."

"So that means they don't have any concrete evidence." I gave him a pat. "I think we're all right. For now, at least."

But Mike only got more freaked the next day, Tuesday. Ernest came in to see *Samson* again that afternoon. At some point during the screening, Mike's secret phone went missing (thanks to a quick visit I paid to his office while he was using the bathroom again), and he just about started bleeding from his eye sockets he got so worked up. At first he wanted to go after Ernest and take the phone back by force, but I convinced him that would only make him look guilty. I told him we should keep cool and trail Ernest after the movie ended. Mike made some excuse to Rochelle, and together we piled into his piece of junk car and trundled after Ernest as he biked down the road.

He made straight for the police station.

We parked across the street, and Mike gripped the wheel with both hands and made soft whimpering noises while he watched Ernest lock up his bike and march inside, his yellow notepad sticking out of his tote bag.

"Oh God," Mike panted, putting one hand to the back of his neck, like he could already feel the noose there slowly tightening.

"I still think we're safe," I said. "They don't have your unlock code, and not even the police can access your phone without that. I mean, unless they put their special police hackers on the case, and I'm sure those hackers have better things to do. Look, let's lie low for a while. See what happens. Keep calm."

Which was exactly what Mike couldn't do. The last part at least. A few weeks passed. Ernest kept coming to the theater, even more often now that Mike had become his project, and every time he'd spot Mike in the lobby or pass by his office, Ernest would give him a serious, significant look. A couple times he even whispered to Mike—with me there to witness it—"Whenever you're ready." Meanwhile, Mike could barely do his job (and believe me, it doesn't take a rocket scientist to manage a movie theater). He kept pulling me into his office for frantic closed-door chats. I kept telling him to hold on.

August came. In a few days I'd leave with my family for Bible camp, and Mike would have to go back to school before we returned, which meant he'd be on his own with Ernest for the rest of the summer. The idea of that had him even more panicked.

Then one day I rushed into his office, shut the door, and said, "I talked to Ernest. He cornered me at church again. He kept digging and digging, trying to get something out of me, until finally I lost it. 'Mike and I know the truth,' I said. 'We know you're working with the police. That's why you've been grilling us.'

"And he admitted it. He said he saw those pictures on your phone, just like we suspected, and he decided you needed to be stopped. I begged him to drop it. I said it would ruin your life, and mine too. I told him you'd never mess around with vulnerable under-age kids again. Because you won't, right?"

He shook his head hard. "No way."

"I asked him what we could do to make this whole thing disappear."

Mike's fingers gripped the armrests of his office chair. Tiny beads of sweat had broken out on his upper lip, like a mustache to go with his billy-goat beard. "What did he say?"

"He said it's not too late. The police haven't unlocked your phone, so right now all they have is his word. He'd be willing to tell the police he made a mistake . . . on one condition. He wants you to make a contribution to our church. 'As proof of your good faith and repentance,' he said."

"For how much?"

"Seven thousand dollars. He asked me how much cash we usually have in the safe, and I'm sorry, I mentioned you haven't been making the bank drops lately."

He clapped both his hands over his mouth and let out a muffled roar.

"It'll be an anonymous donation," I said. "You won't be connected to it, and neither will he. That's why it needs to be cash. He wants you to give the money to me, and then I'll hand it off to him. He thinks a direct handoff would be too risky."

Mike looked up at me, his eyes going narrow. "Wait a second. How do I know you're not just going to take it for yourself? How do I know you're not playing me?" He shook his head. Beads of sweat had broken out all over his face now. A few of them had burst into trickles and run all the way down to dampen his scraggly beard. "I'll give the money directly to Ernest, but I'm not giving it to you."

Don't worry, though, I'd expected this. In fact, I was counting on it. "So you don't trust me? Even after all we've been through?" I made my eyes gleam with hurt. "Fine. I'll see Ernest this Sunday at church. If it'll make you feel better, I'll try to convince him."

I did see Ernest that Sunday during fellowship, and I did talk to him. "I think Mike's finally ready," I told him as he peeled open his croissant. "Your persistence is paying off. He's gone back to using real butter in the popcorn."

"I thought I could taste a difference this week!" Ernest exclaimed.

"Now he told me he wants to talk to you again. He wants to make a confession, and also a donation to our church. All the profits he made on his fake-butter scheme."

Ernest gaped. He dropped the fully dissected croissant onto his plate. "Of course! I'll make another visit to his house this after—"

I shook my head. "But he wants to do it in secret. He still doesn't want his girlfriend or anyone else suspecting. He wants to meet you at the theater tonight, after closing, at midnight. And you're not supposed to let anyone see you arrive."

He blinked at me. I could tell the idea of a middle-of-the-night meeting scared him a little but excited him, too. "Midnight," he said. "Tell him I'll be there."

I didn't work on Sundays—my parents didn't want me to—so I had to call Mike to tell him the news. That might've been for the best. By now I was so full of nervous excitement I didn't know if I could keep the act going if I talked to him in person.

"Ernest's agreed," I told him. Even though Mike couldn't see me, I still tried to hold myself like a femme fatale, sitting in my desk chair with my legs crossed, winding an imaginary phone cord slowly around my index finger. "I said he should rendezvous with you at the theater tonight at midnight. I told him you'd be waiting with the money behind the curtain in screening room one. I'll meet him at the door and bring him to you."

"Okay." The fear made Mike's voice crack and wobble. "Jesus, how am I going to explain all that missing money to my parents?"

"They're gone for the whole summer, right? So you can make the money disappear in the books somehow, can't you?"

"I guess. And Ernest swears he's going to let this drop once I pay him? Like, forever? This'll make it disappear?"

"Yes," I said. "He swears." I gazed at the photo of Lauren Bacall on the wall above my bed. Her face, beautiful but strong and angular. I'd torn the picture of Mike out from under it weeks ago. Crumpled it and thrown it into the trash. "And Mike," I said, "if you really want to make this disappear, there's one more thing I think you should do."

That night I snuck out of the house at eleven fifteen and hurried to the theater by foot. Mike had just locked up for the night. On the floor of his office, we counted the money one more time and stuffed it into a black duffel bag. Then he stationed himself behind the red curtain in screening room one. Just like I'd advised, he wore a button-down shirt, unbuttoned halfway, and a splash of cologne. He'd put some product in his hair and in his billy-goat beard, too.

Before I left him, I said, "Tell me one thing, Mike. It wasn't all bullshit with me, was it? You did like hanging out, didn't you?"

He looked confused at first, but then his face eased into a smile. He gave me a wink, and for a second, he really did look like a young Humphrey Bogart. "Sure I did."

"Thanks. I just needed to hear you say that."

I went to the theater's back entrance, the one that led directly to the parking lot, and let in Ernie, who was just as punctual as I knew he'd be. I led him into screening room one and all the way to the narrow backstage area between the curtain and the movie screen. Mike stood there smoking a cigarette with his shoulder leaned up against the wall. He looked just like he had that first night when he and I met back behind our houses. Except he was a lot more nervous now.

I didn't stay. I had one more thing I needed to do. I went back to the theater lobby, and this time I headed for the front entrance, stuffing my paper hat on my head as I went.

Rochelle stood there, an eager grin on her face, along with even more makeup than usual. She wore a tight red dress, and her cotton-candy hair looked extra poufy. In her hand she clutched the "ticket" I'd printed and hand-delivered to the Morettis' house earlier today. I'd told her Mike had sent me. It had been her day off, but Mike still had work to do. The ticket read: *Good for one admission to a night at the movies you'll never forget. Come to the theater tonight at midnight.*

"This is so exciting!" she bubbled as I let her in and slid behind the snack counter.

"A Diet Coke," I said. "Isn't that your drink?"

"Uh-huh. And a box of Milk Duds, please."

"An excellent choice."

I pushed her treats across the counter and walked her into screening room one. I sat her down in the middle of the middle row, in the very same seat where I'd sat during my date with Mike.

"He'll be right here," I whispered. "He's just getting everything ready for the big show."

I started to go, but Rochelle grabbed my hand and peered up

at me through big, shiny eyes. "Thank you, Cody. I mean it. You've already made this evening so special."

I felt a pang right then. I admit it, I did. Rochelle really was a sweet girl. At least a couple times a week she'd get us all a Burger Bucket at the Burger Barn for lunch. She'd always let me have as many burgers as I wanted and never let me pay her a dime. For that matter, Ernie was a good guy, too, in a judgy, hyper-Christian sort of way. I suppose I should've felt some solidarity with him, considering I was 99 percent sure he was a closet case just like me. But I couldn't let any of that stop me. A femme fatale wouldn't. To get what I wanted, I had to be ruthless. I was a chubby homo living with his Christian nutjob parents in goddamn motherfucking Hellville, West Virginia, and I had no other choice.

I made my way to the front of the theater, off to one side, and peeked behind the red curtain. I flicked a switch on the wall. The curtain hummed open, revealing Mike and Ernie with their mouths locked together, a desperate grimace on Mike's face, Ernie's eyebrows lifted in surprise, his arms thrown wide open and his fingers wiggling, like he was falling from a great height.

The picture only lasted a second. A scream cut through the room, and they lurched away from each other. Mike whirled around to squint at the house.

"R-Rochelle?" he sputtered. "What the hell are you doing here?"

She was already rushing down her row and up the aisle, her hands over her mouth. He jumped off the stage and sprinted after her. I'd pulled back into the shadows at the side of the room so he couldn't see me.

Ernie didn't notice me either. He stared after the others, his fingers still wiggling, his face red with confusion and mortification, before he hurried out through the emergency exit on the other side of the screen.

And then I was alone. Which left me plenty of time to grab the black duffel bag from the stage and, with a swing in my hips Lana Turner would've envied, sashay out of the theater.

"Damn!" Tino said. "Boy's got a dark side. Who'd have thought?"

"Did you really steal that money?" Jenna asked.

Cody didn't seem to know how to react to all the attention.

David was laughing. "No way that happened. But you've got a hell of an imagination. I bet I could make a movie out of that. We should film it when we're out of the Bend."

"I'll pass," Cody said.

We'd found a lake. A motherfucking lake with motherfucking fish in it. Didn't help that none of us had fishing poles. Didn't stop us from talking about all the fish we were going to catch, either. You want a good laugh? Go watch a bunch of city kids wading in a lake trying to snatch fish out of the water with their bare hands. That shit'll keep you laughing for days.

The others had gathered around to listen to Cody's story as we'd walked. Even Tino, though he'd tried to pretend he wasn't listening. I spent some time after Cody'd finished, trying to pick out the shards of truth from the fiction and wondering whether he'd told us what had really happened or only what he'd wished had happened. Sometimes it's easy to spot the truth in a story. Sometimes it's lit-up neon and you can't help but see it. Other times it's not as easy.

I was looking for a nice-size rock, thinking I could beat a fish with it, while Jaila sat by herself sharpening a stick against the side of a boulder. David kept circling her, his orbit decaying until she finally said without looking up, "What?"

"Do you believe in ghosts?"

"I'm kind of busy here, David," she said.

"I know, but still. Do you think they're real?"

"Maybe," she said.

"I saw a ghost once—"

Jaila stood, holding her stick like a spear. "That's great and all, but I'm hungry, so if you'll excuse me."

Turned out, Jaila had the right idea. It took her a solid hour, but she finally managed to spear a fish. It didn't take long for the others to sharpen their own sticks, strip to their underthings, and start making hilarious attempts to spear fish of their own.

Might as well get this out of the way. You're thinking it's weird that our little group was a mix of boys and girls, right? Figure it's strange that Doug and the other camp leaders didn't worry about us having mad orgies or some shit. It wasn't like that, though. Despite the garbage that movies and TV shows try to fill our heads with, boys and girls are completely capable of spending time together without trying to get in each other's pants. The only sex crazed boy in our group was David, and he was too scared of the girls to try anything. Any one of them could have easily knocked him on his ass if he'd gotten inappropriate. And the rest of us would have kicked the shit out of him while he was down.

Plus, there's nothing hot about being dirty and sweaty and hungry. And after you've seen someone take a shit in the woods, all thoughts of sex nope the fuck right out of your brain.

Once we'd caught our fish—three total to split between us—we had to figure out what to do with our freshly dead food. Jaila knew how to clean them, but she didn't have a knife. Luckily, Tino did.

"Where'd you get that?" Georgia asked as she slipped back into her uniform.

"Mind your own fucking business," he said.

Cody stood beside Georgia, clenching his fists. I kept waiting for that boy to pop. Figured it was coming sooner or later, but Jackie snatched the knife from Tino's hand before he could stop her, and gave him a shove back. She handed it to Jaila, who set about gutting our fish.

The sun was starting to sink to the west, but we still had a few hours of sunlight left, and even though we were hungry, Jaila said, and most everyone agreed, that we should keep walking until dark before trying to set up a camp and cook.

"Who the fuck does she think she is?" Tino was saying to David. I'd fallen back to listen to him complain.

"Do you know how to clean fish?" David asked.

"Not the point."

"It's kind of the point."

"Jaila's nothing special," Tino went on. "She probably doesn't even know where we're going."

"I don't know," Cody said, wandering toward them. "I'd put my money on her getting us back to camp."

Tino rolled his eyes. "You didn't steal any cash. A fucking wuss like you? Probably the only part of that story that's true is the part where you got humiliated."

"You don't know anything!" Cody stomped ahead to where Georgia was walking with Jenna.

David was having trouble breathing because of the pace we'd set, and he constantly touched his pocket where his inhaler was, but he hadn't used it in hours. "I got a true story. This one time—"

"Save it for your shrink, perv," Tino said, and moved away, leaving David to bring up the rear alone.

66

We walked until the sun was starting to set, and then found a clearing surrounded by trees to make camp. Tino was barking orders, but I ignored him and wandered out to find wood with Georgia and Cody.

"You should tell it," Cody was saying.

Georgia shook her head and glanced back at me. I didn't say anything, but I got the feeling she didn't like me much. Or maybe she liked me a little and *that* was why she didn't like me.

"It's a good story," he said. "And I bet it would scare Tino so bad he wouldn't sleep until we got back to camp."

"Don't let what he said bother you, Cody." Georgia touched his arm lightly, and he drew back.

"I just don't understand why he's got to be so mean."

"He's scared," she said. "Like we all are. And we all deal with fear in different ways." Georgia gave me another look and lowered her voice.

I went off on my own, keeping Cody and Georgia in view but getting far enough away that they could talk without me hearing. When I got back to camp, Lucinda was standing on one side of the fire pit someone had built, while Tino stood on the other side, Jackie and Jaila holding his arms, and blood was running down his nose.

"You bitch!" he yelled.

"You don't scare me, you limp-dick psycho," she said. "If you knew the reason I was really here, you'd—"

"Laugh?" Tino said. "Probably. Because you're a phony." He looked around the camp. "You're all phonies."

Sunday stepped forward to try to calm the situation while Jenna sat by the fire pit, staring into the empty space, like she was trying to will the flames to life with her mind. But things were getting deliciously out of hand.

"Why do you hate men so much?" I asked Lucinda. "I mean, that's what Tino said, anyway."

"I didn't—"

But Lucinda was already moving toward Tino again, and David and Sunday had to hold her back.

"Do you guys want to hear a ghost story?"

Georgia stood off to the side with Cody, but her voice was loud and carried through the campsite. There was something commanding about it that made the others stop.

"I mean, it's not *really* a ghost story. It's something that happened when I was a kid at summer camp. But I'm pretty sure it wouldn't have happened the way it did if it hadn't been for the ghost stories."

"I want to hear it," Sunday said. "I mean, as long as it's not *too* scary."

"You calm?" Jackie asked Tino.

"Just keep that girl away from me," he said, motioning at Lucinda with his chin.

I was kind of hoping for a real fight. My money would have been on Lucinda kicking Tino's ass all the way back to the Bend. But everyone settled around the fire while Jenna worked to get it started and Jaila unwrapped the fish so we could finally get some food in us.

Georgia sat down last.

"Okay, so this happened the summer before I was in sixth grade," she said. "When I was at an all-girls camp. And none of it was my fault."

"LOOK DOWN"

by Robin Talley

WE WERE ALL OBSESSED with ghost stories that summer.

It was the August before sixth grade. My mom wanted to get rid of me—my mom always wanted to get rid of me for one reason or another—so I was stuck going to the same dumb all-girls mountain camp I'd gone to the August before and the August before that.

But this time I didn't really mind. In fact, that summer, camp actually turned out to be pretty awesome.

Up until all the creepy stuff started happening, anyway.

The awesome parts were mostly because of Hailey. She was my best friend that summer, and she told the freakiest ghost stories of anyone.

The others thought so too. Hailey and I shared a tiny wooden cabin that year with six other girls. Every night, as soon as we were tucked into our bunk beds, someone would turn out the overhead lights and put a flashlight in the middle of the floor, pointing at the ceiling so the room would get all shadowy. Then we'd take turns try-ing to outscare each other.

Most of the stories the girls told weren't all *that* creepy, really. They were the kind you hear everywhere. Guys with hooks for hands who hide in the backseat of your car and try to kill you as soon as it gets dark. Babysitters who get creepy phone calls that turn out to be coming from inside the house. Med students who drug you at a party, then cut out your kidneys and leave you in a bathtub full of ice with a note to call 9-1-1 if you want to live. You know, that kind of thing.

In our cabin on the mountain, with the lights out, though, the stories still *felt* scary, even if you'd heard them before. The camp was basically in the middle of nowhere, and—actually, that camp looked a lot like where we are right now, come to think of it. Weird. I hadn't noticed that before.

But anyway, it can get really, really dark up on the mountain at night, and when there's no one else around . . . Well, it's easy to get caught up in that kind of stuff. You know how it is—you hear a story, and even though you know it can't possibly be true, it still sticks in your head. And then later, when you're out in the dark, and a breeze goes by and you feel that sudden chill on the back of your neck . . . At times like that, even the stuff that you know *can't* be true still feels like it *could* be, somehow.

I never let on when I got freaked out, though. Everyone at camp thought I was impossible to scare, and that was how I wanted it.

I told the goat-man story on our first night there. The goat-man was always my favorite. It was supposed to be a true story—I'd heard it from a counselor a couple of years earlier—but it was obviously impossible. But like all the best ghost stories, it *felt* real when you thought about it later. Even though you knew better.

Back in the 1920s, the story went, the mountain where our

camp was built had been cleared for farmland, and there was this one weird farmer who owned the biggest chunk of it. All the other farmers who lived on the mountain hated him because he was more successful than they were. His harvests were always huge, even when the weather sucked and no one else could grow a thing.

He was getting rich from the land, and the other farmers wanted to know his secret. So one Saturday, two of the neighbors snuck up onto his land and hid all day to watch him work.

They figured they'd see him doing something illegal they could report him for, or at least using some secret farming techniques they could copy. They watched him from sunrise to sundown, but they didn't see anything unusual. He was just planting and harvesting, the same way the rest of them did.

By the time it got dark, the farmer had stopped working for the day, and the two neighbors were ready to give up and go home. As they were creeping back over the property line, though, they heard a strange sound, like someone screaming. It was coming from the barn.

They rushed back across the farm and into the building, thinking someone must be in terrible danger—and saw the farmer holding a bloody ax, with a decapitated goat lying on the ground in front of him. On the wall of the barn, in huge red letters, the words "HAIL SATAN" were written in thick, dark blood.

Well, the two neighbors turned and ran as fast as they could. They made it home safely, and the next day they told everyone in town to watch out for the creepy, Satan-worshipping farmer.

After that the farmer couldn't sell his crops to anyone. His harvests were just as big as they'd ever been, but the whole town knew it was because he'd cut a deal with the devil, and they didn't want to eat food the devil had paid for.

No one really saw the farmer after that. He stopped leaving his land after a while, and then at some point, so much time had passed that everyone assumed he'd died.

He didn't have any children, so there was no one to inherit the farm. Years later, it was turned into a camp. Workers tore down the farmer's house and barn and built new lodges and cabins, and in between them, the scrub and trees grew back until the mountain was covered in forests again. You couldn't tell it had ever been a farm at all.

But every Saturday night, if you wandered deep enough into the woods, you could hear a long, loud scraping sound out where the barn used to be. And if the moon were high enough, you'd see a half man, half goat walking down the trail, dragging a bloody ax behind him.

That was how the story ended. After I was done telling it, I'd pause for a second, so the room was totally silent. Then I made a high-pitched goat-bleating sound. You could tell who was cool and who was a wuss by whether they laughed or shrieked.

Up until that August, the girls I'd shared a cabin with had always said my goat-man story was the scariest they'd ever heard. But everything changed that summer. All because of Hailey.

Hailey loved telling ghost stories too. But the stories she told weren't ridiculous like the ones about hook-hands and babysitters, or bizarre like my story about the goat-man. That was because Hailey's stories really *were* true. She'd heard them from her grandmother, and they were nothing like our stupid made-up kids' stories.

Plus, it was impossible not to believe what Hailey said. She was one of those people. You could tell just from how she talked—she was so warm, so open, so friendly—that she'd never lied about anything in her entire life.

From the moment we met, I trusted her completely. I looked right into her eyes, and she looked into mine, and— Do you know what it's like when you meet someone and you just *get* each other right away? When they always know what you're thinking, without you having to say a word? When you know it's safe to tell them all your secrets because they're going to tell you all of theirs, too?

That's how things were with Hailey, from the very beginning. I'd never felt it that strongly with anyone before.

That summer, the two of us were together pretty much all the time. We didn't really hang out with anyone else, at least not during the day. The other girls in our cabin were nice and everything, but they were a little, well . . . They just weren't as mature as Hailey and me.

Her grandmother's stories, though. I'm not easy to scare, but the stories Hailey told . . . Well, they made me nervous sometimes.

Because Hailey's stories were about ghosts. *Real* ghosts. The kind that hid in dark places and made the whole room turn ice cold. Who could get inside your head and make you see stuff that wasn't really there.

Hailey's stories weren't the kind that made you jump and squeal. They were the kind that clung to your mind all night, even after the flashlight had gone out and you were shivering in your sleeping bag in the quiet darkness.

Her stories didn't let go of you, not even when you fell asleep. They slipped into your dreams instead. The night after one of Hailey's stories, you always knew there would be at least one girl crying in her bunk after she thought the rest of us had gone to sleep.

She never got scared herself, though. Not Hailey. She told them all in this low, even voice. You could just tell there was nothing in the whole world that could ever scare her.

Naturally, I didn't want her to know any of them ever scared *me*. Everyone at camp knew I was impossible to scare. Plus, I guess I just liked her a lot. I wanted her to think I was cool and sophisticated and all that.

You know how it is when you're in middle school. All I could think about was making sure Hailey never found out I'd gotten scared. One night, hours after we'd finally finished telling stories, I woke up while it was still dark out because I had to pee. The bathrooms were up on a hill overlooking the campsite, and to get there, you had to leave the cabins and follow a path down through the woods, past the main lodge house, and up the hill where the trees were super old and thick.

The rule was that if you left the cabin at night, you had to take someone with you. So I woke up Hailey, and we put on our shoes and got our flashlights.

Everything was totally normal at first. Usually, we would've joked around while we walked, giggling about the other girls in our cabin who'd gotten scared listening to that night's stories. But Hailey was still really sleepy and didn't seem to feel like talking, so we were quiet as we followed the path past the lodge house and up the hill. We could hear crickets and birds and stuff. Nothing unusual.

It was pretty out, and I remember looking around that night more than I had before. The path to the bathrooms had basically been cut into the side of the mountain, so the drop-off was steep—that's why we weren't allowed to go up there alone in the dark. Sometimes it could be hard to tell where the path ended and the drop-off began, but that night there was a little moonlight, so we could see down past the edge of the path and into the ravine below.

The little valley was thick with leaves. I remember thinking that it didn't look like it would even hurt that much if you fell. The leaves would cushion you. It might actually be kind of fun. Tumbling down with a nice, soft landing.

But Hailey wasn't paying attention to the scenery the way I was. Instead, she just trudged along half asleep next to me in her frilly pink pajamas and sneakers, yawning the whole way. Once, when we were almost at the top, I even had to grab her arm to keep her from tripping over a tree root in the dark. She was that out of it. I must have been out of it too because I forgot to let go of her arm until we reached the bathroom door.

There was nothing out of the ordinary about that night, is what I'm saying. Even the story Hailey had told before we'd gone to sleep hadn't been as scary as usual. It hadn't even really been a story—just something her grandmother used to talk about from time to time.

Hailey's grandmother, it turned out, always said that on the day you were born, the Spirit of Death wrote a line in its book. It marked down the date of your birth, and the date of your death, too. Apparently, the Spirit already knew when you'd die, how you'd die—all of it.

When your deathday came around, you could try to outrun the

Spirit. You could try to hide from it. You could even try to trick it if you wanted to.

But none of that would matter in the end. Because you were already in the book. The most you could do was make the Spirit of Death angry. And if you made it angry enough, it might decide to take vengeance on you. You could wind up suffering more, and the Spirit might even decide to take someone you cared about ahead of their time.

The moral of the story was: you shouldn't try to cheat the Spirit of Death. Unless you were superdumb. Because the Spirit could be anywhere—it was invisible, obviously—and it didn't care about *you*, not even a little bit. All it cared about was getting its due.

Like I said—not a particularly scary story. It was hard to get worked up about a spirit you couldn't even see. The satanic goat-man was totally fake, but even he was freakier than some invisible Spirit of Death.

But anyway, that night, we finished in the bathroom and then turned around to come back down the hill. Everything still seemed totally ordinary, until we were halfway to the bottom. That was when the sounds started coming.

I stopped walking.

"Did you hear that?" I asked Hailey.

"Hear what?" Her eyes were alert suddenly. She'd stopped yawning.

The mountain around us was completely silent. Until the sound came again.

It was a voice. A whisper. But it didn't sound like a person talking.

It was what you might've expected to hear if the wind could whisper, or the trees could. As if the whole *forest* was whispering.

I couldn't make out the words. Just a low, uneven sound. An empty hiss.

It was coming from just beyond my right shoulder. Even though there was no one on the hill but me and Hailey.

"Who's doing that?" I spun around. Suddenly, Hailey's story flashed through my mind. The Spirit of Death.

"Georgia, what's going on?" Hailey shone her flashlight behind me, down the side of the hill, but there was nothing but trees and dirt and darkness. She stepped closer to the edge, pointing her light down at the fallen leaves. "What is it?"

The whispers came again, right up against my ear. Finally, I could make out two words in all the hissing.

"Go. Away."

I screamed, jerked Hailey back by her shoulder, and grabbed her hand, dragging her after me down the hill. She resisted, and I pulled again, tugging so hard she squealed in pain. She wrenched her arm away, but she came with me, and that was what mattered.

"What's going on?" Hailey's breath was coming fast, her voice pitched higher than I'd ever heard it. "Georgia, what's happening?"

"We have to get away from the hill." I didn't even know what I was saying.

"What is it?" We'd made it to the bottom of the slope. Hailey stopped running. She was holding her arm out of my reach. "Did you get scared?"

"What?" That was when I remembered Hailey thought I was as cool as she was. As far as she knew, I didn't get scared easily, like those crying girls in our cabin. "I mean, no. It was just—"

"Who is that?" A flashlight beam shone in my face. I wanted

77

to cry out, but I resisted, blocking the light with my hand instead. "Georgia? And Hailey? Are you hurt? What are you doing out of your cabin?"

It was Jenn and Vicky, our counselors. They were both in high school, and they slept in the lodge house at the bottom of the hill. My screaming must've woken them up.

"No, we're not hurt." Hailey stepped away from me. Now that the counselors were there, she'd stopped looking anxious. She flipped her hair back over her shoulder and pointed at me. "We were coming back from the bathroom, but then Georgia got scared of the dark."

"I did not!" I couldn't believe she'd said that. Hadn't she heard the same sounds I did?

"Was that you screaming, Georgia?" Jenn lowered the flashlight beam, but she frowned and crossed her arms over her chest.

"No."

"Yeah it was." Hailey jerked her chin toward me.

By then I couldn't hear the whispering anymore, and I was starting to feel kind of dumb. I didn't want to admit to these older girls that I'd heard something in the woods. And I hated the idea that Hailey thought I'd been scared of something stupid. So when Jenn and Vicky tried to ask me more about what had happened, I just shrugged and said I didn't know.

They gave us a lecture, because it was against the rules to be noisy at night. We tried to tell them we hadn't been doing anything wrong, but they didn't believe us. Hailey threatened to call her mom—her mom always got her out of punishments at school—but our phones had been collected the first day of camp and locked away, only to be used if there was a real emergency.

So Vicky said Hailey and I would have to do clean-up duty the next day for lunch *and* dinner. No one ever wanted clean-up duty because you had to scrub out all the pots and pans. The water in the sinks was smelly, and it made *you* all smelly, too. And we were only allowed to take showers first thing in the morning.

Hailey was pretty mad at me for that. Even though I tried to tell her it wasn't my fault. I hadn't made anything up. I really *did* hear that . . . whatever it was.

The next day was miserable.

I'd thought maybe Hailey and I would talk and joke around during clean-up duty. That maybe it would even be fun to have some time to hang out, just the two of us.

Instead, she wouldn't even look at me. And of course we got all gross, just like we'd known we would.

By the time we got back to our cabin that night, I just wanted to sleep. But everyone else, Hailey included, wanted to stay up late telling ghost stories *again*. I wasn't in the mood to tell one that night, not after what had happened, so I said I was too tired.

After everyone else had told theirs—the usual stuff about disappearing hitchhikers and escaped prisoners who stalked couples making out in parked cars and whatnot—Hailey started talking in that hushed, steady voice of hers.

"I realized I forgot to tell you all the most important part of my last story," she began.

"Your grandmother's story, you mean?" asked Anna. She slept in the bottom bunk under Hailey's, and she was one of the youngest in our cabin. She was also one of the girls who tended to fall asleep crying after Hailey told her stories. "About the Spirit of Death?"

"Yeah." Hailey shifted on her bunk. "Right. My grandmother. I forgot to tell you everything last night."

"What did you leave out?" Sydney asked from the bunk under mine. Hailey and I had both claimed the top bunks near the door on move-in day. They were the two best spots in the whole cabin. Plus, this way we could roll our eyes at each other when one of the other girls was being annoying.

"I already told you it's impossible to see the Spirit of Death." Hailey's voice had lowered all the way into its spooky storytelling mode. "But I forgot the end of the story. I should've mentioned that, thanks to the Spirit, there are some people—but only a very few—who *do* see things sometimes, or hear them. When they're about to die."

The skin on the back of my neck prickled.

"It's very, very rare," Hailey went on, speaking into the silence that had fallen over the rest of us. "It's only people the Spirit has specially marked. You see, most people's deaths are straightforward—they die of old age or illness or car crashes or whatever. But there are also a few people the Spirit has selected to die of a different cause. They're the people who die of madness."

It's just a story, I told myself. *No different from the one about the stupid goat-man.*

But as Hailey kept talking, her voice felt like icy fingers creeping down my spine.

"Even the mad—or the soon to be mad—can't see, or hear, the Spirit itself," she went on. "But the Spirit is tricky. It can make you hear things no one else can. Things that aren't really there. That's the first step. Once a person has heard the phantom sounds, their death is only days away, at most. In fact, they might only have hours left to live."

How many hours had passed since I'd heard the whispers? Twenty, maybe? Twenty-one?

"For the rest of their time on Earth, the Spirit will torment them." Hailey's voice had sunk so low we all had to strain to hear. "That's how the madness grows. The Spirit attacks their senses, one by one, until finally, they're eager for death. For anything to put an end to their misery."

Her voice faded into silence.

No one else seemed to have anything more to say after that. We didn't even dare to shuffle in our sleeping bags.

Quiet filled the room after that.

I lost track of time in the hushed cabin. My eyelids had begun to grow heavy.

How long had it been since Hailey had stopped talking? Ten minutes? An hour?

Had she gone to sleep? Had the others?

It didn't matter how many times I told myself not to worry. Those icy fingers on my back never loosened their grip, even as my consciousness faded into sleep.

Then I heard something.

It wasn't words, not at first. Just a low, murmuring sound. Then a voice.

"Do you hear it?"

But it didn't sound like the voice that had hissed at me the night before on the hill. This voice was fuller. Human.

A girl shrieked. Laughter erupted somewhere in the cabin.

A flashlight beam darted around the room like a laser, coming from Hailey's bunk. Then she pointed it underneath her to show Anna sitting up in her sleeping bag, her hand over her face. She was the one who'd shrieked.

Hailey was laughing. I forced myself to join in. A few others did too.

"You seriously bought that, Anna?" Hailey cleared her throat, then whispered, in the exact voice she'd used before. *"Do you hear it now?"*

After that, we were all laughing. Everyone except Anna. She buried her face in her sleeping bag while the rest of us howled.

Laughing felt wonderful. Laughing made the icy fingers release their grip on my spine.

It really was just a story.

I exhaled slowly between giggles. Hailey didn't know I'd been scared. Everything was going to be all right.

Soon, she and I would be back to normal. Best friends again.

I'd missed her so much that day. It hadn't been until then that I realized just how much I needed Hailey.

I'd never really *needed* anyone before. Not like that.

But I had trouble falling asleep after everything that had happened. I kept starting to drift off, then startling awake, thinking I heard the whispers again. The ones I'd heard on the hill mixed in with my memory of Hailey's lilting, mocking voice until I couldn't remember which was which anymore.

Then there was a hand on my shoulder, shaking me.

I struggled to pry my eyes open. The cabin was completely dark. Every flashlight was out.

It took me a minute to make sense of what I was seeing. Then I realized it was Hailey's face, her features blurry in the dark.

"I have to pee," she whispered. It sounded just like when she'd whispered before.

Do you hear it?

I tried to twist my shoulder out of her grip, but she wouldn't let go.

"You have to come with me." She squeezed harder. "It's only fair, Georgia."

The last thing I wanted to do was leave that cabin and go out into the darkness. But I didn't want Hailey to know I was scared, either.

So I nodded and sat up. Hailey slipped down the ladder, and I grabbed my flashlight from the foot of my bunk and followed her down.

We put on our sneakers and crept outside to the path, where the moon shone bright above us. By the time we'd made it to the lodge house, I was starting to feel dumb.

There was no reason to be scared. Everything outside was totally normal.

I probably hadn't even heard anything the night before on the hill. I'd just let all those stupid ghost stories get to me. What a loser.

We got up to the bathroom, and everything was still perfectly ordinary. When we were coming back down the hill afterward, we passed the place where I'd thought I heard whispering the night before. This time, of course, nothing happened.

By that point I was feeling *really* dumb.

When we were halfway to the bottom, near the little shelter with the outdoor sinks, I was trying to think of how to apologize to Hailey for getting us in trouble over nothing when I saw something move behind the trees.

At first I thought it was Jenn and Vicky coming to yell at us again, even though we really weren't breaking any rules. But I didn't see either of the counselors. Just their shadows, moving in the middle of a grove of trees at the bottom of the ravine.

Or . . . they *looked* like shadows. At first, anyway.

They were these tall dark shapes, with sharp edges. The closer we got, the larger they loomed in the trees. Until they were far over our heads—way too tall to be a person's shadow.

I stopped walking. So did Hailey. She was staring into the trees too.

"Do you see that?" I whispered.

Hailey didn't answer. Her face had gone still and pale.

That's when I remembered the Spirit of Death.

It would make you hear, or see, things that weren't there. Things that would drive you mad.

I shivered, but then I shook my shoulders back. The Spirit of Death was just a story. This was real life.

I fought past my fear and called out. "Jenn? Vicky?"

No one answered. But the shadows moved.

That's when I knew.

I wasn't making it up in my head this time. Something—something *big*—was moving in the dark, right behind the trees.

I was so scared I forgot to be embarrassed.

I couldn't even scream. All I could do was step backward and grab Hailey's arm.

84

Then, suddenly, I felt cold. I was trembling all over, despite the sweltering August heat.

"What *is* that?" Hailey whispered. I didn't know if she meant the temperature drop or the dark thing behind the trees. But then it didn't matter because the shadow moved again.

It was coming toward us. I stepped forward, in front of Hailey, to get a better look.

The shadow was growing taller. So tall it almost reached the tops of the trees.

Then the whispers returned.

Move. Go. Go!

I screamed then. I screamed louder than I'd ever screamed in my life.

"What is it? Georgia, Georgia, what *is* it?" Hailey was practically shrieking.

Then Jenn and Vicky were running up to us again. And when I looked back, the shadow was gone.

This time I didn't hold back. I told them exactly what I'd seen. Jenn and Vicky stared at me like I had three heads.

Then Hailey rolled her eyes. And suddenly, I wanted to cry.

I'd been sure she'd seen the shapes moving too. But she was acting like I was just as dumb and boring as the other girls in our cabin. The ones who cried over a stupid story.

What if I'd imagined her reaction up on the hill? What if I'd imagined *everything*?

What if I really *was* going mad?

It was clear that Jenn and Vicky didn't believe me. Even so, they got their flashlights and searched the place in the trees where I'd seen the shadow. Of course, nothing was there. I tried to explain that the thing had gone away before they'd found us, but they only sighed.

"Look," Jenn said, "for tonight, just go back to bed. But we can't have this keep happening, so starting tomorrow, both of you will have to sleep down here in the lodge house where we can keep an eye on you."

Hailey basically wanted to kill me after that. The whole point of camp was having fun in the cabins with your friends at night. Sleeping in the lodge house with the counselors was like being grounded.

Hailey didn't speak to me for the rest of the night. Or all through the next day, either.

I had no choice but to eat breakfast, lunch, and dinner at the corner of a table by myself while Hailey sat with Anna and Sydney and the other girls from our cabin. They spent every meal leaning in close together, whispering and laughing. Every so often one of them would look up at me, then look away with a muffled giggle.

It was the worst day of camp so far. Maybe the worst day of my entire life.

Hailey had been everything to me. It had been the two of us, together, against the whole world. Now she was treating me like I was no better than any of the others.

But we were still stuck sleeping in the lodge together that night. Somehow, I thought, this *had* to get better. Maybe, before we went to sleep, I could explain what had happened, and Hailey would understand. Maybe things between us could go back to the way they'd been.

"This is so stupid," Hailey whispered when we were setting up our sleeping bags. The lodge house was where our whole group of campers gathered to do crafts and stuff, but at nighttime it was just a big, open room lined with tables and benches. Jenn and Vicky slept on the floor near the back door, so Hailey and I had put our stuff as far from them as we could get, near the front. "If either of us has to go to the bathroom tonight, we should just pee in our sleeping bags. It'd be better than going out *there* again."

I agreed. I'd already made sure to go to the bathroom before bed that night, and Hailey had too. Going before lights-out was fine—there were always tons of other girls going up and down the hill at the same time—but there was no way I was going up there again before dawn.

It turned out we couldn't really talk after that, though. Not without Jenn and Vicky hearing. So I climbed silently into my sleeping bag, trying not to let my disappointment show.

It took me forever to fall asleep that night. In our cabin you could always hear people rustling in their sleeping bags, or talking in the other cabins near ours. Down in the lodge, though, it was totally quiet. There wasn't a single sound except the crickets outside and Hailey breathing softly next to me. I couldn't even hear Jenn and Vicky.

"Are you awake?" Hailey whispered all at once. Her lips were so close to my ear I nearly jumped.

"Yes," I squeaked.

She laughed softly. "Sorry. Didn't mean to scare you."

"You didn't scare me."

She laughed again. "I just wanted to see if you'd like to hear the rest of the story. There's only a little more."

I rolled over to muffle my voice. The only way we could talk without Jenn and Vicky hearing us was to put our faces right next to each other, our lips practically touching. "You said the story was over."

"I thought it was, but then I remembered there was something more. The other girls in the cabin don't need to hear this part, though. Just you."

I looked away. I refused to let her see me shiver. "Whatever."

"What? You don't want to know?"

I shrugged. She laughed again, then started to turn her back to me.

"Wait." I gave up. Tears pricked at my eyes. "What is it?"

She laughed again and rolled her face back to mine. "Last night, when we were coming down that hill, for one second I really did think I saw something there in the trees. But then I realized it was just moonlight. You were so scared you almost made me get nervous too! But the thing is"—Hailey lowered her voice, her tone growing serious—"it made me realize something else, too. I'm sorry, Georgia. Because I could tell, from the way you were looking down, that you really *did* see something. Or you thought you did, at least. The Spirit, Georgia—the Spirit's marked you. You're destined to die of madness."

I blinked, trying to keep back the tears, but they fell anyway.

Hailey shrugged in her sleeping bag. She didn't look away, even though she must've seen me crying.

"I mean, it's not like there's anything you can do about it," she whispered. "I just wanted to tell you so you knew what to expect. Sorry. Maybe you'll live long enough to go home and see your family one last time after camp."

She rolled back over. She didn't seem especially sorry.

After that, there was no way I was going to sleep.

I didn't *believe* Hailey, exactly. The whole story about the Spirit of Death . . . It all sounded like something out of a cheesy horror movie.

But what I'd heard—and seen—on the hill wasn't cheesy at all.

Plus, even though I knew better . . . I couldn't shake the idea that I'd been marked.

The whispering voice had kept telling me to *go*. To leave that hill. What if something bad really *was* going to happen to me there?

And if there hadn't really been a voice—if I really had imagined everything, two nights in a row—did that mean I *was* going mad? With or without help from any spirits?

All I remember from the first part of that night was staring at the dark ceiling of the lodge house, freaking out and crying. I definitely don't remember falling asleep. But I guess I did. Because the next thing I remember, I groggily opened my eyes to a pitch-black room and realized I couldn't hear Hailey's soft breathing anymore. She must've gone to the bathroom after all.

The lodge house was probably two stories high with the way the roof sloped, but there was only one light in the whole place, and it was out. Being in there in the middle of the night, with no one around, was like being in a huge, empty cave.

But there wasn't *no one* around. Jenn and Vicky were in their sleeping bags down on the far end of the room.

I felt stupid for being afraid, but I wanted to see the counselors. Just so I'd know I wasn't all alone. So I got out of my sleeping bag and made my way to the back of the room, feeling my way along by gripping the edges of the long tables. I waited for my eyes to adjust to the light, but the pure black emptiness in that room never faded.

"Jenn?" I whispered as I got closer. "Vicky?" But I was so quiet they probably couldn't hear me.

Finally, I felt my toe hit the edge of a sleeping bag, and I relaxed. I bent down to shake the counselor's shoulder.

But when I reached down into the darkness there was nothing under my hand but a flat, empty sleeping bag, and the hard floor below.

I reached over to the next sleeping bag. It was empty too.

"Vicky?" I spoke out loud this time. No one answered. "Jenn? Hailey?"

There was no sound at all. Even the crickets had shut up.

By then I was so scared I could barely think. I knew the back door was nearby, and all I wanted was to get outside, where at least there would be light from the moon. I felt around for the door and started to panic when all I felt was empty air. Finally, I reached the wall and ran my hands along the rough wood until at last I reached the door. I yanked on the handle and swung it wide open.

A rush of air hit my face, and I started to relax. But there was only more blackness. If the moon was out, it was hidden behind the thick trees.

I knew the cabins were nearby, but I couldn't seem them. Just the rough wood of the wall behind me, the dim outlines of tree trunks, and the dirt path that wound away from the lodge house and up the hill toward the cabins. I was desperate to see someone, *anyone*, so I started creeping slowly down the path.

"Hey!" a voice shouted.

I jumped so hard I almost screamed. Then a hand clapped over my mouth, and I really *did* scream—but no sound came out.

"Relax, weirdo." It was Hailey. She took her hand off my mouth.

I tried to breathe, but my throat felt frozen. "Where are Jenn and Vicky?"

I shook my head. My vocal cords were starting to function again. "I don't know. Did you come out to look for them?"

"Yeah." Hailey shifted, like maybe that hadn't really been what she was doing out here, but the truth was, I didn't care. I was just so happy to see her. "Do you think they went up to the bathrooms?"

"Probably." I didn't want to go that way again. I kept following the path to the cabins. Hailey walked with me. "What if they—"

That was when the whispering started again.

It was so close this time. It was inside my ears. Inside my head. And this time I could hear it more clearly than ever.

Go away! You don't belong here!

I swallowed my scream.

"Did you just—" Hailey started to say as we turned past the grove of trees.

And saw Jenn and Vicky.

They were on the ground near the woodpile, with Jenn lying on top of Vicky. They were kissing. Vicky had her hand up Jenn's shirt.

I screamed for real that time.

Hailey saw them too, but she didn't scream. At first she just stared while Jenn and Vicky leaped up and straightened out their clothes. Then she turned and ran back into the lodge house.

Jenn and Vicky were both talking at once, tripping over their words, trying to ask me what I'd seen and if I was going to tell anyone. I didn't really care about that, though. I was just glad that now, I knew what all those strange whispers had been, and the shadows in the trees.

I guess we forgot about Hailey in the awkwardness of the

moment, until a couple of minutes later when she came out of the lodge house with her phone. Our phones were all supposed to be hidden somewhere, but Hailey must've figured out where they were because she was already talking to her dad. Telling him he needed to come get her, because two of our counselors were sinners, and Hailey wasn't about to have sinners taking care of her.

Well, that was the end for Jenn and Vicky. Hailey's dad must've called someone else right away because it couldn't have been more than half an hour before the camp director rolled up in her car with a couple of other leaders.

They brought Jenn into the lodge house first. Vicky had to wait outside with Hailey and me. Vicky was crying by then, and I felt kind of bad for her, but Hailey stood as far away from us as she could, doing something on her phone.

"You should've just said for us to go away in your normal voice," I told Vicky because it was embarrassing just standing there, watching her cry. "We would've left you alone. It's not like we *wanted* to catch you."

"Yeah, right." Vicky sniffed and glared down the path at Hailey.

"Well, either way, you didn't have to whisper all creepily like that. You scared me. *That's* why I screamed that first night, you know. I didn't even see you guys then."

"What are you talking about?" Vicky scrubbed at her eyes. "All I knew was you two kept showing up, screaming like weirdos, every time we—"

"Vicky?" The camp director was on the back steps. One of the other leaders was getting into the car with Jenn. "Come inside. We're ready for you."

The other leader told Hailey and me to go to our regular cabin for the rest of the night, so I don't know exactly what happened to Jenn and Vicky after that. I only know they were both gone before we came down to brush our teeth that morning. Instead, there were two new counselors at the lodge, grown-ups who told us Jenn and Vicky had gotten sick and needed to go home early.

Well, Hailey wasn't about to let that story stand. Over breakfast, she told everyone what had really happened. She'd decided not to leave camp, since Jenn and Vicky were gone, but all through the day, she took every opportunity to tell the other girls how revolting it had been finding them the way we did.

Every time she told the story, it got worse. By the time dinner rolled around, I heard her whispering to someone that Jenn and Vicky had been totally naked when we caught them. And that they didn't stop, even after they saw us, until Hailey called the camp director. She even said Vicky had tried to grab her. Everyone was shocked, and they all kept saying how sorry they felt for Hailey and talking about how gross the whole story was.

That night, in our cabin, I tried to tell the other girls what Hailey said wasn't true, but that only made Hailey mad. So instead of telling ghost stories, she told everyone about how I'd been going outside and screaming every night because I was that scared of the stupid Spirit of Death, which she'd only made up in the first place.

Then she told them the reason I was defending Jenn and Vicky was because *I* was a lesbian too.

Which was just totally absurd. But that didn't matter. Now everyone in the cabin thought I was a big paranoid lesbian weirdo. They all kept whispering things I couldn't quite hear, then giggling when I looked their way.

It really sucked, to be honest. And the way Hailey looked at me after that sucked most of all. As if I was nothing. As if I'd been a complete waste of her time.

I didn't think I'd ever fall asleep that night. But I'd barely slept the night before, so I guess I nodded off eventually.

When I woke up it was still dark, and the girls were whispering at me again. That's what I remember the clearest now. Whispers and giggles. Then footsteps. A door opening and closing.

I was only half awake, but I'd already figured out what was happening. I'd been coming to camp for years.

The girls were playing a prank on me. They'd waited for me to fall asleep, and when I opened my eyes, they were going to jump out and try to scare me, or something dumb like that.

Well, I'd show them. I started to get up, ready to tell them they couldn't scare me.

But when I sat up and opened my eyes, the whispers and giggles were gone.

The cabin was empty. It was dark—not a single flashlight was on—but I could see the bunks around me.

No one was there. All the other sleeping bags were empty. It was totally silent, too.

I reached toward the foot of my bunk for my flashlight. It felt too light in my hand, though, and sure enough, nothing happened when I turned the switch. My cabinmates must have stolen the batteries on their way out.

What a boring prank this was. When I'd played tricks with my friends in other years, we'd always stayed in the cabin. That was the whole point of pranks—to laugh at the girl when she woke up and saw that we'd put her hand in a glass of water, or written on her fore-head with markers, or whatever.

I climbed down from my bunk and reached for the light switch by the door. But when I flipped it on, it was still just as dark in the cabin as ever.

That was weird. The light had worked the night before. The girls couldn't have climbed all the way up to the ceiling to mess with the lightbulb. It must have burned out by coincidence.

Whatever. Hailey and the other girls were probably hiding right outside the cabin, waiting to jump out at me when I went outside.

I opened the door and shouted, "You guys can cut it out! I'm not scared!"

But there was no sound in response.

There were no lights, either. No flashlight beams bouncing around. No lights from the other cabins or from the lodge house up the hill.

And there was no moon. Everything looked just as it had the night before. Dim and gray and empty.

"Hailey?" I shouted. No response. "Anna? Sydney?"

Still nothing.

But I'd just heard them leaving the cabin. They couldn't have gone far.

The hair on the back of my neck prickled. But that was stupid. There was nothing out here except girls playing a mean trick. The only scary things that had ever been at this camp were the lesbians by the woodpile, and they were long gone.

A breeze picked up and blew against my cheek. A warm summer breeze. At first.

But it kept blowing, and after a minute or two, I realized the air around me was growing cooler. Soon I was shivering again.

I didn't see how Hailey and the girls in the cabin could've done *that*.

"Hailey?" I said again. But I couldn't shout anymore. I could barely even get the word out.

That was when the whispering came back.

This time, there were no giggles. No furtive shushing.

This whisper sounded exactly as it had that first night. On the path down from the hill.

But this time, it didn't tell me to go away.

Georgia, the voice whispered. *Look down. Look down. Look down.*

The repetition went on and on and on. I shook my head and held my hands over my ears, but the whispering never stopped.

Look down. Look down. Look down.

It wasn't coming from just one side, the way it had before. These whispers were coming from all around me.

Look down. Look down. Look down.

I wanted to scream, but my throat was frozen. My whole body was immobile. I could only move my eyelids.

So I shut them. Maybe shutting my eyes would shut out everything else, too.

And it worked. It actually worked. With my eyes closed, I couldn't hear the whispers anymore.

The breeze had stopped, too. The cold had begun to let up. The goose bumps that had formed on my arms were fading.

It was over.

I tried to relax, to shake it off. I still couldn't move, but I was sure that when I could see again, the world would have gone back to normal.

I opened my eyes.

The first thing I saw was Hailey. She was standing right in front of me. So close our noses were almost touching.

I tried to gasp, to back up. But I couldn't.

She lifted her hands toward me. For a second I actually thought she was going to kiss me.

I didn't know what to think. My heart was racing. I was scared, but I was also . . . not.

Then she reached for me. And wrapped her hands around my throat.

She squeezed her fingers, closing in, choking me.

I couldn't breathe. I tried to claw at her hands, but I couldn't lift my arms.

I couldn't scream. I couldn't even close my eyes. But the world was turning black, anyway.

Hailey tipped her head backward, her eyes rolling up, her mouth opening wide. The blackness down her gaping throat was coming forward to swallow me whole.

She began to laugh. Huge, bellowing laughs, the sound rocking the earth under my feet. I was falling, falling—

My eyes flew open. It was still dark, but awareness flooded into my limbs.

I was gasping, reaching for my throat.

The hands were gone. I could breathe.

I didn't see Hailey anymore.

"She's awake!" someone hissed.

97

Something felt sticky on my fingers and my neck.

I was in my bunk bed, down inside my sleeping bag. That was why I couldn't see. I reached up, but I couldn't find the opening at the top of the sleeping bag.

A flashlight beam shone bright behind the dark fabric covering me. I reached up again to pull the bag down off my face, but I still couldn't get to the top. In the process, whatever was making my hands sticky got on my cheeks, and then my face was sticky too.

And all around me, everyone was laughing.

It had been a dream. The girls tiptoeing out, Hailey choking me in the dark . . . It was nothing but a stupid, pathetic nightmare. God, even my *dreams* were embarrassing now.

I reached up again. I still couldn't find the opening at the top of the sleeping bag.

Was there an opening at the top? Maybe I'd somehow flipped myself around backward. I tried to wriggle around so I was facing the other direction, but the bag was too narrow.

The laughs in the bunks around me grew louder. Bolder.

"Look at her!" someone whispered.

"Has she figured it out yet?"

"Shhh!"

My heart was racing even faster than it had in my dream. What the hell was going on? I reached up, yanking on the fabric of the bag, but it just came down harder on my head. The bag was hot and stuffy. It felt like I was running out of air.

The laughter in the room around me got louder, then louder still, as my breath started to come out in pants. I was trapped in here, in this dark, sticky place, and everyone else was just *laughing*, as if—

"Shhh!" one of the girls whispered, but she was still laughing. "The new counselors will come in here if we're too loud."

"Those old ladies? They wouldn't come out of the lodge even if we were down here killing her."

"Shhh!"

Then I understood what had happened. They'd tied my sleeping bag shut.

I reached up again, forcing myself to inhale the stale air, and found where fabric was bunched up. That was where the opening was supposed to be.

The girls must've waited for me to fall asleep and then tied it shut from the outside, with . . . what? A lanyard or something? It couldn't be very tight. I tried to work my hand up into the opening, but my fingers were sticky and slimy, and even smelled kind of *minty*. . . .

Toothpaste.

They'd filled up my sleeping bag with toothpaste. Then they'd pulled it up over my head and tied it shut.

My hands, my neck, my face. Everything was covered. The girls must have emptied out every tube they'd brought with them.

Gross. And stupid. So, so stupid.

I choked back a sob.

"I think she's trying to get out of it," one of the other girls whispered through the laughter.

"Shhh!"

My fingers finally squeezed through. A moment later I pushed my whole hand out. Then my other hand, until I could wrench it all the way open. The trickle of fresh air made the sticky wetness on my face itch.

But it was still air, glorious air. I jerked the fabric of the sleeping bag down until my head and shoulders were out.

All at once the flashlight beam was bright in my face, and the laughter in the cabin had crescendoed into howls. I reached up and realized the toothpaste was covering my hair too.

"Oh my God!" someone squealed. "It's like a scene out of a horror movie."

I turned my back on them, focusing every ounce of energy I had on *not* crying as their peals of laughter filled the room.

I'd been wrong about Hailey.

I'd thought she was the only one who really understood me. I'd thought I understood her, too. But she'd been lying to me the whole time.

Well, I couldn't let her think she'd gotten to me now.

"Shut up, Hailey," I yelled, still facing the wall.

"Hailey's not here," someone said with a giggle. The light was still shining right on me. I could see it out of the corner of my eye. "She went to get water."

"And missed the fun part," someone else said. More giggles.

I had to get out of there.

I unzipped my sleeping bag the rest of the way, smearing toothpaste over every inch of it that wasn't already covered. The others kept barking out laughter.

I reached for my flashlight, but it turned out someone really had taken my batteries. I pretended not to notice, left the flashlight where it was, and climbed down the ladder to the floor. My pajamas were so sticky I'd have to throw them out.

My hands shook as I pulled on my sneakers. I'd have to go to the sinks to clean up. Then maybe I could ask the new counselors to let me sleep in the lodge house for the rest of the night. Anything would be better than staying in here.

"Where's she going?" someone whispered, still giggling. I ignored them and opened the door.

Outside, it was warm. The moon shone overhead. Crickets chirped all around me.

Nightmares, kid pranks, random lesbians—it was time I grew up and stopped letting every little thing freak me out. The girls in my cabin were losers. I didn't care about any of them. Or what they thought of me.

Hailey, though. It was different with Hailey.

She wasn't just a loser. I *hated* her. I hated everything about her.

We'd been having the perfect summer. And then she'd ruined everything.

I trudged up the hill. The sinks were partway up the path to the bathroom just past the trees where I'd seen Jenn's and Vicky's enormous shadows the other night. As I passed the lodge house the moon must've gone behind a cloud or something because it got dimmer all of a sudden, and the crickets started getting quieter, too.

I ignored it all and kept walking. I was through worrying about dumb stuff like moonlight and weird sounds in the darkness.

I was almost at the sinks when I heard the whisper.

Look down, Georgia.

Great. The girls from my cabin had followed me outside. I must've heard them during my dream, too. Telling me to look down at my stupid toothpaste-covered sleeping bag.

"Quit it, you guys!" I turned around to look for them.

I didn't see any of the other girls, but I wasn't about to wait for them to jump out from wherever they were hiding. I bypassed the sinks and started up the only path that led away from there—the path up to the bathrooms.

Look down, Georgia! The voice was louder now. Not really a whisper anymore. *This time, you're too late.*

Too late? For what?

I whirled around. The girls had gotten so loud there was no way they could be hiding anymore.

But I didn't see them. I didn't see anyone.

The air around me was completely still. There wasn't even a breeze.

There was no moonlight above, either. Just a few pinpricks of stars.

What had the voice been talking about? What was I too late for?

And what did it mean, "*this time*"?

I'd climbed that hill night after night. And I'd heard something, or seen something, every time.

But I hadn't *done* anything. I'd only screamed and run, dragging Hailey with me.

Then the voice came back. Just like in my dream, it was coming from all around me, even though there was no one else on the hill.

Look down. Look down. Look down.

"For real!" I shouted. "Stop it! I'm not scared this time!"

Look down look down look down—

"*Stop it!*"

But I gave in. I looked down, into the ravine.

At first all I saw were tree trunks. And the big piles of fallen leaves that were always at the bottom.

Then I noticed something else. A strange shape in the leaves. It was a lighter color than the other piles.

I squinted in the faint starlight until I could tell the shape was pink.

The same shade of pink as Hailey's pajamas.

I tried to step back but stumbled, my sneaker catching on a rock. I fell backward, catching myself with my hands before my head could hit the ground.

I didn't want to look again. But the whispers were still coming.

You were too late this time, Georgia.

That first night. I'd pulled Hailey back from the edge of the ravine. She'd been sleepy, and not watching where she was going, and—

Georgia. Look down.

The voice wasn't coming from all around me anymore. It was coming from the ravine. Maybe it always had been.

It was so dark I could barely see anything.

I had to go down there. I had to look.

I scrambled down the slope. I wasn't being as careful as I should've, but my feet landed squarely on solid ground with every step.

It wasn't my time yet. The Spirit hadn't been coming for me after all.

It had been Hailey all along.

Look down, Georgia.

I reached the bottom of the hill and tore through the heaped piles of rotting leaves. Now that I was closer, there was no way to pretend it was only a trick of the light. There was definitely something on the ground.

Suddenly, it was right in front me. *She* was right in front of me.

It felt as if the earth was falling out from under my feet. As if I were sliding down the slope, too. As if I'd broken into a hundred pieces, and now I didn't know where they were supposed to go.

It was Hailey. It was definitely Hailey. But it wasn't the Hailey I knew.

This Hailey's eyes were black and empty. Her neck was bent at an angle like something out of a scary movie. Her body was limp, frozen in the leaves. I didn't have to check her pulse to know that the blood had stopped flowing through her veins.

She was dead. But I could've sworn her lips were moving.

She was whispering, still. Somehow. I could even hear the sound they formed.

Look down, Georgia. Look down. Look down. Look down.

"So you're into girls, huh?" Jackie said.

"What?" Georgia's eyes were just a little too wide, her movements a little too precise. "When did I say that?"

Jackie shrugged. "No judgment here. Just an observation."

None of our bellies were full. We'd each gotten some fish, which hadn't even tasted particularly good, but barely enough to take the edge off the hunger earned from a day spent hiking.

"Leave her alone," Jenna said. She was staring into the fire she'd built, though she didn't look proud of her creation the way any of the others might have.

"That was *not* a scary ghost story," David said. He'd settled in against a log he and Tino had dragged by the fire, his legs sprawled out in front of him.

"It was plenty scary," Jackie added, "but not because of the ghosts."

"How do you figure?" Lucinda asked.

Cody scooted closer to Georgia, who hadn't said anything since finishing her story. "Drop it, guys, all right?"

Jackie held up her hands. "I'm just saying the scary shit was how Hailey went all Westboro Baptist on the girls they caught sucking face."

Tino had calmed down a little, and Jaila had given him his knife back, which he was playing with. Opening and closing the blade, probably unaware he was doing it. "So what? Who gives a shit who's banging who?"

"Whom," Jaila said.

"What?"

"Who's banging whom."

Tino tensed. "I don't need a fucking grammar lesson."

Jaila shrugged.

"I'm not gay," Georgia said in a quiet voice.

David piped up. "It's cool if you are. I'm bi. This one time, my friends Ryan and Tony and I—"

"I'm not!" Georgia stood and stormed away from camp.

Cody moved to go after her, but Sunday waved him off. "Let me talk to her," she said. He nodded, and Sunday moved off into the woods to find Georgia.

"You think that girl Hailey really died?" Jenna asked when Sunday was gone. She was looking at Cody, but her question was for everyone.

Jaila was using her pack as a pillow and was stretched out near enough to the fire to keep warm but far enough away not to roast. The days might have been warm, but it had started to cool rapidly once the sun had set, and all we had were our shitty, thin sleeping bags. "Probably not," she said. "Sounds like Georgia wished Hailey had died, though."

"Great," Tino said. "So we've got a pyro, a liar or a thief—my money's on liar—a closeted lesbian with mean-girl issues, and I don't know *what* your problem is."

"I don't have one," Jaila said. "But *you* might if you don't shut your mouth."

"If y'all are going to fight," Jackie said, "I've got ten bucks on Jaila."

"I'll put twenty on that," Lucinda added.

Jenna let out a groan. "How about no one fights? Can we do that? Maybe? If I've got to be stuck in the woods with you people—"

"'You people'?" Jackie said. "And what's that supposed to mean? You think you're better than us?"

106

"I think that's exactly what she was implying," I said, slipping my voice into the fight without drawing attention to myself.

"You don't know anything about me," Jackie kept going. "Oh no, you like to set fires because you're just another entitled suburban girl who thinks she's got problems. Your problems don't mean shit out here."

Jaila sat up on one elbow, staring at each of us like she was the only adult in a room full of bratty children. "Everyone just calm down, all right?"

"I've got a story," David said. "A real ghost story, you know?"

Lucinda glared at him. "I swear to God if this is a sex story, I'm going to cut off your balls."

David could barely resist looking at his crotch. "Uh . . . it's a ghost story. Sort of. There's also cake."

"Quit telling you're going to tell it," Jackie said, "and just fucking tell it already."

"You know, a recent study showed that eighty-six percent of people admitted that they masturbate regularly, and fourteen percent of people lied about not masturbating. Everyone masturbates. I think the more interesting question is *why*? Let's see a show of hands, huh? How many of you masturbated this month? This week? *Today?* I'm the only one? Yeah, sure."

Lucinda growled low. David cleared his throat and said, "It's relevant! I swear."

"Get to the ghosts," Cody said.

"Yeah, okay," David said. "But the story starts with a video."

107

"BIG BROTHER, PART 1"
by E. C. Myers

YOU KNOW THAT "Invisible Hand" video that went viral a couple of years ago? Of course you do. Everyone's seen it. As of last month, the last time I had Internet access, it had over two-and-a-half billion views—almost as much as "Gangnam Style." I bet if it were shorter and had music, it would be number one. Missed opportunities. On the other hand, people have cut it down and remixed it with everything from the *Ghostbusters* theme (too obvious) to *Hamilton*'s "Satisfied" (strangely satisfying), and there's just no beating the original. Pun intended.

Okay, so if you haven't seen it, you've probably heard about it, unless you've been living under a rock, or living without Wi-Fi, which is the same thing. The original video's really long, about six hours— six hours, seven minutes, forty-two seconds to be exact. Sure, most viewers only watch a certain seventeen minutes near the beginning, but the length of the video helps make the case for its authenticity.

You really haven't seen it? Okay. The video shows a pretty average teenage girl's bedroom and a pretty average teenage girl sleeping in bed. The light's on, which, yeah, maybe seems weird. A lot of people have pointed to that as evidence that it's a hoax, but there's a reason for it, trust me. And she's sleeping on top of the covers with gym shorts and a tank top. There's a book next to her, but you can't quite make out what it is. It's *The Martian Chronicles*.

Yes, the book could explain why the light's on, if she fell asleep while reading it. But that's not knocking the book. I've read it; it's a good book. Sometimes even a good book will make you fall asleep if you're tired enough. If you've been staying up late, night after night. Trying to stay awake, night after night.

The picture quality's embarrassingly low, like it's been recorded through the webcam on a laptop. Exactly like that because it was.

You see her sleeping for a few minutes, and it's around then that people start fast-forwarding, or they check out and switch to the latest episode of *The Psychic Twins*. Watching a random girl sleeping either makes you feel like an Edward Cullen–level creep or it turns you on, but if you wait for it—yeah, people have remixed it with that *Hamilton* song too—then you'll see something start to happen.

She starts to move a little bit, kind of a shimmy, kind of a wiggle, and she smiles. Then she opens her mouth, and her breath hitches, she gasps, and— Do you want me to go on? Do you need a moment?

Okay. Then she arches her back a little, and she moans. Yeah, the way you think, all sexy-like, like she must be having the best. Dream. *Ever.* You wish you were having that dream. Maybe you wish she were dreaming about you. By the end of the video, she's doing full-on *When Harry Met Sally*, and please don't tell me you haven't seen that classic film either. I don't want to know.

That's basically it. Seventeen minutes of a teenage girl having mind-blowing orgasms, or faking them, depending on how you want to look at it. Shouldn't be anything unusual about that; should be an everyday occurrence if there's a kind and loving god out there, unless he's the kind of god that frowns on orgasms outside of marriage. And I want no part of that religion, thank you very much. So here's the really strange thing, why everyone's talking about it: it isn't clear *why* she's coming. She isn't moving her hands, which stay out of her shorts the whole time, and she's alone. That's why people have been talking about "the invisible hand." But there's a lot more going on behind the scenes than that.

Yes, I do know a lot about that video. I've studied it obsessively. Unhealthily. But so has everyone else, right? What I'm saying is there's a reason for everything if you look for it, and before I go on with this story, there are three things you need to know.

Number one: the girl's name is Allison Kim. Allie. It wasn't listed on the video, but there've been a ton of articles, and it wasn't long before she was outed in the video's comments.

But don't read the comments. Never read the comments.

I knew her name before everyone else did because that's number two: I recorded the video.

I don't blame you for not believing me, but why would I lie about something you can confirm easily when we get back to civilization? My username is dayofthetentacle. My channel has over two million subscribers since everything happened. But it may have fallen some since I haven't been able to update it while under this rock.

Oh yeah, number three: Allie's my sister.

If that makes you think I'm a bad person, that's fine. Everything's fine. I've seen that look before, from people I care about a lot more than you lot. I'm not interested in winning friends and influencing people. I'm just going to tell you my story, Allie's story, because I have to. I have to. Because no one else will listen.

I promise you, everything I'm saying is the absolute truth, and it's not what you think. But hold on, there's one more thing. I wasn't completely honest before when I described Allie as a "pretty average teenage girl." She is—was—astonishing. Top of her class, world-class swimmer, future doctor, overachiever. There was nothing average about her. That was all before the video, naturally, but I don't deserve all the blame for what happened to her.

I'm still trying to understand what happened to her. Maybe you can help me figure it out. But first, let me ask you something: Do you believe in ghosts and aliens and things that go bump in the night?

So how did my sister, a popular A student and a model Christian daughter, end up as a viral video? End up the sexual fantasy of millions of strangers, the soundtrack for thousands of lonely, horny losers getting off every day? Worse: How did she end up mocked, bullied, bitter, and ultimately missing?

As with most tragedies, as for most of us here right now on this survival trip, it was all an accident. It wasn't supposed to happen this way.

See, I didn't build my YouTube following with spy cameras and voyeurism and good intentions. I made short films, videos that no one watched, that ironically were planned to have the best chance at being the next viral sensation. But that's not how these things work. The next Internet meme is the video that no one saw coming.

Sorry, didn't mean that pun. Really.

It's the video that should never have existed, that some people later wished hadn't been recorded. It's the video that was never meant to be seen by anyone, let alone two-and-a-half billion someones. Certainly not by your parents. Especially not your sister, the unsuspecting subject of said video.

It began in the middle of the night. I was up late editing a short film starring my friends Ryan and Tony. Ryan's a girl, and Tony's a guy. Kind of confusing, I know, but gender can be complicated, and speaking of complicated: I've slept with both of them. No, not at the same time. Technically, it was just blow jobs with Tony, once when we were drunk. And while you might call Ryan and me "fuck buddies," no strings attached, the truth is . . . There are a lot of strings. Tangled, messy strings. I'm in love with that girl.

The film is a little comedy piece about the last slice of cake in the cafeteria. In the story it turns out it's all happening after the apocalypse, and the cake is really a brick, and Ryan's character is dead, and Tony's character has been trying to survive in the high school eating the remains of his friends and hallucinating the whole thing. *Dark* comedy, okay? It needs work.

It was taking longer to edit than usual because I was distracted watching Ryan and Tony interact, especially during outtakes when they thought the camera was off—when I told them the camera was off. I was trying to decide if there was something going on between the two of them because they had been acting chummier than before, and awkward around me.

The three of us have starred in all my videos, sometimes with Allie. That was kind of my thing, my signature, the way Tim Burton always works with Johnny Depp and Helena Bonham Carter, and Joss Whedon is always going to find something for Amy Acker, and Christopher Guest films are all basically the same movie with the same people. It makes it a lot easier to work with your best friends. Less drama. Or so I thought.

I'm editing and watching Ryan and Tony, and for some reason I start getting really turned on and wondering if they're fucking now and if there's a chance at a threesome and if they'd let me film it. Soon I'm jerking off, thinking about Ryan's perfect little breasts and Tony's warm mouth on my dick, and Allie—

Whoa. *Allie?* And I pause the video and realize that I'm thinking about sex because I hear moaning. Not on the recording; it's coming from the other side of my bedroom wall.

Did I finish? What do you think?

Another thing you need to know about my sister: she's fifteen. She was thirteen then. And I'm not saying that's too young to be fooling around and having a good time. I'm the last person to suggest that, believe me. But she's my little sister, and I know her better than I know myself. Specifically, I know three important facts:

She doesn't have a boyfriend. Or a girlfriend. She barely has any friends, to be honest.

She's a virgin. She doesn't have time to think about that kind of stuff. Sex stuff. Relationships. People.

She doesn't masturbate.

Forget what I said before about how everyone masturbates. There are exceptions to every rule, at least there are when it's a thirteen-year-old girl and she really really really believes in God the way that I believe in Sasquatch, and our parents would be murderous if they could hear the way she's carrying on. Fortunately, they're on the other end of the hall—Dad's a loud snorer and Mom's a heavy sleeper. I think that's the only reason they're still together because it's the only way they perfectly complement each other.

But my sister. My sister! She's doing the heavy panting thing and the whimpering and the grunting and holy shit what the fuck, it's my sister. I think maybe she's watching porn—that would be a first too, and almost as shocking—but no, I'm pretty sure it's all her.

And I can't help but be weirded out and a little turned on, and I don't know what's going on, so I do what I always do when I face something unbelievable: I start recording. My expensive, awesome microphone gets the whole thing while I sit there listening for ten minutes, completely conflicted over what my body is doing and my brain is telling me and wondering whether I should storm over and . . . do what?

Here's another weird thing I noticed that I didn't think much of at the time: when she was done, she just . . . stopped. Like someone flipping a light switch. I crept to her room and listened at the door, but I could hear her snoring lightly; she gets that from Dad. No voices from her room, and only one person breathing as far as I could tell. She was alone.

The next morning her alarm went off seven times before I heard her get up and go to the shower. When she came down to breakfast, she dragged herself to the table, like her limbs were weighed down. She slumped into her usual chair across from me and splashed milk into a bowl of cereal. I kept watching her until she looked up.

"What?" she said, dribbling milk down her chin.

"Sleep okay?" I asked.

"I guess."

"Any strange dreams?" I asked.

"Not that I remember." She put down her spoon. "Why?"

"No reason," I said hurriedly as Mom entered the kitchen. "Probably nothing."

"That's not nothing," Ryan said. She pulled my earbuds from her ears and fanned her face exaggeratedly. "Can I have a copy of this?"

"Ryan!" I said. "It's *Allie*." I shoved my iPod back into my pocket, wondering if I'd made a mistake playing it for her. But I needed to share it with someone and figure out what to do.

"Uh-huh. I've seen the way you look at her."

"What the hell do you mean by that? She's my sister."

"I know, but . . ." She shrugged. "She's cute. I wouldn't blame you for noticing, as long as that's all you do."

"Ew. You must have me confused with Tony," I said.

Ryan glanced up and down the hallway. "Have you seen him today?"

"Not yet," I said.

"You going to play that for him too?"

"Any reason I shouldn't?"

"No, I just want to see the look on his face when you do."

We caught up with Tony at lunch. His eyes widened when I played the file for him.

"This is *Allie*?" he asked.

I nodded.

"Damn, girl," he said. "She must have been in a good mood this morning."

115

"She was exhausted," I said.

"I guess she would be," Tony said.

"So what do we do about it?" I asked.

"Nothing. It's her business," Ryan said.

"You know what you have to do, bro," Tony said. "Hide a camera in her room. Find out if she's sneaking someone in at night or going it alone."

"That's disgusting," Ryan said. "Aside from the fact that it's unethical to record someone without their knowledge, it's almost certainly illegal. Definitely illegal since she's a minor."

"Yeah," I said. "And she's my sister."

Tony snorted. "I've seen you check Allie out."

"I have not!" I glared at Ryan. "Did you get him to say that?"

She held up her hands and shook her head.

"Relax, Day. No judgment. She's hot," Tony said. "If she were my sister—"

"She's thirteen," Ryan said. "Here's an idea. Before you lie and break the law, how about you try talking to her?"

"That's gonna be an awkward conversation," I said.

"Don't be a coward, Day. Be a good big brother."

You know in cartoons, when someone has a crisis of conscience and a little devil shows up on their shoulder to tell them the naughty thing to do? That's Tony. The angel on my other shoulder, always guiding me true? That's Ryan.

I was worried something was going on with them and I would either be left out or lose one of them as a friend. Devil or angel, I needed both of them, or who knew what kind of a mess I would get myself in?

* * *

There are a few stages we go through when we hear something we don't want to be true. You're probably experiencing them right now.

Stage one: shock and disbelief. When I confronted Allie in her room after school, it took me a while to get around to what I wanted to say. But after small talk about her school project and her next swim meet, after trying to talk around the question by asking her if she was interested in anyone at school—which got me the standard-issue thirteen-year-old's eye roll—I finally came out with it.

"Did you have a, um, friend over last night?" I asked.

"What?" Allie asked. She was concentrating on building a collage on poster board for her social studies class. She had cut images out of magazines in the shapes of each of the fifty states and was building a map of celebrity faces and ads for expensive cars, gizmos, and gadgets. One of them caught my eye: a fancy, bullet-shaped vibrator.

"Whoa, is that . . . ?" I pointed.

"Oh!" It took Allie a moment to understand what she was looking at, bless her pure, innocent heart. Then she grabbed it, her face blushing. She turned it over to hide it, and Kim Kardashian stared up at us.

"I didn't notice that on the other side of the page!" she said. "I just took a bunch of old magazines and newspapers from the school's art supply room."

"It was probably just a mistake," I said, unsure whether I was referring to the magazine scrap or what I'd heard last night. That kind of thing could cause a scandal at St. Elijah's Preparatory School, the kind of thing that could get someone expelled or fired.

"David, I have homework." Allie blew her bangs away from her eyes in frustration. "So much homework." Her voice was high, the way it sounded when school was getting to be too much. Maybe she'd finally found a healthy way to relax from all that stress. Better than taking drugs, right? This really wasn't any of my business, but I needed to know she was safe, and that included not letting our parents find out about whatever this was.

"Okay." I took a deep breath. "Last night I heard, um, sounds coming from your room. Kind of, um, *sexual* sounds?"

You know me, I'm not too shy to say whatever comes to mind, no matter how dirty or disgusting it might be. But not with her. Not with Allie. And maybe that was the problem. I didn't want to have this conversation with her.

"You're wrong," she said.

"Nope. Like, maybe you were dreaming?"

She shook her head. "Maybe *you* were. Why would you think I . . . ? How could you . . ."

I held up a hand to stop her. "Hold on, Allie. First of all, sex isn't something to be embarrassed about."

"I know, it's a 'beautiful thing that two people do when they're in love. And very married.' Direct quote there from Mom when she gave me 'the Talk.'"

"I got the same thing from Dad, except he phrased it as a beautiful thing I was absolutely forbidden to do if I want to continue being his son. But it's almost completely wrong. Sex is kind of ugly and messy and gross, if you want to be honest, but it's worth it because it feels so good! And it can kind of be beautiful if you're with the right person, and definitely if they are particularly beautiful. Just being honest here. Also, love is entirely optional, and it's more accurate to say 'two or more people,' and maybe some toys."

Allie looked stricken.

"Which is to say, I know what sex sounds like, and I heard it coming from this room."

"No," she said. "Impossible. You'd think I would be the first to know about something like that." Her cheeks flushed.

"I have, um, proof."

Stage two: denial.

"That isn't me," Allie said when I played the file—low, so our parents wouldn't hear it. "You faked this."

"That'd be the first time a guy faked a girl's orgasm," I said. "Why would I do that, anyway?"

"You make stuff up all the time to get people to click on your videos."

"*Allie,*" I said.

"I didn't mean that." She covered her face. Then she covered her ears while the moaning went on and on and on. "Turn it off! Please!"

Stage three: anger.

"You pervert!" she shouted. "You thought it was me, and you started recording?"

"Shhh! I only recorded it because I couldn't believe it. And you're lucky Mom and Dad didn't hear you too."

"And they never will. Delete it," she said.

"Sure. Whatever you want." I deleted it.

"And the backup?" she said.

"Okay. Come watch me do it if you want."

She followed me into my room and watched over my shoulder as I pulled up the file on my computer, deleted it, then emptied the trash. As far as I was concerned, I hoped that would be the end of it. If she was lying about it—because she was embarrassed or whatever—then she would try to be quieter next time so she wouldn't get caught.

Allie sighed with relief after I deleted the audio file. A moment later she said in a low voice, "You really heard that last night?"

"Allie, I have no reason to lie about something like this."

She nodded. "If you hear it again, come wake me," she said.

"You're sure?"

"Yeah," she said. "Promise me, okay?" Her voice shook.

Stage four: fear.

"I promise," I said.

Lucinda threw a rock at David that hit him in the arm. "I told you what would happen if it was a sex story." She looked at Tino. "Give me the knife."

"That's really messed up," Cody said. "She was your sister."

David rubbed his arm where he'd been hit. That rock was definitely going to leave a bruise. "It wasn't like that!"

Sunday and Georgia had returned while David was telling his story, and they'd sat with Cody, still whispering to each other. I kind of wished I'd been able to hear what they'd talked about in the woods.

"Anyway," David said, "you didn't let me finish."

Jaila motioned at Tino, who'd fallen asleep and was snoring on top of his sleeping bag. "Yeah, I think we've all heard enough. We should get some sleep."

As we each laid out our sleeping bags, Jenna and Lucinda kept forming a wall that forced David to lay out his pack away from the rest of us. Neither said anything, but they made it clear he wasn't welcome near the fire.

When we'd all settled in, Cody asked, "Do you think we'll make it back to camp on time?"

No one answered. The Bend might have been built on a philosophy of teamwork and strength through unity, but we were no team, and we definitely weren't unified. If I had to guess, I'd have wagered most of us were wondering if we'd manage to make it back to camp at all.

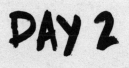

DAY 2

BREAKFAST WAS A MEAL of grouseberries that Jaila assured us definitely weren't poisonous, though we were each so hungry that I doubt it would have mattered if they were. Striking camp was a quiet affair. Tino and Lucinda gave each other a wide berth, and Cody clung to Georgia, except when she went off to take care of business. No one wanted much to do with David, and he wandered around with a hangdog expression on his face that might have earned him sympathy if he hadn't started telling us a story about how he recorded his sister doing something no guy is supposed to want his sister doing.

David hadn't actually slept much, which I knew because I'd followed him when he'd gotten up in the middle of the night to walk into the woods alone. I thought at first that he was going to take a leak, but he wandered a good ways off and then stood by a tree talking to himself for a while. He kept saying how he knew *they* were there and it was okay if they took him too. Then he cried for a while before finally returning to camp. I don't think he noticed me watching.

"Are you sure we're going in the right direction?" I overheard Jackie asking Jaila when I came back from taking care of my own business.

Jaila shrugged. "Think so, but it's hard to be sure. Doug got me all turned around driving out here. I'm pretty sure the Bend is northeast, but we could walk right past it and never know, so . . ."

I wasn't the only one eavesdropping. "You don't know where we're going?" Lucinda came out from behind a tree, speaking loudly enough for the others to overhear.

Tino, who was sitting with his back to a tree and had looked like he was trying to catch a few more minutes of sleep, opened his eyes. "That fucking figures. I knew we shouldn't have listened to you."

Jackie frowned at Lucinda and clenched her fists. "Is that what she said? Maybe you need to clean your ears out and listen better."

"Can we not do this so early?" Georgia asked.

"No," Tino said, rising to his feet. "I want to know if we're lost or what."

"We're not lost," Jenna said before Jaila could.

Then Sunday went, "Says the pyro," and it was an all-out war of words that had everyone shouting at each other. Tino got in Jackie's face, and Jenna covered her ears with her hands, and Cody stood in front of Georgia, like he was going to protect her, though I might have been mistaken in my first impression of her because I didn't think she needed any protecting.

Finally, David shouted, "Can we please, please just start hiking? Anywhere? Please?"

"Whatever," Tino said. "But I'm leading today."

"No one's following you who doesn't want to get lost," Sunday said. "Jaila's the only one of you who actually knows what she's doing!"

"You think you're better than the rest of us, don't you?" Tino said. "We're nothing but a bunch of fuckups, every one. We got a girl lighting shit on fire, a guy who gets off watching his sister, a closet case who probably pushed her friend off the side of that mountain, and you probably tried to blow up your school or something." He shook his head.

"I'm *not* a perv—" David started to say.

Jaila cut him off. "We're not lost," she said.

"How do you know?" Cody asked. His voice wasn't accusing the way Tino's had been, but simply curious.

"Because," Jaila said, hanging her head low, "I know something about being truly lost."

"THE SUBJUNCTIVE"

by Alaya Dawn Johnson

IT WAS DARK when the girl arrived, at last. She had come from far away—never mind how—and she had arrived too late—never mind why. But she was here now, with dandelion seed–hair, wild and dusty from days on the high and twisting roads that cut through the valleys and low hills covered in cactus and mesquite and the occasional flowering agave. She walked through the sleeping town slowly, the soles of her shoes scraping the broken cobblestones of the main road. A passing dog barked a question at her, sniffed, and cocked his head in recognition.

Been a while, he seemed to say.

The girl nodded and winced. "Too long," she whispered, because of the night and the quiet but also because the words had burned to embers in her mouth, and she was afraid that if she spoke too loudly they might go out forever.

She continued past the dog and the sleeping turkey hens and the low houses with their open porches and swinging hammocks,

FERAL YOUTH

illuminated only by the silver light of a gibbous moon. It smelled still of woodsmoke from the fires that had heated the evening meal; it smelled of dust and dry grass and the muddy creek that passed just in front of the church. *Home,* she mouthed silently, and tasted its tiny spark.

She made her way to the church. The large wooden front doors were closed, but she knew the side entrance would be unlocked for the townspeople who sought religious solace after sundown. She walked around the old eighteenth-century building familiar in its cared-for decay, and ducked under the low-hanging lintel of the doorway. Someone else had left it open. Inside, half-burned candles flickered against the vaulted ceiling of the nave. They had been left in front of the figure of San Antonio Abad, that kindly white man with his shepherd's crook and matted beard. There were carnations by the candles and little papers folded by his feet—prayers and supplications for the lost.

"You came back."

The girl recognized the voice; she didn't flinch or turn around. It was a ghost; it was her sister; it was the only person who could have felt her return to this place that had once been their home.

"He hasn't returned?" the first asked.

The second girl took a step closer. The girl with words like dry tinder in her mouth, with dusty dandelion hair—she didn't turn around.

"You know he hasn't. You can feel it, can't you?"

"Feel what?"

"The pressure."

"I don't know what you're talking about," said the dandelion girl, though she did know.

"You've been gone too long," said the other, and her voice was as long and twisty as a valley wind. "They found a coyote in the decline by the path up to the sacred well. An hour from town, Jaila." That was her name, the dandelion-hair girl, the girl whose words were slowly going out.

"It could have just been an animal. Any old coyote, dead in a ravine."

"With a patch of orange fur at its throat. With a scar by its eye and a knife in its ribs."

Jaila closed her eyes and swayed. "What did they do with it?" she asked after a moment.

"Nothing. Left it there to rot. It's just an animal, after all."

"Just an animal."

"Everyone suspects and no one will say. He hasn't come back."

"Who? The flowers here? The candles?"

"I was waiting— I didn't want to go alone—" The second girl stopped abruptly. In the distance a dog barked, then two more, and they woke the roosters who started crowing to one another, louder and louder, just to see who would win.

"Ursula," whispered Jaila, and the din smothered the hot, dangerous flame of the name—because that was her name, the other girl. She had a rope of black hair down to her waist and a huipil embroidered with feathers, and a wide, happy nose, the better to keep the wind in it. Ursula had always been friends with the wind—the only one as good at following a trail was the boy both of them loved.

And he wasn't here to help them now.

Jaila put her hands in front of her mouth; her fingers seemed to glow where they touched her lips.

"What happened to you?" asked Ursula.

Jaila thought. Her gaze shifted from Ursula's face to the shadowy murals tucked into the cupola of the church to the serene image of the saint standing in his niche. She had belonged to this place once; it had been familiar and kind to her. She had dreamed herself here so many nights. Was this another dream? How had she found herself, at last, upon the road? And if it were a dream, *why was she still too late*?

"I tried," Jaila said.

Ursula frowned. "I *needed* you, little sister."

"I tried!" And this time Jaila's voice was a roar that burned her lips and singed the little hairs beneath Ursula's windy nose. She quieted the flame again; she hoarded the embers. "They wouldn't let me."

"And now? How did you get away?"

They stared at one another, Ursula expectant, and Jaila distracted, confused by the question. She was here, the dirt in her sandals was the dirt in her hair, and it was like no other dirt in the world. And yet, she couldn't remember . . .

Very near them, just behind the church, or just by Jaila's elbow, a coyote yipped. The dogs whimpered and quieted. Ursula gripped Jaila's hand. They ran outside to the open plaza in front of the church.

"Was that—" Jaila started, but Ursula broke away.

"Brother!" Ursula roared. "Vete a la chingada, hermano, is that you?" The wind blew down from the hills, blew down the howl of a coyote, distant now, and brushed against the church bell so that it rang just once. The world was still; the world held its breath; the world waited, as the two girls waited, for what that bell had rung into existence.

Now, behind Ursula, muddy tracks crossed the broken cobblestones, heading away from the gate. They had not been there a moment before. Jaila bent down and touched one of their crumbling edges.

"Coyote," she whispered.

Ursula knelt beside her and sniffed. "The woods. The track to the sacred well. He's still out there. We have to find him."

"I can't," Jaila said. "I've only been there once. They don't like it when I go."

"We won't go to the well, just around it. But he's out there, Jaila! You won't abandon him again, will you?" And Jaila heard, unspoken, all the holes that they had ripped in each other's lives when she left.

Jaila nodded. Her lips were burning, her tongue was a twisted wick dipped in the oil of conflicting vocabularies and aspectual grammars. Maybe Ursula understood. She just took Jaila by the hand and led her away from the church toward the creek. They followed it silently until the town dropped away behind them. They climbed the hill and entered the path through the woods, dark and forbidding— darkened and forbidden.

The path was a slim red dirt line looping through patchy forest up here in the hills. In the dark, with the moon sinking rapidly in the west, it held different dangers than the winding desert roads below. Only the wind in Ursula's nose, chasing and testing her, told them where to go when the trees blocked even the stars overhead. An owl hooted, three low beats. They flinched.

"We won't die tonight," Ursula said. Because that's what the owl's call meant on a night like this: an omen of death.

Maybe we won't, Jaila thought, and then froze. Though she hadn't opened her mouth, she had heard it, a voice not quite her own murmuring with the leaves and the wind.

"Did you say something?" Ursula asked.

Jaila's mouth was burning again. She shook her head. After a moment Ursula shrugged and started again down the path. They continued for an hour like that, using roots and outcropping rock for handholds as the path got steeper. Jaila had to stop twice to catch her breath. She had a pack with a bottle of water still half filled, though she couldn't remember where she had bought it. She offered it to Ursula, who took a swig and then let Jaila drink the rest. It had been too long; Jaila could see it in Ursula's eyes. That pity and impatience, as though she were truly a foreigner.

"I'm trying," Jaila snapped, unthinking. Her words lashed out like a whip and sizzled in the air between them. They smelled of sulfur and burning rubber.

"What did you say?"

Jaila realized that she'd spoken in the other language, the one that Ursula didn't understand. She pulled out other words, placed them gently on the tip of her tongue, and let them fall with lazy sparks to the dirt and dry leaves at their feet. "Harder than I remember."

A wind blew between the two of them, blew the sparks into the air where they were extinguished like fireflies. Ursula's nostrils flared wide. "I smell it," she said. "It's down the slope there. The body."

Jaila's heart started pounding, fast enough to break. Ursula put her hand on Jaila's shoulder.

"The body of the coyote," Ursula whispered.

Jaila nodded fast. "Not him," she said, and this time the words that slipped out were in the other language, the one that the trees and the rocks and the wind and the rain spoke up in these hills. Their fire was pure and blue and smelled of rain.

Ursula frowned at it. "How long have you been able to do that, Jaila?"

But Jaila didn't say anything, because Jaila didn't know. She followed Ursula as she veered from the path. In the dark Jaila would have stumbled straight over the edge of the decline, but Ursula hauled her back by the collar.

"Wait here," she said. "I'll go down."

Ursula secured her machete in its scabbard on her belt and clambered over the edge. Her head quickly disappeared from view. Jaila waited. She wanted to join her friend and not let her face whatever was down there alone, but she knew that she'd never be able to scale the cliff safely in the dark. Ursula and the boy had always been better in the hills than Jaila. The wind rushed past her, spinning the leaves in circles. The owl hooted again, closer now. And then another animal, maybe a dog, growled softly just behind her. She spun around. The trees were quiet; even the mosquitoes seemed to be sleeping. She was alone.

The dog—or whatever it was—growled again. The sound came from deeper in the woods, farther from the path. She couldn't see it for the shadows.

"Ursula?" she tried to call, but fear had banked the flame in her mouth. Her voice was the heavy smoke of wet kindling, and the wind blew it away before it could reach her friend. The animal shrieked, and now she recognized it for what she had feared: a coyote. And she was alone, undefended in its territory, with her back to a ravine. She couldn't see well enough to run, so she unslung her pack from her shoulder and searched inside. She couldn't remember how she got it any more than she could remember how she found herself on the road back to her most beloved home. Maybe it had a light or a gun or— Her hand wrapped around the hilt of a knife. She'd have been better off with a machete, but a knife was good; a knife she knew how to handle. The coyote howled. She wondered if it was alone; she wondered if it just meant to threaten her off or attack her. It howled again; from below them, as though from the middle of the rock itself, a howl answered. The two calls twined into a song, not as inhuman as it ought to be. Like horns at a funeral playing in mournful diminished fifths. And then, for a moment, like boys at four in the morning drinking Victorias and listening to sad ballads, a cry of pleasurable despair.

His name slipped from between her lips. She didn't mean for it to. But she was staring into the dark of the woods, holding a knife, and she wanted so much for him to be there that she couldn't hold it back.

She thought it was a bomb at first. It lit the trees, the hills, the cliff where Ursula had disappeared. Birds screeched and flew away, squirrels and moles and snakes scrambled from the underbrush. The closest leaves caught fire, which spread down the branches. She froze, staring at the damage she'd unintentionally caused. Where was Ursula? She couldn't hear her friend anymore. She didn't dare call out. The fire was high now, burning the hairs on her arms with its heat. Her lips, though . . . Her lips felt as cool as the bottom of a well.

A coyote walked from the fire. He was large, his head nearly to her hip, with a blond triangle of fur by his neck and a drooping right eye cut by an old scar. He bared his teeth. The knife fell from her grip and speared the earth by her foot. Ashes were raining around them like fat snowflakes; she had dreamed of snow once, back in the days when they had all loved one another.

The coyote nodded once and then turned around and left the circle of the burning trees.

She chased after him. She wanted to call out, but she knew the woods might not survive it. She'd go back to the cliff, she'd find Ursula later. Ursula would agree. She couldn't let him go this time. Not if it really was—

She leaped over the thought just as she leaped over the roots and overturned trees in her path. The coyote kept just ahead, fast but not so fast that she couldn't follow. Periodically, he'd stop to look back at her and jerk his head as though to say, *Faster, string bean. Did you forget how to run while you were away?*

They were climbing the hill, where the trees gave way to outcropping rocks and scraggly shrubs. She wasn't sure where because he had left the path, and all she saw were stars and sky and dark blobs of trees in the distance.

They paused just at the edge of some kind of clearing. She stopped. Ursula was there, facing her across the darkness of the open space, as though suspended above it. The wind ran its fingers through her hair, brought the smells of the burning forest and wild coyote fur and the dried flowers crunching beneath her feet, right beside puddles of wax from long-expended candles.

"It brought us here," Ursula called. "Why?"

"Where is here?" Jaila whispered, so that her intention could be discerned more by the pattern of smoke leaving her lips than the thready sound of her words.

Ursula laughed, and the wind kicked a spray of brown-orange petals into the void.

"The well," she said, and the wind said, and the coyote said, just as Jaila felt sharp teeth—*his* teeth—bite hard into the back of her leg. She stumbled forward, but instead of rocks, her right foot encountered cold, dead air. She was on the edge of the sacred well after all. She hadn't marked the edge, and so she overbalanced, and she fell in.

Ursula screamed. Her face receded more slowly than it ought to, as though Jaila were sinking into water and not miles of empty air. Then Ursula took a breath and dove in after her.

Jaila had only ever been to the sacred well once. It was meant for rituals and sacrifices, solemn processions winding their way for hours through mountain paths until they reached the edge of the world. A hole in the earth, a navel in the belly of god, so wide and so deep that no one could see the bottom, or hear an offering crashing against it. It did not end—or at least, where it ended was not a place the way the hills and the rocks and the trees were a place. It was a conduit to the gods, a between-space, where in the right time and after the right rituals, the mundane world could communicate with the divine.

In the old days they had sacrificed humans above the well and then thrown their bloody bodies inside. They did it at the start of the rainy season, to give the gods their due and rebalance the scales of the universe, so that the rain might fall and the harvest might be good, and fertility of the earth renewed again for another hard year. These days they sacrificed turkeys and chickens, but it meant the same thing. The gods understood. A boy would fast for months beforehand, purifying himself for his brush with the gods. Jaila had come to the ceremony when she was eleven. He had been thirteen then, dark skin and long bones and a rib cage like a wooden box you keep fruit in. He had already been skinny, but as he fasted he grew into something else—frail and ferocious, like a sapling clinging to a cliff face. She had loved him before, but in an ordinary sort of way. He showed her how to knock down paper wasps nests and collect the honeyed combs; he brought her back the first young corn from the maize field; he called her "string bean" to her face and stupid names to impress his friends and then apologized after.

But on the day of the ritual, she saw him transformed. He didn't look at her once, though he was nearly naked, and before it would have embarrassed him to be seen that way in front of the whole town. He stood calmly through the blessings, so still that she had nudged Ursula to ask if he was still breathing. His eyes were so wide, his pupils so black; even before the sacrifices, all he could do was stare at the sacred well.

The blood splattered him when he killed the chickens and turkeys. Jaila flinched, though not because of the death; she was used to that. It was because at that first moment, he had stared straight at the two of them, and something moved behind his eyes, something great and inscrutable and *not him*.

She had loved him truly after that. He'd never gone back to being the boy he was. He chased power, chased whatever it was that had called him on the edge of this precipice. He chased it even when it became dangerous, when it destroyed him, when everyone begged him to stop.

Those people deal in death, brother, Ursula had told him during the last fight that Jaila had witnessed, *there is nothing holy in it.*

And he had turned to her, his eyes blasted black with something more substantive than divinity, and said, *There is nothing more holy than death, sister.*

Jaila heard him again now as she fell. *There is nothing more holy than death.* The light of the stars and the moon and the first wisps of dawn were fast receding.

Ursula reached her, crashed into her chest and held on, and then they spun together, down and down to their deaths, as the coyote had commanded.

"I'm sorry," Jaila said in the language of the trees, and the flames singed her dandelion hair and illuminated the inky black perfection of the rock around them.

Ursula hugged her. She didn't say anything. It was okay—the wind rushed around them now, and Jaila couldn't hear anything at all. She waited.

But they didn't crash. They just kept falling. They were bunched up inside the wind, as though it were a net. Jaila knew they ought to have died already, but without any light to see, it felt more like floating through a tunnel. Ursula lifted her head from Jaila's shoulder and then reached out her arm.

"What's happening?" Jaila asked. She chose the weakest words, lobbed them past where she guessed Ursula's head would be, and the fire unfurled like two flowers spinning around their heads. They were a meter away from the black wall. Ursula's eyes were narrow with concentration, and her nostrils flared.

"I called the wind," Ursula said.

"You can do that?" Jaila asked.

"Your grammar can catch fire?"

"I don't know how that happened. You two were the powerful ones."

"He always said that's how it would be with you. That you'd have to find your power to come back to us. That you would when you wanted it enough. But you came too late for him."

"Don't say that. Didn't you see the coyote? He brought us here."

Ursula snorted, and the air surrounding them bucked and twisted. Jaila flung herself forward to keep her balance, and her hand brushed the wall. She shrieked, anticipating pain. But it didn't hurt. Her fingertips had passed through, creating oily currents as she floated down. She snatched her hand back, but in the lingering light of her shriek, she saw weird figures in the slick.

A procession—a hundred people in brightly woven huipils and capes, walking behind men dressed in costumes of jaguars and eagles and fanged gods. Then a pyramid, an ancient temple with steps gleaming white and a chapel at the top painted blue and red. Ursula—it had to be Ursula, she had her nose and her hair and her mocking, mischievous eyes—but she was wearing the same clothes as the women in the procession, with golden plugs in her ears and lower lip. She was painting a figure on an accordion scroll of cedar bark paper.

"Ursula?" Jaila said. The girl's head jerked up. For a moment their eyes met.

The image broke apart, spilled its constituent colors down the wall and re formed again, briefly, into something more familiar: the woods of the surrounding hills. Jaila was running through them, her hair on fire, her laughter leaving a trail of ashes behind her. In the deep shadows of dusk, a coyote kept pace beside her.

The images faded as the wall regained its stillness.

"Where are we?" Jaila asked. She was gripping Ursula's hand so tightly it had to hurt, but Ursula didn't complain.

"Haven't you figured it out?" Ursula said with that familiar curve of her lips, one a lip plug could do nothing to disguise. "We're in between."

"In between what?"

"Worlds. Our world and the gods' world. Your world and my world. Real worlds and unreal worlds and almost-real worlds. He never talked to you about it?"

Now Jaila got bitter, and it threaded her flame with a sickly green. "He said dangerous things like that weren't for sweet girls like me."

Ursula snorted again, but this time Jaila kept her balance. "Machista fool," she said.

Jaila laughed, and burning flower broke apart on the gleaming black behind them. A thousand rivulets swarmed and gathered until they outlined a coyote walking in the dark. It limped. As more lines converged, Jaila could see some kind of spear lodged in its side. It panted, glanced behind itself, continued down the path. It seemed to wind closer, or at least the coyote got bigger, near enough for them to see the blood matted to the fur by its hip and in front of its neck. It looked up and yipped.

They shouldn't have been able to hear it. They hadn't heard the other strange visions in the slick, but the coyote's call came at them as though from underwater. It approached them and howled. Jaila leaned forward. Its eyes were clouded with pain, but they bored into hers, yellow and fierce with recognition. It wanted to tell her something. It had come back to tell her something.

"Tizoc?" she said.

It rushed from her lips with a roar that deafened her, with a shine that blinded her, with a heat that seared her skin. It poured onto the slick, poured until the fire burned a little bit of it away.

The coyote stepped through.

The coyote wheezed from the pain in his side. He was real, or real enough for his fur to smell like blood, for his breath to stink of river water.

The fur by his right eye was cut by an old scar, from when the three of them had gone to the river to fish and he'd waded in too deep and been carried out by the strong current of the late rainy season. They'd waited in an overcrowded emergency room for hours while blood soaked the rag he held there, and Jaila had shivered with alternating waves of horror at the misery of the place, and jolts of pleasure at being so near to him.

It was around that time that he found a chamán with a bad reputation from a few towns over—not respected but feared—who taught him how to find his nagual, to become a coyote. He drifted away from them then—became less Tizoc, the older brother and truest unspoken love, and more Tizoc, the sicario who did unspeakable things in the desert and came back with another tattoo and a habit for first-harvest cane liquor. He spent some nights on his knees, clutching the icon of San Judas Tadeo to his chest while he cried over a pain he swore was an enemy poisoning his soul.

You're poisoning your soul, Jaila had wanted to tell him, but she had never dared. All her words had burned out around him, had fallen out of her mouth, as white as wood ash, and dusted his perfectly polished hand-tooled leather boots.

Go back to bed, Jaila, he'd growl at her. *You don't belong here. You shouldn't be out at night.* And he'd look at her, and she would know: he no longer trusted himself.

He hadn't been dangerous before. He pretended it was his power, his nagual, his wild coyote that made him dangerous now. Even Ursula had tried to believe that for a while, before they found the photos on his phone. Dead men with their throats ripped out, faces slack, eyes wide with terror. One of the men clutched an icon of the Virgen de Guadalupe, now drenched and wrinkled with his blood. Oh, a coyote had done it, that much was true. But it was not the coyote that was dangerous.

It was the man.

Jaila had left not long after. She had left, or she had been dragged away—it depended on your perspective. Ursula had screamed at her, at the end—*Why don't you fight? Why don't you tell them you don't want to go?* But Jaila was choking with ashes, with fear and regret. At what he had become, at what would happen to them all if they stayed here in the desert and the hills, invoking the bounty of Mother Earth with flowers and candles and the blood of dead turkeys. Maybe she had believed him when he said that she didn't belong here, where the earth spoke in the only words that had ever felt at home in her mouth.

She had tried to come back when she heard the news of him, when the wind whispered that he had disappeared. But they had stopped her. Just when she had decided to fight, they had stopped her.

So how had she found herself here, on the road back home at sunset, with water in her bag and a flame in her mouth?

"Is it you?" she asked the coyote now. "You brought me here?"

"Jaila," Ursula said, urgent. "Jaila, don't talk to him. He can't be real. Do you see that spearhead in his side? It's like something out of a museum. . . ."

He tilted his head and snorted a little. He lifted a bloody paw and smeared her arm with it.

Dead men don't do magic.

Ursula stiffened against her. "What did you say?"

"Nothing. I just heard—"

"Heard what?"

"Him," Jaila whispered, and the flame didn't burn her anymore; it just gave her light and kept her warm.

You brought yourself here, the coyote said.

"Did you hear that?" Jaila asked.

Ursula looked at her and the coyote, then closed her eyes and exhaled. The wind bucked, tossed them high and dropped them low—in this in-between place, everything seemed to go in two directions at once—and Jaila grabbed the two of them, her two greatest loves, and held on.

The wind steadied again. "Will you let go a little?" Ursula said, muffled against Jaila's shoulder, in the language of their sisterhood, their friendship, the language that had always connected one little outsider girl to these people and this land. They hadn't spoken it before now.

Jaila released her. They were both covered in the coyote's blood. His eyelids were sinking and then opening, as though he were about to pass out. Ursula gazed down at him, her eyes fierce and almost as yellow as the coyote's in the lingering light of Jaila's words. "And tell him he was a fool and a murderer, and he broke his sister's heart, too—not just yours, Jaila; he broke mine too."

"He can hear you," Jaila said quietly. "And he's not dead. Look! We have to get back to the woods, find where his human body is, and take him to the hospital. He'll survive if we hurry. . . ."

They both turned to her. She fell back against the cushion of the wind, made dizzy by the familiarity of it: the brother and the sister turning those uncannily similar gazes upon her in the moment they realized that they understood something that Jaila, the perennial outsider, didn't.

"Jaila," Ursula said, "I found his body. His *human* body. In the ravine. Someone had stabbed him and then rolled him over the edge. They wrapped him in a goddamn blanket, Jaila, and I found him like that."

It was Ursula's eyes that made Jaila believe her. They were so steady and so full of pain, so sorry for everything they had seen. "But didn't he lead you to the sacred well? Didn't you see him bite me to push me in?"

"It wasn't him," she said. "His nagual is dead too."

The coyote looked as though he were dying on her lap now, panting and groaning in an effort to stay conscious that Jaila didn't understand.

"Then who are you?" Jaila asked softly.

Tizoc, he said. *Not the same one but not a different one, either.*

"And where are we?" she asked.

She got a faint grimace, which she took for a smile. *The subjunctive tense.*

"Shoulda, woulda, coulda," she said in her first language, the one that the two of them didn't understand, and she laughed so hard that she cried.

"It *is* him," she told Ursula through her tears. They turned Jaila's flames beautiful shades of purple and blue, but the fire held. "He's dying again, but it is him."

We cross paths with our other lives, with our other selves when we pass through here. We are in between our own possibilities.

Now Ursula gripped Jaila's hand hard enough to hurt. "Tell him he could have been brilliant—tell him he could have been loved for his real self, not that power he chased until he died."

The coyote gasped a laugh. *I didn't deserve it, but I was loved. You never told her?*

Jaila remembered that one night—the blanket in the desert, the stars like sand strewn across the sky, the promises he'd whispered, the money he was saving, the plans he had. But she hadn't seen the photos then. She hadn't known the money was rotten, like those bodies in a hidden grave that their families would never find.

She shook her head, and the coyote sighed and was still.

They floated for a while afterward, heavy and pendulous with the dead weight of the coyote.

Ursula broke the silence. "We have to leave."

Jaila nodded. "But we'll never get back to where we were before."

"We can't stay here forever. We have to try."

"We can't go back together?"

Ursula hugged her. "No, little sister. You know we can't."

"You'll find me?"

"Will you find me?"

Jaila gripped her shoulders. "Always," she said, and the flame leaped from her mouth, blue and gold. It burned through the slick with the ferocity of an oil fire, and left a hole just large enough for her to jump through.

"Go!" Ursula shouted.

"But what about you?"

"Don't worry about me. The wind will find me a way through. I have a debt, anyway, to the coyote."

They met each other's eyes one last time. Jaila caught herself smiling. Then Ursula pushed and Jaila tumbled, and she fell through the hole her heart had made.

She landed in a gas station bathroom in Pearsall, Texas, on broken tiles that had once been white. She recognized that sink, the broken pipe gushing water from fifteen seconds before, when she had tried to climb it to reach the window. She was wet. Her arm hurt from where she had fallen.

Federal agents were waiting for her outside. They had caught up to the bus, and she wasn't going to escape them this time. She wasn't going to make it to Ursula.

Jaila stood up. She peeled off her wet hoodie. It smelled, very faintly, of dried marigolds and coyote blood and the desert wind that blows down far away hills at night.

An officer pounded on the bathroom door.

"Always," Jaila said, in the language of that place, and let him in.

"Aw, hell," Jackie said. "You sure you didn't eat some bad peyote or something?"

We'd been walking for a couple of hours, slowly making our way over increasingly rougher terrain. The woods had given way to rocky ground and boulders, and we'd had to backtrack a couple of times to find a path down that wasn't so steep. Tino was out front again, but he was following Jaila's directions, even if he wouldn't admit it. He was a control freak, but he wasn't stupid. Even if Jaila didn't know exactly where we were or where we were going, she knew the general direction we needed to hike, which was more than the rest of us could say.

We picked some roots that Cody swore were wild onions, which he said he remembered from one of Doug's lectures on what we could and couldn't eat in the woods. Jaila said we had to be careful they weren't death camas, but they smelled like onion, and that was good enough.

"Believe what you want," Jaila said. "It's just a story."

"Did Tizoc or the coyote or whatever he was," Georgia asked, "did he really die?"

"I said it was only a story!"

Tino started laughing. It was a dark, bitter sound that carried through the woods. "Girl falls down a well or some shit and thinks she knows how to get us back to camp." He was shaking his head. "Come on, Jaila, talk to the wind or whatever and figure out where we are."

Georgia shouldered up past Cody. "Leave her alone, Tino."

"Mind your own business."

"You really think Doug would miss you if you didn't make it back with us?" Lucinda said. "Is there anyone back home who wouldn't be happy if you disappeared? Keep talking and maybe we'll find out."

Tino snorted. "One rich girl defending another. I'm shocked."

"Why don't you tell us why *you're* here?" Jackie said. "What'd you do? Rob a convenience store or something?"

"Why I'm here's none of your damn business," he said. "But I got a story for you. I got the winning story right here."

"A CAUTIONARY TALE"

by Stephanie Kuehn

I WAS ON THE BEACH when I met him. Dover Springs was throwing its annual Feast of Avalon party to celebrate the autumnal equinox. This tradition involved hundreds of wealthy college students playing pagan for the night. Gripping lit torches and armed with cases of beer, they'd marched off campus and down the hillside as a unified force to flood Dover Cove, that narrow sliver of beach carved along the southwest end of our midsize California coastal town, where they'd promptly set a massive bonfire ablaze. Everything after was flicker-flame and hedonistic persuasion. A drum circle pounded away near the water's edge, a rhythmic invocation urging the toga-draped crowd to lose themselves in the sand and the darkness, to dance, drink, fight, and fuck, all beneath the bone-colored moon.

They were more than happy to oblige.

My job that night was simple enough: I was working as a student safety escort. That sounds boring, I know, but someone had to do it. It was a two-mile return hike back up to campus; Dover Springs was like a fortress, built high on a hill, overlooking the water, sequestered from the rest of the world by geography, by privilege—hell, even by iron gates. If someone felt unsafe walking alone in the darkness, I was meant to go with them and ensure they arrived back at school without getting mugged, abducted, or—the most likely scenario— passing out in their own puke before rolling into a drainage ditch to die. Of course, I wasn't armed with a gun or pepper spray or anything other than a bright orange vest and a heavy-duty flashlight, so my role was one of illusion more than genuine protection. But that, I suppose, could be said about a lot of things.

Despite my role—or likely, because of it—I might as well have been invisible on that beach. No one bothered to speak or look at me, and the party was pretty much going full throttle by the time the stranger stumbled from the darkness. I didn't get a chance to see where he'd come from or what he'd been doing—pissing in the sand dunes, no doubt—but I watched as he weaved his way in my direction before his legs gave out, sending him crashing to the ground, not five feet from where I was.

I didn't say anything. My initial impression was that the guy was both extremely tall and extremely drunk; he had a half-empty bottle of Maker's Mark gripped in one hand. He was also a Dover student, that much was obvious, but not like the others. His heavy blond hair had been styled into a Kennedy-esque swoop, and he wore ridiculous clothes for the occasion: a tweed jacket and dark tie and brown leather oxfords, all of which were the antithesis of the equinox celebration, both in overall spirit and basic common sense. Who the hell wore oxfords to the beach?

It took a moment before the stranger became aware of my

presence, but when he did, he sprawled his large body across the sand like a walrus, rolling onto one side with a grunt so that he was facing me. He reached his hand to shake mine.

"Hollis English," he boomed.

"I'm C. J.," I replied.

"C. J. what?"

"Perez."

"Well, C. J. Perez." He offered me a roguish hint of a smile. "As luck would have it, you're just the person I've been looking for."

This was about the last thing I expected to hear. "You've been looking for *me*? Why?"

The stranger pushed himself up to sitting, so that we were both facing the ocean, the swell and suck of the rising tide. "Because tonight of all nights, I need what you're offering."

"And what would that be?"

"Safety."

"Oh." I relaxed a bit. "Well, sure. Yeah. Whenever you want, we can walk back up together. That's what I'm here for."

Hollis held up his whiskey bottle and shook it. "In the interest of self-disclosure, you should probably know that I'm really fucking drunk."

"That's okay. It's sort of expected."

"Want some?" he asked.

"No, thanks."

"What? Don't you drink?"

"Nah."

He scoffed. "Why the hell not? And don't start in with some

virtue argument. I see that gold cross hanging from your neck, C. J. Perez. If you're guilty of one sin, you're guilty of them all. And we're all fucking guilty. Even you."

"I just don't like it. Plus, I'm working."

"Boring." Hollis waved a disinterested hand. "Tell me what year you are. I've never seen you around before."

"I'm a freshman."

"Figures. I'm a sophomore, by the way, so my wisdom about this school is infinitely greater than yours. Anything you need to know, I'm your man. What house are you?"

"None."

"None?"

"I'm not pledging."

His eyes gleamed with boozy admiration. "Then you're one smart fucking kid. First year, and you already know there's no sense fighting tradition in a place like this. Hell, I only pledged Pike because my asshole dad did it before me. He really is an asshole, by the way. Guess that means I'll be one too. But such is life, right?"

I didn't answer.

Hollis leaned back on tweed-covered elbows. "How old does that make you? Eighteen? Seventeen, even? Tell me you're a goddamn adult."

"I'm twenty," I said.

He snorted. "Who the hell goes away to college when they're *twenty*?"

"A lot of people."

"Really?"

"Sure."

"Why?"

I pushed my fingers into cold sand, savoring grit. "For me, it was mostly a matter of money. I spent a couple years working after I graduated. My family, well, we were going through a hard time. I couldn't afford to leave. Until now."

"What happened?"

"My father died."

"Shit." Hollis frowned, pushing his perfect hair back. "Well, that fucking sucks. I'm sorry, man."

"Don't be. He was in a lot of pain."

"But I am," he insisted. "Losing a family member like that . . . It changes everything. It's not easy to keep going, to keep doing what you're supposed to do, when something happens to make it all feel pointless."

"True. But you don't always know *how* tragedy'll change things. Because, in a way, my father dying was lucky."

"Lucky?"

"I don't mean it wasn't awful. I just mean, well, we had nothing, really, after what happened, so I ended up working down at the yacht harbor, trying to save money. But it was my boss there who nominated me for this citizen scholarship program. That's why I was offered the spot here at Dover Springs. Full ride. Room and board. It wouldn't have happened otherwise. So, you know, fate, mysterious ways, and all that."

"Still," Hollis breathed, "that's a steep price to pay for college."

"Everything has a price."

"I guess. What was he like, your dad? Were you close?"

"He was brave," I said after a moment. Then: "Yeah, we were close."

"Did you grow up around here? In Dover?"

"Yup."

"Me too."

Of course he had. This fact didn't surprise me, even though our paths had never crossed. Hollis and I came from different worlds, after all. Like everyone I'd grown up with, I was the product of both public schools and public housing, whereas he'd clearly been raised on prep school and trust funds. Dover was funny that way, a dimorphic sun-baked beach town, populated mostly by working poor struggling to hold on to declining jobs in tourism, agriculture, and manufacturing. But there was also the Other Dover, the part that sat separate from the rest of us, an oceanfront enclave of gated communities that housed the ultra wealthy, the powerful, the influential. The people living in those communities rarely ventured to other parts of town. They never had to. And when it came time for their Ivy League–rejected offspring to flee the nest—or more accurately, hop out of it—Dover Springs was the obvious choice. Never mind that the school's notorious exclusivity was based solely on tuition price, not reputation—the end result was the same; they could afford what others couldn't.

"Hey, look at that," Hollis said.

I turned to see him pointing at the hills above us, at the exact spot where the school sat, high on a distant bluff, hidden behind trees.

"What am I looking at?" I asked.

"The fog," he said a little breathlessly.

Hollis was right. Dover Cove faced south, which meant the wind rattled our backs, blowing down from the north. Heavy gusts pushed swirling sheets of fog straight off the ocean and into the hills, where it would gather in clumps and cling to the earth until sunrise. This soupy claustrophobic gloom was a defining feature of our town. It seeped into your pores and through your mind, and even if you lived in a place with triple-pane windows and an air-purifying system to keep the fog from slinking inside and playing host to mold spores and chronic illness, there was no way to escape it completely. It was pretty much the one thing everyone in Dover had to reckon with on a fairly regular basis.

"I like the fog," I said. "I know it's shitty to drive in, but it always feels so *familiar*. Like it's meant to be here. Like it has purpose. Yet at the same time it reminds me of things I couldn't possibly know. A different time period, perhaps. Or a different life."

"You mean déjà vu?" Hollis asked.

"I guess. It's weird, but it's something I feel a lot. This sense that I've been here before, on this beach, watching this fog."

"Maybe you have," he said softly.

I turned to look at him. "What's that supposed to mean?"

"Maybe there's more to the fog than people realize. You've heard of the Dover Phantom, haven't you?"

I laughed. "Of course. Everyone's heard of the Phantom. He's our local legend. Our town monster. Our cautionary tale."

"But a tale against *what*?"

"You tell me."

Hollis's eyes glittered in the moonshine. "You don't believe he's real, do you?"

"The Phantom?" I asked. "Yeah, sorry for the shocker, but I have a hard time believing there's a serial killer who can materialize from the fog stalking the town of Dover."

"Well, you should believe it because I can assure you he's

absolutely, one hundred percent real. And by the way, it's not *Dover* he's stalking."

"It's not?"

"Oh no," Hollis English told me. "It's *us*."

I watched as he downed more whiskey. "Us?"

He gestured at the party, at the staggering hordes of college students.

"You mean everyone on the beach?"

"I mean our peers. Our fellow students. You and me. All of us. You think 'cause you're at some fancy private school now, you don't have to worry about watching your back?"

"I didn't say that."

"Yeah, well, our precious school's not as safe as it's made out to be. Doesn't matter how much our daddies pay to send us here. There's some dark shit going on. Did you know someone broke into the admin building last night and stole some stuff?"

"What'd they take?"

"Don't know. But the point is, even with people like you around—"

My spine stiffened. "What do you mean, *people like me?*"

Hollis gestured at my vest. "This. This whole useless thing you're doing. You're a goddamn *safety escort*. You're supposed to make me feel good about being drunk and stupid and letting my guard down, but let's be real—the world's not any less dangerous just because you're in it."

"Then stop drinking," I snapped. "And while you're at it, find your own way back to campus."

riddle

"Fuck you."

Whatever. I turned my back on him and the fog and the murky hills and instead set my gaze once again on the ocean, that rippling vastness stretching toward the horizon. The drum circle—now accompanied by wasted students howling at the moon—pounded on, and while the water was somewhat calm, everything on the beach was pure chaos. The Feast of Avalon was intended to honor the balance of light and darkness, that fleeting moment of harmony on Earth's wild tilt around the sun. But for Dover students, most of whom had never known true darkness, it was their chance to throw harmony to the wind, to raise as much as hell as they dared, so long as they woke up the next morning with their gilded futures still intact.

I'd had enough. I jumped to my feet, brushed sand from my knees. Began to walk away.

"Wait," Hollis called after me. "Where are you going?"

I paused long enough to stare down at him, at his perfect hair and stupid oxfords, which were soaked and ruined and cost more than anything I'd ever owned. "I'm getting out of here. I'm sick of this shitty party. I'm sick of everything."

"But you can't leave me."

"Sure I can."

"Your job is *literally* to help me."

"Oh, so now you care about my useless job?"

"Yes!"

"Why?"

"Please, C. J.!" The haughty expression on Hollis's face had shifted into one of sheer panic. "I'm sorry I said that, all right?

159

I told you I'm an asshole. But I *need* you. I do. Or I need someone—anyone—who's willing to keep me safe tonight!"

It's fair to say I can be swayed by emotion. I guess that goes a long way in explaining how I was able to shove aside my resentment toward Hollis and the fact that he genuinely believed *his* safety was worth more than my own. That he genuinely believed I might agree with him. But it was the Dover way, after all, to assume that things like financial aid and scholarships would generate gratitude, not enlightenment, on the part of the recipient. In that sense his attitude was hard to take personally. So Hollis English and I ended up walking back to campus together, although he refused to tell me what it was he was afraid of and why he didn't want to be alone.

"You have to tell me *something*," I said as we left Dover Cove, walking up the rickety beach steps and past the boardwalk and the tributary that was lined with pussy willows and croaked with peeper frogs. From there we cut through the north end of town, zigzagging through the fog-hazed streets, heading for the access trail that would take us into the woods and back up to campus. "It's going to be a long walk if you don't talk. And I already told you about my family."

Hollis dipped his head as we strode across the macadam. Something was jumpy and odd about him—he kept looking over his shoulder—but slugging more whiskey and smoking a clove cigarette seemed to lift his mood. "You like horror films, C. J.?"

"Yeah, sure. Sometimes, I guess."

"What are some of your favorites?"

I thought about this. "Well, I don't like gore. So nothing with a lot of blood."

"Seriously?"

"Yes, seriously. I guess what I like are stories that don't just make you scared of what's out there, waiting to get you. I like the ones that make you scared of what might be hidden somewhere inside of yourself. Not knowing one's own secrets, never mind anyone else's."

"Give me an example."

"*Jacob's Ladder*. Also *Stoker*. *The Invitation*. *The Exorcist*, even."

Hollis offered a begrudging nod. "Decent choices. I approve."

"But you know, I think *Psycho* might be my favorite of all. I figure if someone can make you empathize with a killer, they must've done something right."

"Empathy," Hollis echoed. "Can't say that identifying with a killer is ever what I'm looking for in a film. Or in anything."

"What are you looking for?"

"Justice."

I laughed. I couldn't help myself. "When has *justice* ever been the source of horror? Isn't it usually the opposite?"

Hollis scowled. "I don't mean law-and-order-type justice. I mean more of a spiritual kind of thing. Karma or whatever. Like *The Ring*. Or *I Spit on Your Grave*."

"You're talking about revenge," I said. "That's different. Those aren't stories about fairness."

"Then what are they about?"

"Punishment, I guess. Retribution."

He shrugged. "Sounds like justice to me."

I didn't answer. We'd reached the dirt trail that would take us into the trees and out of the town proper. The fog haze grew thicker, the shadows darker, gloom closing in on all sides. I switched on my flashlight.

Hollis grabbed for my arm. "Hey, turn that off!"

"What?"

"I said turn it off!"

"But I can't see!"

"I mean it!"

"Fine!" He kept grabbing at me until I shoved him back; Hollis was significantly larger than I was, but he was too drunk to be very coordinated. I held on to the flashlight but finally switched it off like he asked. "What the hell?"

"I don't want anyone to see us."

"Like *who*?"

Hollis peered over his shoulder again. "Like anyone."

"What?"

He walked faster, leaving me to catch up with him. Soon I was sweating from the effort, the trail growing steeper as we trudged upward through the night.

"You ever hear about Danielle Bradford?" Hollis asked after a moment.

I glanced at him. "She someone you know?"

"Not exactly. She was a student here back in 1915. That was the fourth year Dover Springs was in operation."

"What about her?"

"Well, Danielle was a local, like us. She came to study music— played flute and cello, although from what I've learned, she wasn't particularly talented at either. Anyway, when she was in her sophomore year, on a foggy September night, just like this one, Danielle finished practicing and left the conservatory. She was trying to make it back to her dorm before the ten o'clock curfew, according to witness reports. Only . . ."

"Only what?"

"Only she never got there. They found her body the next morning, in the bushes right outside her own room. Her throat had been slashed with a razor."

"Jesus. Who did it?"

"They never found out. Two years later . . . it happened again. Only this time the victim was a guy. Samuel Forsythe. Also a sophomore. He didn't show up to class after visiting with his family for a weekend in March. I guess his friends assumed he hadn't returned to campus. Well, two days later he was found hanging from a tree in the woods behind the chapel, which used to be on the north side of campus, by the way, down by the stream. They moved it in 1956 due to flooding."

"So he'd been murdered too?"

"That one was harder to tell. But a third student, Graham Keller, was killed the year after that, also on a night with particularly dense fog—this time in September again. He'd gotten separated from his girlfriend while hiking and was found in a clearing the next morning. He'd been stabbed in the neck repeatedly with an ice pick—so clearly murder. This sparked rumors of a serial killer in Dover. Our very own Jack the Ripper, but someone with a taste for college students, not prostitutes. And because of the fog and the mysterious nature of the deaths, it wasn't long before the killer was given a name."

"The Dover Phantom," I said.

"Exactly. But you want to know what happened next?"

"What's that?"

"The murders stopped."

"Stopped?"

He nodded. "For over twenty years. The next killing wasn't until March 20, 1939. Mary Downing. She was found strangled near the tennis courts. And there were two more murders. In 1941 and '42. They stopped again until '65, and it's been like that ever since: three murders approximately every quarter century. We're up to thirteen dead students now, including one a few years back, which means we're due two more for this cycle. And sure, people know about some of these deaths, obviously. Maybe they've even heard of the Dover Phantom. But no one's put all the pieces together the way that I have. No one sees it for what it really is. A *pattern*."

"A pattern?"

"Yes! It means something. This is all happening for a reason. And not only do we get three killings every generation, but they all take place in late March or late September. Do you know why that is?"

"There's a lot of fog?" I ventured.

"It's the *equinox*."

"What?"

"I'm serious. The vernal equinox is March 20 and the autumnal is tonight. September 22. Those are the two times of the year when day and night are equal, and all the killings have taken place on or within a day or two of these dates. That can't be a coincidence."

I was beyond baffled. "So you think these deaths are connected— both to each other and to a specific celestial event? But why?"

"That's what I'm trying to figure out. I mean, it's a whole century of murder, but because it's been happening over such a long period of time, no one cares. Except me."

"So why *do* you care?"

His voice hardened. "Are you saying you don't?"

"No, but you want me to believe in a killer who strikes every twenty-five years or so, exactly three times, only on these dates, and that he's been around for over *a hundred years*?"

"That's right."

"How could that be?"

"I've thought about that." Hollis licked his lips. "A lot. Because the killings being random would be the most obvious explanation. Dover has crime. Hell, we've had our fair share of murders around here; it's no wonder not everything is front-page news. Did you know that during the seventies, there were at least three active serial killers in this general part of California?"

I nodded because I did know. Dover, for all its gated excess and idyllic seaside beauty, was known for its drifting population and increasing drug trade. Loose morals and New Age fetishism. Beneath our summer tans and salt-spray ease, darker urges lingered. Violence. Racism. Cultish ideologies. Utter greed and dirt-cheap pleasures. "But that doesn't answer the question about how he could be around for such a long period of time."

"Well, what if the killer's not a *he*?"

I cocked my head. "You mean, what if the killer's a woman?"

"No, I mean, what if the reason the killings have been happening for so long is because the killer's not a *who*, but a *what*?"

* * *

I gaped at Hollis, but before I could respond, the roar of an approaching car engine made me jump. We'd reached the junction where the wooded trail joined with the main drive leading up to the school, and I whipped around in time to see a pair of headlights careening out of a hairpin turn and rocketing up the hillside.

I stumbled back at the sight, reaching to pull Hollis with me, only to find him not reacting to the vehicle at all—he just stood there, staring at me in that strange way of his. It was creepy, really, so I hissed: "What do you mean, the killer's a *what*? Like a tree?"

"No, not like a *tree*," he snapped peevishly. "You're an idiot."

"Then what are you talking about?"

But Hollis refused to answer. Instead, he folded his arms and set his jaw, like I'd offended him in some way. I didn't get a chance to ask more questions because the approaching vehicle—which turned out to be a silver pickup, its bed filled with a crowd of shouting students—blared its horn and came to a screeching stop beside us. The air reeked of burned rubber.

"Hollis English!" The driver of the truck leaned out of the window. "Holy shit. What the hell are you doing out here?"

Hollis said nothing, but I stepped forward, put on my friendliest smile. "We were just heading back to campus. Want to give us a ride?"

"Who are *you*?" a girl from the back asked me. She wore a Giants hat and knelt on the wheel well. "I've never seen you before."

A guy seated beside her shone a flashlight at me—the reflective piping on my vest lit up in an embarrassing way—and he hooted. "Look at that! He's a *safety escort*, Z. Hollis needs a grown-up to walk around with him."

The girl clapped her hands. "That makes total sense."

"Doesn't it?"

She looked at me again. "So how long have you been working here?"

"Huh?"

"You're one of the new hires for the grounds staff, right? That's why you got stuck doing this?"

Her friend rolled his eyes. "Jesus, Z. He's a *student*. Probably doing work-study or something."

I nodded.

"Come on," the driver said impatiently. "I don't give a fuck who the kid is so long as he doesn't jack us. Get in the back already. Let's *go*."

We scrambled into the truck bed, where I promptly thanked everyone and introduced myself. Hollis, on the other hand, remained a sullen heap, pulling his knees to his chest and refusing to say anything, despite the fact everyone appeared to know who he was.

"You coming to the after-party?" The girl with the Giants hat squeezed between us. She seemed to want to make things up with me. "Or are safety escorts not allowed to have any fun?"

"What after-party?" I asked.

"At Pike house. Hollis knows about it. He's supposed to be helping host the damn thing, but you know how he is."

"Not really. We just met tonight."

The girl grinned. "He hasn't tried to convince you to go ghost hunting with him, has he?"

"Uh, that hasn't come up."

Her eyes sparkled. "But he told you about the ghosts, didn't he?"

I glanced at Hollis, who looked more miserable than ever. "I don't know what you're talking about."

"Oh, he told you," the girl said brightly. "I can tell. And look, we all think he's nuts, but who knows? Maybe he's right. Maybe we're all being haunted."

"Haunted?" I echoed.

She pinched my arm. "He's not going to puke, is he? He looks like he's going to puke."

"He might. He's had a lot to drink. More than he should've, that's for sure."

Hollis lifted his head, just enough to glare at me. "You know, I can hear you, Perez."

"Sorry," I muttered.

He kept up with the glaring long enough to pull his whiskey bottle from his pocket and drink more.

The girl whispered in my ear, "Don't worry about him. He's always like this. He's been strange ever since . . ."

"Ever since what?" I asked.

"Never mind. He just needs to have fun. And you know, after that shitty thing I said to you earlier, maybe you do too."

I hesitated. "Yeah, maybe."

The truck rocked through a pothole, sending the girl bouncing against me. She laughed at my startled expression. "Well, in that case," she said. "There's no excuse. You *have* to come to our party."

The truck paused briefly at the security gate before finally rolling on to campus. The ground fog beneath us had grown so dense the road had all but vanished. Everything else still twinkled with beauty, with seclusion; the Dover Springs property was a lush woodland oasis consisting of almost two hundred acres of tree-lined trails, quaint classrooms speckled among the redwoods, and swinging footbridges that stretched across burbling creeks.

Clustered on the east side of campus, a row of stately frat houses sat far from the freshman dorms, close to the trees, and after we'd parked in the nearby student lot and were walking up toward Pike house, the girl with the Giants hat pulled a pair of devil horns from her purse. I watched as she slipped them on over her baseball hat before digging around for a glittery silver halo that she gently placed on top of my head.

"What's this for?" I asked.

"You're going to need it where we're going."

"I am? What kind of party is this?"

"You still don't know?"

"No."

The girl grinned as she trotted up the front porch steps ahead of me. "Heaven and hell."

Part—all right, most—of me longed to follow her, but when I turned to look for Hollis, I felt a twinge of guilt. Or shame, really, for having abandoned him. While everyone else from the truck was flooding into the frat house, he remained standing off to the side, in the shadows, with his broad shoulders slumped and his hands in his pockets.

"Nice halo," he muttered as I walked over to him.

"I bet I can find you one."

He shook his head. "Go get laid if you want. You don't need to take care of me."

"I don't want to get laid."

"Everyone wants to get laid."

"Well, I don't," I insisted.

He pouted. "I'm *not* hunting ghosts, by the way. Zoe hears what she wants."

"Yeah, well, you were the one who said we were all in danger from a killer who wasn't a person. What're people supposed to think?"

"We *are* in danger!" he cried. "All of us! Right now. Well, technically, *you* aren't. But the rest of us are."

"Why not me?"

His eyes flashed. "You really want to know?"

"Yes!"

"Then I'll show you. Come on." Hollis turned and beckoned for me to follow, leading me up onto the porch, through the frat house front door, and straight into hell.

Once inside, I stopped and stared. Then I couldn't *stop* staring. It was impressive, really, to see how quickly the party had moved from beach to home. Unlike Hollis and me, everyone else apparently must've driven back to campus after the eleven p.m. bonfire cutoff. The entire downstairs of Pike house was currently decorated in flames and pitchforks while a black light lit the living room with swirls of neon and the crush of painted bodies. Iron Butterfly's "In-a-Gadda-Da-Vida" thundered over the speakers, set on hellish repeat, and the line for the keg stretched from the kitchen, winding down a long hallway.

I probably would've kept standing there for all eternity except Hollis tapped my shoulder and pointed to a staircase. Spell broken, I nodded and trailed after him, departing hell and ascending into a world bright and glittering—the second floor of the frat house had been transformed into a cloudy fog machine–generated sort of paradise. Every surface was covered in aluminum foil and flickered with candlelight. Glitter and angel wings fluttered from the ceiling while Sia sang passionately.

The party's theme, it dawned on me, was a direct nod to the Feast of Avalon—that other celebration of light and dark, good and evil, those warring forces of our world. But there was no time for any deeper theological musing; dragging me down a confusing twist of corridors, Hollis quickly pulled me into a filthy bedroom and shut the door behind us. Then locked it. I looked around. The place was disgusting. It resembled a rat's nest more than anything else—papers were tacked to the wall, clothes strewn everywhere, dishes piled in a corner, including dirty ones crusted with bits of food.

"Nasty." I pointed at a small cloud of fruit flies. "Don't you eat in the dining hall ever?"

"Not anymore," he said. "Now look at this."

"At what?"

"Right here." Shoving a bunch of crap onto the floor, he switched on a desk lamp and flipped open his laptop. Huddled beside him, I watched as he got online and pulled up the Dover Springs website, navigating to the page titled "Our History." "Tell me what you see."

I squinted at the screen. The page described information I already knew: how the site of Dover Springs had originally housed a private mental asylum that had been in operation from 1886 to 1907, at which point the hospital had tragically burned down. Rather than rebuild, the doctors who had operated the asylum decided it would be better and more charitable for the Dover community to start a private university instead.

"Okay," I said when I was done reading. "So what?"

"Did you look at the picture?"

I hadn't, but on the page was an old black-and-white photograph of a group of stuffy-looking old white guys—the school's founders. They were standing on the main campus's lawn, flanking a large sign with the Dover Springs crest carved into it.

"How many people are in that photo?" Hollis asked.

I quickly counted. "Thirteen."

"Do you consider that a good number or a bad one?"

I paused. "An unlucky one."

"Fair enough," Hollis said. "Well, I've been curious about the real history behind this place, so I did some digging into who these guys were and especially the asylum that was here before. The one that burned. And despite all that charitable talk, it was a pretty fucking awful place. There were reports of abuse. Neglect. People claimed they were wrongfully held for years on end. Families were broken up. Spouses couldn't get their loved ones out, even when they wanted to leave."

I frowned. "But that's just how it was back then, right? People with mental illnesses weren't treated fairly. Or humanely. I mean, it's shitty, but I don't know that it means the Dover Springs Asylum was any more cruel than any other place."

"Maybe not. But they were definitely more corrupt. Did you know that the town of Dover used to have a special committee that had the power to determine if someone needed to be institutionalized? And their decisions were legally binding. There were no hearings or means of recourse; they had complete discretion. This committee called themselves the Commission of Lunacy."

"No way," I said. "That can't be a real thing."

"It *was*. And from the records I found, those same thirteen doctors who ran that hellhole, who got subsidies from the state for every patient they housed, were the exact same doctors who made up the commission."

I pointed at the photo. "These guys?"

He nodded. "It's all on record, if you know where to look. With the commission's power, they were able to have Dover citizens committed for the most ridiculous reasons: being distraught over a breakup, losing faith in their religion. Even for getting fired from a job or protesting unfair work practices. Usually, it was poor people. Or women."

"Jesus."

"The worst of it is, when the hospital caught fire, all the staff and doctors got out safely, but they didn't go back for a lot of the patients. And you know how long it must've taken the fire department to get up that hill. By the time they arrived, nineteen patients had died, locked in their rooms; some in restraints, waiting for help that never came. Can you imagine? Being shut in there for no reason in the first place—or because someone wanted you locked up and out of the way—and then dying like that, completely helpless?"

"I really can't," I said, although I wondered if he knew anything at all about our country's current issue with mass incarceration. "It's disgusting. But, Hollis, these doctors, the school founders . . . When you said the killer wasn't a *who* but a *what*, what did you mean?"

"I meant, what if the killer's not a person at all, but a whole *group* of people?"

My mind spun. Thirteen. He'd said there'd been thirteen doctors.

"What kind of group?" I asked cautiously.

"What else?" Hollis said. "A coven."

A coven. I stepped back from his desk. "You can't actually believe that."

His face colored. "Sure I can! It makes sense, doesn't it? They were the *Commission of Lunacy*, for God's sake. They essentially murdered nineteen innocent people who *they* wrongly locked up, and as a result, they were rewarded with this school, where they profited even more. If that's not evil, I don't know what is. And so maybe that coven is still around. Maybe those same thirteen men weren't men at all, and they have to keep killing every so often, in order to . . ."

I stared at him. "In order to what?"

"Stay alive," he whispered.

I blew air through my cheeks. "That still doesn't explain the time period. I haven't seen any hundred-and-fifty-year-old men wandering around Dover recently."

"But what if they don't look old? What if that's the *point*? Think about it: If you needed a constant stream of young people to sacrifice for your own eternal youth, and you couldn't run your asylum scam anymore, what better plan could you have than building your own elite university and inviting those young people to *pay you* for the privilege of coming here?"

I was speechless. This wasn't just drunken rambling. This poor guy really believed what he was saying, that those same thirteen men still lived up here, still walked among the students, in some youthful form or another.

He kept going. "It's the equinox. That's the key. I thought it was ghosts at first; you know, some sort of specter. But that was wrong.

174

The celestial event is definitely part of the ritual, which means there's a good chance someone here on campus is going to die tonight. Before sunrise. Although *you* don't have to worry about being targeted."

"Why's that?" I asked.

"You're too old. Everyone who's been killed so far has been nineteen."

"Nineteen?"

"The same number as those who died in the fire."

"Ah." Then it hit me. "Wait. How old are you, Hollis?"

The smile he gave was a grim one. "I'll be twenty next week."

There was no talking sense to him after that. Hollis really and truly believed what he was saying, and nothing *I* said changed his mind. Apparently, a coven of witches was running the school and sacrificing its own students on the nights of the equinox in some black magic blood rite so that they could live forever. It was a terrifying thought, sure. But not one I could bring myself to believe.

At all.

"So what're you going to do?" I asked after we'd gone back and forth for a bit. It was clear our opinions on the matter were deadlocked. It was also clear he resented my skepticism.

Hollis paced the room. "I *told* you. Tonight's the best shot I'll ever have, so I'm going to find the Phantom and I'm going to stop him."

"Him?"

"*Them!*"

"How?"

"I don't know!"

I went for the opening. "See! That's just it. You don't even know what you're looking for, which means you won't find it and you won't disprove it, and that means you'll just keep—"

"Shut up!" Hollis stopped to seethe in my direction. "I already know you don't fucking believe me. You've made that pretty god-damn clear."

"It's not that. . . ."

He walked toward me then. His hands were curled into fists. "You don't get it, do you? I don't *want* your opinion. I never wanted it, C. J. It's worthless to me because you don't know shit about any-thing. So just shut your mouth. Okay?"

"Okay," I said.

Hollis sneered. "You're pathetic."

I didn't argue with him on that point. Instead, I shut my mouth and stood there, staring at the floor, waiting until Hollis had grabbed his coat and his whiskey bottle and stormed from the room.

Slammed the door behind him.

I stayed like that for a while, unsure of what to do or how to do it or if I should even do anything at all. But in the end I couldn't do *noth-ing*. So after a few minutes, I left Hollis's room, winding my way back through heaven and down the staircase into hell, where I found the party had grown more crowded, more out of control. Iron Butterfly's seventeen-minute psychedelic dirge droned on while someone lined up shots of Fireball on the dining room table. I couldn't see Hollis anywhere, but I did spot Zoe, the girl from the truck who'd given me my halo. She was leaning against the wall, still in her Giants cap and devil horns, and I couldn't help myself. I went to her.

"Hey," I said.

She smiled. "It's the safety escort."

"My name's C. J."

"How 'bout a drink, C. J.?"

"No, thanks."

"You know, I still think it's weird," she said.

"What's weird?"

"That I've never seen you before. You don't look familiar at all."

"It's a big campus," I said.

"It's really not."

My cheeks warmed. "Yeah, well, it's pretty easy to be invisible when everyone wants to pretend you don't exist."

Her brow furrowed. "Why would anyone want to pretend that?"

I opened my mouth, but before I could say anything else, the music cut off. The overhead lights came on, too.

"Oh shit," Zoe whispered, and pointed behind me.

I turned and groaned. Hollis English was standing on a coffee table in the middle of the living room. He looked more disheveled than ever: his hair a greasy mess, his eyes wild and bloodshot, his oxfords somehow missing. In one hand he still held on to that damn whiskey bottle, but in the other he gripped what appeared to be a large hunting knife, the kind with a long jagged-edge blade. He definitely hadn't had *that* before. I held my breath, watching in horror as Hollis staggered, almost fell, then raised the knife high above his head with a roar of fury.

"One of you here," he screeched, "is a killer! You're worse than that, even. You're a *monster*. I know what you're planning, so you can quit hiding behind whatever mask you're wearing. Show

177

yourself! Come after *me* this time and stop being such a goddamn coward!"

In response, the crowd around him began hooting and laughing, as if this were a performance they'd seen before.

"Maybe it's me tonight!" someone called out.

"Or me!" yelled another.

"Maybe we all want you dead!"

"Or undead!"

"No . . . definitely dead!"

"Should I do something?" I whispered to Zoe. "This is bad."

She shook her head. "The best thing to do is ignore him. He won't remember any of this tomorrow."

That seemed a reasonable tactic, except a guy who I recognized from earlier as the driver of the silver pickup, elbowed his way through the crowd right then and swaggered up to Hollis. The expression on his face was one of pure disgust.

"Let's do this, English," he said. "I'm sick of your paranoid shit. If it weren't for your dad, I would've kicked your ass out of this house by now. So yeah, tonight, I'm all for doing whatever the hell it is you want. If one of us is looking to kill you, let's just be done with it. Okay?"

Hollis shrugged. "Okay."

The guy snapped his fingers.

And the lights went out.

For the first ten seconds there was silence. Zoe reached for my hand, and I held hers. Then I heard a thud, like bodies colliding. Followed by what sounded like a piece of furniture tipping over. Someone screamed and glass shattered, and that was when panic set in because everyone was shouting and moving, and someone shoved me from behind. I wrapped my arms around Zoe, to keep her from being run into, and more screaming started and—

The lights came back on.

Hollis was nowhere to be found.

"Hey, where is he?" a voice shouted.

"What the hell?" The truck driver guy lay on the floor, rubbing his cheek. "That asshole sucker punched me."

"Look!" A girl with feathery angel wings pointed at the carpet next to the now-tipped-over coffee table. A dark stain covered the gray shag. It hadn't been there before.

"Oh shit." Everyone closed in.

"Is it blood?" someone whispered.

The first girl crept closer, her face ghost white. She put her fingers in the stain and sniffed them.

"It's just wine," she announced loudly. "Red wine."

"Fucking Hollis." The crowd stepped back. Turned away. The party quickly picked up where it had left off. Iron Butterfly crooned once more about walking the land, and the bottle of Fireball returned to the table, along with the shot glasses.

"Where do you think he went?" Zoe asked me.

"No idea. You know him better than I do."

"Not really. I mean, we went to school together growing up, but he was always such a snob. He changed after what happened with his sister, of course, but that's to be expected, isn't it?"

"What happened with his sister?"

Zoe touched her horns. "You don't know?"

"No."

"She died. It happened a few years back. Up here, actually. She hung herself in the woods down by the quarry. It was around this time of year, and from everything I heard, it was definitely a suicide, but Hollis always thought otherwise."

"She hung herself?"

She nodded.

"He had a *knife*, Zoe."

"I know."

"Have you seen him with it before?"

"No."

I fretted. "This isn't good. His sister dying like she did, it's—"

"It's what?" she pressed.

"Well, one of the risk factors for suicide is a family history of it."

"How do you know that?"

"I just do."

"So you think he might hurt himself?"

"I don't *know*. But I'm worried. I should go find him."

Zoe bit her lip. "You want me to come with you?"

I *did* want that, of course, but knew better than to say so. "I'll be fine. I can take care of it on my own."

A hint of relief sparked in her eyes. "Good luck."

"Thanks," I told her. "I'll need it."

Then I was in the fog again, running, moving, as fast as I could. I fled the frat house, tearing down the porch steps and sprinting for the trees, away from the noise and the party. Once on the main foot-path, my shoes pounded the earth, as fast I dared to go. My flashlight was useless in the soup, and it was only my studied knowledge of the winding circuit of trails that carried me across the far edges of campus. Toward my destination.

I kept going, navigating on pure faith and desperation, crossing over no less than two clattering bridges in the process. The Dover River churned beneath me, and the deeper I ran into the creeping tendrils of fog and clinging haze, the greater my sense of déjà vu grew. I'd made this breathless journey before, it seemed—perhaps in some other lifetime or some other world, but I'd been filled with this exact same swell of fatalism.

I knew how this story ended.

Didn't I?

Reaching the quarry at last—the spot where Hollis's sister had lost her life—I stumbled my way around the perimeter. The air reeked of moss and stone, and with the way mist had gathered on the water's surface, the entire area resembled a frothing cauldron.

I cupped my hands together. Called out: "Hollis! Hollis, where are you?"

No answer.

I kept stumbling, kept calling his name. Until there, finally, on the far edge of the water, perched high on a boulder and hidden beneath the swaying branches of a large willow tree, I found him. Air slipped from my lungs, and I hurried forward on grateful legs, only to have my gratitude veer toward panic as I realized just how close he was to tumbling into the frigid water.

"Hey, C. J.," Hollis said as I approached, although he didn't bother lifting his head. His words were slurring worse than ever. "You look like a goddamn angel."

The halo. He meant my halo. "Why'd you run away like that?"

"I had to, man. I had no fucking choice."

"You *do* have a choice, Hollis. I promise you."

"I really don't." His voice cracked, taking on a plaintive tone.

"Hey, hey, why don't you give me those." Climbing up, reaching him at last, I gently plucked both the hunting knife and whiskey bottle from his hands. Hollis absolutely did not need either.

"I puked," he told me, gesturing at the ground. "A lot."

My nose wrinkled. "That's okay. But maybe you should come in a little closer from the edge. You don't want to fall in. You'll drown."

"I know you don't believe me," he said sullenly. "No one does. Everyone thinks I'm crazy."

I sighed. "I don't think you're crazy, Hollis. Just sad. Zoe told me about your sister."

His eyes brimmed with sorrow. "They killed her. I know they did. She didn't fucking kill herself."

"Maybe someone *did* kill her. I don't know. I really don't. But I do know it wasn't a coven that did it. Or a witch. Or anything at all like that."

"How can you be sure?"

"Because evil is a man-made commodity. One hundred percent. Do you remember what I said earlier? The most frightening thing is the knowledge that true evil lays within. Not in magic or the supernatural. But in ourselves."

Hollis waved at the cross I wore around my neck. The one that had been my father's. "You really believe that?"

"I'm not saying there aren't things in this world we don't understand. But those doctors you were talking about? The Lunacy Commission? They were just *men*. Bad men, who died many, many years ago, the way that all men do. Yes, they used their wealth and status to profit off the suffering of others, and yes, when that hospital burned down and killed those nineteen patients, it was a tragedy. But a *human* tragedy. Of the most unjust and unfair sort. But you want to know what else I believe?"

"What's that?" he asked.

"That while man doesn't endure, the evil he creates does. There are men alive today with different faces, who wield different power, but that old Lunacy Commission still exists. It never went anywhere. It may take on different forms, but its function is always the same. So the pattern you should be looking for is one of exploitation, not magic. Because those deaths you're so interested in aren't the reason. They're the reaction."

"But a reaction to what? Why would any of this *happen*?"

I crawled closer to sit beside him on the rock. "Maybe I can explain it this way: you and I, we both grew up here in Dover, but our lives, the way we see the world, couldn't be more different."

Hollis let his head loll in my direction. "You think?"

"I *know*. And see, first off, the Dover Phantom, this killer you're so obsessed with, well, when I was a kid, I wasn't taught that he was a monster. Or anything to fear. In part, of course, because people like me didn't come to places like this. We were never the ones in harm's way."

"Well, you're here now."

I smiled. "But I'm really not. Just because I was offered a scholarship doesn't mean I took it. Like you told me, this school's not as safe as it appears. For example, last night, it wasn't hard for me to break into one of your admin buildings and steal this vest. Or to sit on the beach and wait for the school drunk to find me."

His face clouded with confusion. "Huh?"

"Look," I said soothingly. "I know you've thought a lot about this. But sometimes, to see the whole truth, you have to step back from what's personal in order to take in the bigger picture."

"What picture is that?"

"What does your father do, Hollis?"

"He works for a pharmaceutical company. TriGen. He's the CFO. But what does that have to—"

"Did you know my dad worked for that same company? In one of the manufacturing plants. And when he got injured on the job, TriGen wouldn't pay his workers' comp claim. Not only that, but they fired him and countersued in order to set an example for their other workers. My dad stood up to them—I told you he was brave—but between his medical bills and legal fees, he never had a chance. He lost everything in a matter of months. So when he drove to the beach on a clear night when the stars were shining and shot himself, it was his gift to us. TriGen dropped the suit and paid his bills. Not because they cared, obviously, but even they knew better than to bring a grieving widow into the courtroom."

"Jesus. Fuck. I'm sorry, man. That's terrible. I had no idea."

I kept smiling. "Yeah, well, there's a lot of terrible in this world. Because there are a lot of things people like you don't want to see. Or change. It's what you've been taught, but it doesn't have to be your destiny."

Hollis shot me a dark look. "What do you mean, *people like me*?"

"I mean, people who refuse to accept that a force they've always seen as monstrous is actually something different altogether."

"Like what?"

"Like a hero. A human one, but a hero nonetheless."

His eyes bulged. "What are you talking about? I don't fucking believe that."

"You sure?"

"Yes! I'm absolutely sure!"

"Then I'm sorry to hear that," I said. And I *was* sorry. I'd done what I could. Like so many heroes before me, I'd looked to the equinox and strived to bring balance to an unbalanced world. But balance was more fleeting than I'd realized. If Hollis had already gone so far as to create his own mythology in order to avoid having to point the finger anywhere but at his own values, there wasn't much I could've done to persuade him in the first place. He didn't want logic; he preferred tilting at windmills.

So maybe I really did know the ending to this story.

"You know those nineteen people who died here? In that fire?" I asked softly.

"Sure. Of course."

"Well, they weren't the only ones who suffered. Their loved ones did too. Maybe *their* suffering was even greater—having to live in the aftermath and watch those killers profit and get away with murder."

"Yeah, maybe. What does that have to do with anything?"

I leaned close to whisper in his ear. "It has to do with the fact that you were right, Hollis. The Phantom isn't a he. Or a who. The Phantom is all of us who haven't forgotten or forgiven that one moment of agony and injustice. Who are still called, every generation, in the name of equity, to try to meet our counterpart from the other side halfway. But when justice isn't given—and it never is—that's when we're forced to take something else."

"What's that?" he demanded.

"Retribution."

Disbelief became terror when Hollis saw me raise the knife and understood what I planned to do with it. He recoiled, scrambling back to get away from me, but with the steep drop and the water behind him, there was nowhere to go.

"C. J.!" he cried out, holding his hands up. "Why? Why are you doing this? What did I do?"

I moved in swiftly then. Gripping the hunting knife, pinning him down with my knee, I felt no anger in my heart, no wrath or vengeance, just the cool breeze of certitude. Hadn't I known this was how it would be? Monsters never understood they were the ones in need of slaying.

"Cautionary tales aren't meant to be told," I whispered before I brought the knife down. Before the blood began to spray. "They're meant to be heard. So we'll keep telling this one, over and over, for as long as we have to. Until someday, somehow, you finally begin to listen."

No one said much after Tino finished his story, but I think we were all glad Jaila had the knife and not him.

Water was running pretty low, so we looked for somewhere to refill our canteens, which took us an hour out of our way. The stream we found was barely a gurgle of a thing, but it was enough.

Everyone had broken down into their little cliques again. Except Tino. He was by himself, leaning against a tree when I noticed Jenna approach him.

"Sorry," she said.

"Yeah you are."

"We've all been through . . . stuff." Jenna's shoulders were rolled forward, and she wasn't looking Tino in the eyes. "Just, if you want to talk, I'll listen."

Tino laughed. "You think I'd want to talk to you?"

I'm pretty sure if he'd spoken like that to Lucinda, she would have cut off his balls, but Jenna just offered him a shrug. "Maybe. And if you don't, that's fine too."

Then she walked off again. I was expecting him to keep laughing, but the moment Jenna was out of sight, Tino's bravado fled. It was like the iron in his spine melted, and the tree was the only thing holding him up anymore.

"You think he killed someone?" Cody was asking Sunday and Georgia when I wandered back to where they were sitting on the ground.

Sunday shook her head. "No way. He's full of it."

"But all that stuff he was saying about Lucinda and me being rich?" Georgia said. "I mean, my parents have money, but we're not like that. We give to our church, and I volunteer and—"

"Don't take it personally." Sunday laid her hand on Georgia's, but Georgia pulled it away immediately.

"I'm not—"

"She's just being nice, Georgia," Cody said.

Georgia scrambled to her feet. "We should get going. Let's go." And then she stormed off the way we'd been walking earlier, leaving Cody and Sunday to gather their things and follow.

I should have gone after them, too, but I couldn't help wondering what else I could learn listening in on conversations when no one was looking for me. Jackie and David were discussing their favorite TV shows—Jackie's, of course, was that werewolves in space show that was full of good-looking twentysomethings who were supposed to be teenagers—and David's was some online show I'd never heard of. I was thinking Jackie was going to give David a black eye for suggesting her favorite was garbage, but she kept her fists holstered. Jaila and Jenna were discussing how much farther we could walk before nightfall and whether we'd actually make it to camp by the end of the third day. Jenna could do all the calculations in her head, like she was some kind of human calculator. It was amazing. And despite what Tino thought, I had faith that Jaila could get us back to camp on time, even if she was faking the faith she had in herself.

Truthfully, I didn't give a shit when we returned to camp. I didn't have anything there worth going back to, and nothing waiting for me at home when we finally left the Bend. I might have been hungry and filthy and exhausted, but this was the most fun I'd had since my uncle had dropped me off, and I wasn't ready for it to be over.

I didn't hear the yelling at first, but I saw Jaila's head jerk up, and then I heard what sounded like Cody screaming in a panic. I followed Jenna and Jaila to where the others had all gathered around Georgia. She was bleeding from her head, and her right ankle was bent in a way ankles weren't meant to bend.

"She was trying to climb down those rocks and she slipped and I think her foot's broken and—"

Georgia was awake and crying about how she couldn't play soccer with a broken ankle and what was she going to do now, and I couldn't figure how she was worried about soccer when she was hurt and we were in the middle of nowhere.

David knelt beside her, stripped off his shirt, and pressed it to the cut on her head. He pulled the makeshift bandage back and poured a little water on it. "It's not deep," he said. "Just bleeding a lot."

Everyone looked to Jaila for what to do, but she'd gone pale and backed away. Tino growled at how useless we all were and got down on his knees to examine Georgia's ankle. He untied her boot and peeled off her sock. Her foot was already turning purple and swelling up."

"Shouldn't you leave the boot on?" Jackie asked. "So it acts like a splint or something?"

"Won't do any good if her foot swells up inside and cuts off circulation," Tino said.

"Here." Jenna handed Tino a first-aid kit that I hadn't known she had.

"Is it broken?" Cody's face had gone paler than Georgia's.

"How the hell should I know?" Tino said. "I'm a delinquent, not a doctor." But he wrapped her ankle with a roll of gauze to immobilize it the best he could. "She's not walking anywhere."

"I could use the flare," Jaila said.

We all turned to look at her. "What flare?" David asked. "You have a flare?"

Jaila nodded. "Doug gave it to me for emergencies. Told me to use it if anyone got hurt, and they'd come get us."

"This is a big fucking emergency," Cody said. Even with all of us crowding around Georgia, he'd stayed by her side, holding her hand.

"Shit," David said. "I would have broken my leg yesterday if I knew we had a way out of this."

Everyone was talking over each other, most telling Jaila to use the flare, and I doubted it was because they cared about Georgia.

"I don't want to quit," Georgia said.

Lucinda, who hadn't given her opinion yet, said, "I don't think we have a choice. If you can't walk, we'll have to carry you, and I don't think we'd make it back on time if that were the case."

Jaila was already digging around in her backpack. "That settles it, then." She pulled out the clunky flare gun. "Sorry, Georgia."

I knew why I liked being out in the woods, but I didn't understand why Georgia was crying about going back to the Bend early. Hell, being hurt likely meant Doug would call her parents to come get her. We were *all* supposed to leave two days after we returned from our survival trip, but she'd get to leave even earlier. Her parents would probably charter a private plane or some rich-person shit to rescue their little girl if that's what it took.

Jaila popped the cartridge into the gun, clicked it into place, raised it over her head, and pulled the trigger.

Nothing.

She pulled the trigger again.

Nothing.

"Shit." Jaila pulled out the cartridge, replaced it with another, and tried again.

Tino swiped it from her and opened the compartment where the flare went in, trying to fix it, but it was no use.

"Figures Dipshit Doug would give us duds," Jackie said.

"What're we going to do?" Cody asked, his voice rising high with panic.

"We'll have to make a stretcher," Jenna said at the same time as Lucinda said, "We'll carry her."

We spent an hour pulling the frames of our packs apart and using the rope we had to strap them together to form a litter to carry Georgia. It wouldn't have won any awards, but it was sturdy enough to hold her weight. Tino and Jackie got into an argument about who was going to have to carry her, but Lucinda and Cody volunteered almost immediately.

The mood of our clusterfuck had taken a nosedive. Jaila couldn't be entirely certain we were walking in the right direction, Georgia was hurt, we were all hungry and thirsty and itching from not having a real shower, our emergency flare gun was useless, and we only had a day and a half to find the Bend. And then it started to rain.

"I bet Doug gave us bum flares on purpose," Tino was saying. "Probably thought it'd teach us a lesson about relying on ourselves."

"Twenty bucks says he still lives at home with his parents," David said.

"I don't know," Sunday said. "He's not so bad." Even Jackie glared at her for saying that, so she added, "You know, for a middle-aged momma's boy."

Cody started struggling with his end of the litter after only an hour, so Sunday switched out with him. David offered to take Lucinda's place, but she said she could keep going all day, and I believed her.

The rain made it even more difficult to find our footing, and it seemed like we were going nowhere fast.

"Someone please tell another story," Georgia said.

David's face brightened. "I can finish mine."

"Hell no," Jackie said. "I'm depressed enough as it is. But I got one."

"JACKIE'S STORY"

by Justina Ireland

EVERYONE KNEW THAT there was nothing beyond the Alderus asteroid belt. It was the kind of thing kids learned in their first year at school: how to avoid space sickness and that beyond the Alderus asteroid belt was nothing but Void, an edge of space so dark that nothing could exist beyond that edge.

It was the perfect place for the Williamson brothers to hide out.

Sean Williamson piloted his beloved spacecraft through the rocks, swearing anytime one came too close. They'd nearly run out of fuel by the time the ship had reached the rock field, and even though he had a back-up tank of Ore to power the craft, there was no use for it. The goal was to drift through the rock field long enough to confuse the Leviathan ships chasing them. Using all his fuel now would only put the second half of the plan in danger.

Daniel Williamson, Sean's younger brother, cleared his throat. "Maybe you should swing her around a little to the left—" A hollow boom echoed through the ship as another boulder bumped off the hull.

"Dammit, Danny! I don't need your help crashing. I've got this all taken care of myself. Why don't you see if you can raise Cass on the secure channel? Surely she's heard something by now. And maybe change out of those coveralls while you're at it."

Danny gave his brother one last withering look before moving through the ship to the communications console. They'd been waiting for a ping from Cass on their private channel for days, waiting for the one last piece of information that would help them accomplish their lifelong mission to destroy Dr. Mags, the woman who had torn them from their family and changed them forever into monsters.

Danny brushed his dark, disheveled hair from his eyes and began searching for Cass's frequency. Both of the Williamson brothers were incredibly good-looking, but while Danny was tall and rugged, Sean was shorter with spiky blond hair. They didn't share much beyond their chiseled jaws, steely gazes, and the occasional willing partner. Their temperaments as different as night and day.

"Hey, is this fan fiction? Fan fiction doesn't count as a real story," said David.

Jackie rolled her eyes. "Yes, it does. This is a totally original story that I wrote."

She continued.

Danny found Cass after a couple of tries, connecting to her frequency with little trouble. He was the brother that could fix any technical issue. It was Sean who could fly them out of a tight situation, though. However, the asteroid belt was giving even him trouble.

"Danny! Where are you guys?"

"Alderus asteroid belt. Outrunning a pack of the Corporation's Leviathan cruisers. You got any news for us?"

"I do. Big news. There's something going down with the Corporation. Can you and Sean meet me on Finicus Prime in two days?"

Another asteroid scraped across the hull, causing the ship to lurch and Sean to curse loudly. Danny cleared his throat. "That might be difficult, but we'll do our best."

"Great! See you then. Oh, and Danny?"

"Yeah, Cass?"

"Tell Sean that we have unfinished business," Cass said, her voice getting husky. "Of course, you're welcome to join us as well. I know you're a fan of teamwork," she said before signing off.

Danny signed off as well before yelling to Sean in the front of the ship. "Cass has something. You think you can get us to Finicus Prime in two days?" He didn't mention Cass's very welcome invitation. No need to distract Sean any further.

"Oh, sure! Because it's not like I don't already have enough miracles to work," Sean said.

Danny took that as a yes and headed to the engine room to make sure that the ship would actually get them there.

Finicus Prime wasn't the kind of station anyone ended up on by choice. A backwater satellite light-years away from shipping lanes and proper technology, it was the kind of place smugglers and freaks landed to grab supplies or sell hot merchandise or find a quick hookup.

It was the kind of place the Williamson brothers loved.

"I'll have a bacon cheeseburger and a berry pie," Sean said, leaning back in his chair.

"*Um, tossed salad and vegetable protein loaf, thanks,*" *Danny told the order droid. The bot trundled off, and Sean snickered.*

"*What?*" *Danny asked.*

"*It isn't alive. You don't have to be polite.*"

"*No one knows exactly how much they know. There's no reason to be rude,*" *Danny said.*

Cass slid into an empty chair without a word, laying a clear diskette on the table. "*Danny is right. Studies have shown that bots are twenty-three percent more accurate when they're treated like a person.*"

Sean sighed heavily. "*Cass.*"

"*Sean. Danny. Story is that the Corporation is up to something new. Something bad. This disk outlines everything I know.*" *Cass flipped her dark hair over her shoulder and looked around the food counter.* "*It isn't looking good, though. There's something afoot. Something bad.*"

"*We got it, Cass. We'll take care of it,*" *Sean said just as his food arrived.*

Danny nodded. "*It's what we do.*"

Cass leaned forward, her breasts heaving, nearly escaping the top of her shirt. "*So when are you boys going to take care of me?*"

"This is literally the plot of a *Space Howl* episode. I saw this one. They end up going to some planet and stealing a vial they think is the antidote to their werewolf disease, but it's really a serum to help farmers grow crops on some small planet. They end up giving the serum to the scientist working for the farmers so they can grow crops," said David.

"It's sort of like that, but different," Jackie said, chewing at a thumbnail until it bled.

Tino rolled his eyes. "No way she gets to win for something she stole from TV."

"Really?"

Several folks nodded.

"Okay, fine." Jackie took her hair down and readjusted her ponytail as she spoke. "So, since no one wants to listen to my *Space Howl* story here's another one. This is a story my dad told me when I was a kid. It was always my favorite tale."

The city?

The city. Well, it changes you.

When my brothers and I went there we were just a bunch of kids, fresh-faced and full of dreams. We had no clue how the world worked, and no way we ever thought we'd end up how we did.

Mostly, I never thought *I'd* end up like this. Broken and broke, not a penny to my name. I've done terrible things. Things I'm not proud of. I've hurt people and ruined lives. And I did it all for them.

My brothers.

The three of us were all born on the same day. Triplets. Maybe that's why we were always so close. We were united by blood and a birthdate.

More on the blood later.

Phillip was first, and he came into the world squealing at the top of his lungs. *Wee, wee, wee.* They say he didn't shut up until our mother put her teat into his mouth.

Next was Peter, who was so big that our mother labored for over an hour just to push him out. He didn't say a word as he lay there in the straw, waiting for Ma to tend to him. He just looked around, taking everything in, silent and stupid. More than one man would underestimate him because of his big, lumbering quiet.

I was last. Paul the Runt, smallest of the litter. I didn't squeal, and I wasn't large enough to remark upon. I was completely unmemorable, an afterthought to the birth of my brothers.

And so it went. The three of us grew up in a small town, and we each gained a peculiar sort of notoriety. Phillip was the talker, the guy who could charm a girl out of her bloomers or a friend out of his pocket money. Peter was big, and those who messed with him quickly discovered that it was a bad idea. And me? I was the thinker. I could sit back and find a solution to any problem. Chances are I could have been a scientist or something else prestigious. Maybe a doctor.

Maybe. If Peter and Phillip hadn't been my brothers.

When we were barely on the cusp of adulthood, Phillip had the bad luck to fool around with a woman who was spoken for. When the husband found out, he came sniffing around the farm, looking for my brother. The cuckold found Peter instead of Phillip, much to the jilted man's dismay. Peter lay a beating down on him, but the damage had already been done.

"It's time you boys got a move on," my mother said, hauling her girth from one side of the barn to another. "I can't have you boys fighting and carrying on like that. It draws too much attention. 'Sides, it's time you boys made your way in the world. It's unseemly for boys to live with their mama for too long."

So we left.

That night, after tying our meager possessions up into a bindle, we jumped a train to the city.

* * *

New Pork was nothing like any place we'd ever been before.

The city was a terrifying and exhausting place. Cars raced along the streets, horns honking incessantly. Buses threatened to mow down unwary pedestrians, and there were people everywhere, clogging the sidewalk, flowing in and out of the buildings like a trail of ants to an overturned soda can. And underneath it all was a current of desperation and urgency that made me anxious.

Phillip, of course, loved it.

"This is it, boys! This is where we'll make our mark on the world." His snout wiggled with excitement. "We will make this city bow to our demands. She'll be our mistress; she'll cradle us to her bosom, and we'll make her scream out our name."

I winced at Phillip's melodramatic speech, but he didn't notice. He looked around, adjusting his bow tie and cocking his hat at a jaunty angle, the tip of his pug nose wiggling in excitement. Peter said nothing, just stood on the sidewalk and watched as people tried to inch around him.

I scratched my chin as I considered Phillip's words. "I dunno, Phil. It doesn't seem safe here. Maybe we should make a bid for the next town. We aren't used to city life." I hated the way my voice sounded: whiny, weak. But I missed our safe, small-town life already. All I wanted was a reasonable facsimile of it, and something told me the city wouldn't provide that.

Phillip threw his arm across my shoulders and wheezed a laugh. "Come on, Pauly. Give it a go. I bet you'll love it in no time."

I looked around, and a girl passing caught my eye. She saw me looking, her cheeks pink and round. But she didn't look away shyly like the girls back home did. She met my stare dead-on, raising her chin a little in defiance.

I shrugged. "Well, okay. A month. I'll give it a month."

Phillip squeezed my shoulders and gave me a grin. "A month. Sounds like a plan."

Our first month in the city was miserable.

We lived in a flat with two other guys, both of them hogs. They drank too much and passed out in the living room, snoring loudly. They frequently left their stuff all over the place and ate all the food in the icebox whether or not it was theirs. It was a terrible place to live, but we didn't have much choice. It was the only place we could afford.

Phillip had a job as a waiter in one of them buffet-type places called the Trough, but no one ever left him much in the way of a tip. Peter got work down at the wharf, and although he made a decent wage, most of his paycheck went to cover the shortfall from Phillip and me. As for me . . .

I got a job as a bookkeeper in a sketchy office building. It was there that I first got the idea for the straw purchase.

Would that I'd never thought of it.

Firearms were highly regulated in the city. Only certain folks could get licensed, and it all rested on an intelligence test. This had the effect of driving the price of the guns up, even those that were available for sale illegally.

A man in my office, Mr. Crenshaw, began talking wistfully about how he'd like to buy a gun. "I've been saving every last grunt I've made for the past year. A hundred grunts just to take the test, and another hundred for the gun. But I keep failing the damn thing. I'm almost a thousand grunts into buying a gun, and I still don't have one."

That gave me an idea.

"Mr. Crenshaw, why don't you give me three hundred grunts, and I'll give you a gun."

Mr. Crenshaw was an elderly sort, and his eyes watered as he peered at me. "Say what?"

"Well, if I take the test and pass, I can buy a gun. I can buy as many as I'd like, right?"

He considered me. "Well, I s'pose."

"No one knows who the gun belongs to once it's bought. No one cares. So if I buy the gun and give it to you, you get a gun and I get enough money to take my girl out somewhere nice." There was no girl, and the money would go to the rent, but the old man was so happy that he forked over the dough lickety-split.

When I got back to the flat I told my brothers my scheme in a low voice, so our roommates wouldn't hear us. Peter gave me a slow nod; his way of agreeing it was a good idea. But Phillip had bigger ideas.

"Pauly, why stop at one old man? Why not buy a hundred guns?"

I blinked at him. "What?"

Phillip began to pace. "There have to be dozens of suckers like him in the city, just aching for a chance to get their grubby mitts on a gun. A gun means protection; it means power. Every girl wants to be with a fella who can keep her safe, and every man wants a gun. Nothing makes a man more foolish than a loaded gun." Here Phillip paused and elbowed me to make sure I caught his double meaning. "And a fool and his money are soon parted. So why not make some grunts? I can chat these guys up, and you take the test and get them their merchandise. It'll be brilliant."

I looked at Peter, who was now doing his slow nod for Phillip.

"What's Peter going to do?" I asked.

Phillip grinned, showing his teeth. "Peter is going to keep everyone honest."

For the next year we lived a life of leisure. The straw purchase racket was pure genius, and all three of us quit our jobs and moved out on our own. Phillip moved to the north end of town, near the poker clubs and bars he loved. Peter met a nice girl and moved with her into a small house on the outskirts of the city.

I moved into a nice high-rise building with a security guard. Although I'd been in the city for a while, it still made me nervous. Especially with our less-than-legal enterprises.

Phillip had big plans for us, and the straw purchase soon grew into a full-fledged criminal empire. I came up with the ideas, and Phillip and Peter implemented them. Prostitution, racketeering, illegal gambling, moneylending. If it paid well and it was illegal, we dealt in it.

And we were good at it.

Phillip was the mouth of the operation, using his gift of gab to cement alliances with other rackets and to smooth the way with the local cops. Peter was the muscle, and whenever a payee was late or someone didn't want to play nice, he broke into their house and hurt their feelings.

And I was the background guy, the idea man. Phillip looked like he was in charge of things, but I was the one running the show from the shadows. I kept my ear to the ground and applied the rumors and gossip I heard to our business, moving poker parlors before they were raided, paying off minor nuisances, and ending those who were thinking about talking to the feds. We cut a bloody swath through the city, taking what we wanted, killing anyone who got in our way.

The three of us were unstoppable.

That's when I started to hear the whispers about the Wolf.

In the old days the Wolf had owned this city. He was big and he was bad, but no one had seen or heard from him in years. There were rumors that he took a chunk of the pie from every operation, and those that weren't willing to play nice risked having their houses blown in, so to speak.

Phillip tsk-tsked away my worry when I mentioned the rumors I'd been hearing; stories of a bushy-haired fella kicking in the doors of some of our smaller operations. We were in the back room of the bar my brother owned, the liquor sales and good-time girls up front a cover for the games in the back. Those days, Phillip spent more of his time playing cards than running things, so more and more of the day-to-day operations fell to me.

"There's no such thing as the Wolf, Pauly," Phillip said, throwing a card down on the table. "We would've met him long before now if he was a real thing. Quit worrying," he said. "You're gonna give yourself wrinkles." Then he did that thing where he grabbed the back of my neck and shook me a bit.

I pulled free and gave him a nod as he went back to his card game, his hat cocked at a jaunty angle and a girl on his knee, that fearless grin I'd come to hate plastered across his face.

The next morning Peter found Phillip dead, his eyes staring wide and surprised. He'd been closing up, restocking, when someone had come in and iced him. No one knows what was said, and the drink straws scattered across the bar floor weren't talking.

Peter and I gave Phillip the best funeral money could buy, and at the wake afterward, I pulled my brother aside.

"We need to look into this Wolf thing, Pete. You and I both know he offed Phil, and the last thing I want is this guy huffing and puffing all over us."

My brother shook his big dumb head and drained the beer from the bottle in his giant mitt. "Never you mind, Pauly," he said, his voice deep and rusty from disuse. "I'll get him. The boys and I are gonna go out and rattle a few cages, see what shakes loose. You just keep everything running smooth like. Phillip woulda wanted it that way." Then Peter went off to comfort his girl, who was standing in a corner crying pretty tears for a man she didn't know.

I shook my head, feeling a dark sense of déjà vu. Phillip hadn't listened to me either, and look where it had gotten him. But I knew better than to argue with big dumb Peter, and I let him do what he wanted.

Peter took out his grief on the city. Shopkeepers trembled in fear at the sound of his heavy boot steps, and the women in the markets whispered about whose husband had taken a beating recently. Peter worked his knuckles bloody trying to get answers, but he came up with nothing.

"Maybe it was an inside job," he said one night as he sat on the couch in Phillip's old office. It had been two months since Phillip's murder, and I sat behind his big fancy desk, going through the day's take.

With my brother gone I had started meeting with the cops on our payroll and the bosses who ran some of our smaller operations. Although I wasn't as good at it as Phillip had been, I was holding my own.

"It wasn't an inside job, it was the Wolf," I told Peter. "We need to find this guy and offer him a deal; otherwise we're going to be next."

My brother just shook his big dumb head and sighed. "I told you, there ain't no such thing as the Wolf. It's just an old rumor. Phillip was axed by someone in the organization. We just need to find out who." My brother stood and put on his flat cap. "I'm goin' home. I'll see you tomorrow."

But I never saw my brother again.

They said it was a bomb, and that someone had snuck into Peter's house during the day while his girl was out and planted it in the kitchen. When the thing went off it completely devastated his house and part of the neighbor's. The cops never really found all of Peter's body, just bits and pieces of it mixed in with the sticks of his destroyed house. Peter's girl wasn't home at the time, and for a little while the cops tried to pin it on her, but she wasn't a killer. When she came home from her bridge game and saw the condition of the house, she broke down. The only damning bit of information the cops got out of her was that she'd been seeing Phillip on the side before he bit it. The poor girl was destroyed. Here she'd lost the two greatest loves of her life within a span of a couple months.

I paid for her to go upstate for some relaxation in a facility and thanked my lucky stars I was smart enough to leave the skirts alone.

But now I was all by myself, and I knew that the Wolf was real. Any day now he'd be coming for me, and I'd be ready.

I bought the building I lived in and evicted all the other residents. I fired the guard downstairs, giving him a nice bonus so he wouldn't be too out of sorts, and I put my own boys in the front. I installed bars on all the windows and bricked up all the entrances except for the main lobby. Now there was only one way in and one way out, and you had to get past my boys to see me.

I was ready.

The bosses and dirty cops who reported to me thought I was losing it, that it had been an inside job, both Peter's and Phillip's murders. I took out hits on all of them. Then I found new guys, ones I could trust. I let them move up through the organization. I rebuilt my enterprise from the ground up.

And I waited.

Six, seven, eight months passed, and no sign of the Wolf. I relaxed my guard a little, started going out more. Dinner once a week. A show every once in a while. My enterprise flourished, and I was rich. I deserved to enjoy a little bit of that.

The Wolf found me one night while I was out at dinner.

I sat in the center of the restaurant, the only patron. I had taken to buying out the entire establishment when I dined so that I could eat alone, since people made me jumpy. I was less paranoid, but the Wolf could still be out there, waiting for his chance. I was enjoying a bowl of slop, the specialty of the house, when a bushy-haired man walked in. Both of my boys stood up, ready to escort him out, but he mowed them down without a word.

I jumped up from the table and ran, through the kitchen and out the back alley. I could hear the Wolf's shoes pounding as he chased me down, and I gasped for breath, squealing as I ran. I was soft and large from too much food and too little movement, and there was no way I could outrun the monster I'd glimpsed back in the restaurant.

I skidded down an alley, coming up on a dead end. I searched around for an exit, but the only thing there was a pile of bricks and a few overflowing trash bins. I grabbed a brick and ducked down behind the garbage can, trying to quiet my breathing and hoping the Wolf hadn't seen me.

Footsteps paused at the end of the alley and then began to approach. "Little pig, little pig," a gravelly voice called, and chills ran down my spine. "You owe me."

"I don't owe you nothing!" I yelled.

The Wolf chuckled, voice low. "Just because you already paid me to do the job don't mean you ain't gotta pay me again. What would your associates say if they knew you were the one who had your brothers snuffed out? Your own flesh and blood. That you killed all your old boys just to cover your tracks. Nothing but a parade of death and sorrow all the way home."

I squeezed my eyes shut, and thought about my brothers. I thought about the way we'd played together in the mud when we were small and how hard our first month here in the city had been. But mostly I thought about how they were always there for me, fighting my battles, talking on my behalf. And how, later, they'd always taken the bigger cut, how I'd done all the hard work, but they'd kept most of the gains.

And now here was the Wolf, trying to do the same thing.

It wasn't about the money anymore. It was about the principle.

I opened my eyes just as the Wolf walked by. I gripped the brick with my mitts and brought it down on the back of his head. He fell to the ground, but I didn't stop. I brought the brick down again and again until the Wolf stopped moving, his bushy tail limp.

I'd killed the Wolf, me and my brick. And I felt no better for it.

I stumbled home and washed the blood off me. I felt so old and so drained. I was sick of the city and tired of my life. I'd had my brothers killed and killed the Wolf, but there would always be more of his kind, scavengers looking for a taste of blood. The city had broken me. It had turned me into a murderer, a criminal, a parasite on society. I couldn't even stand to look at myself in the mirror.

So I fled.

I took all the blood money I'd accumulated and left the city. I bought a small brick house out in the country and found a girl who didn't mind when I got quiet and stared off into space, thinking about the old times. It was a good life.

But every once in a while, in the dark of night, when the wind would blow through the rafters of the attic, I'd think I heard footsteps and a voice crying, "Little pig, little pig, you owe me." And now, as an old boar with nothing to occupy his days, I think I hear that voice calling to me more and more.

I know it's all in my head. The Wolf is dead, and I killed him. It still scares the bejeezus out of me.

So if you've got your heart set on going to the city, kid, go. You can find success there, even though hopefully, you travel a more honorable path than I did. Just remember this one thing:

Beware the wolf inside your heart.

Cody giggled at first, and then he started laughing so hard he had to stop because he almost dropped his end of the litter, and Georgia along with it. "Did you really just give us 'The Three Little Pigs'?"

Jackie shrugged, smiled. "Maybe."

"Genius," Sunday said. "But I kind of want to know what happened to the brothers in space."

"Maybe some other time," Jackie said.

The rain had slackened off and finally quit altogether as the sun was starting to set. We hadn't figured out what we were going to do for food, and if the others were as hungry as I was, people were going to start getting cranky before too long.

"How much farther do you think we have to go?" Georgia asked.

"What do you care?" Tino said. "Not like you have to do any of the walking."

"That's not her fault," Cody said.

"Like hell it isn't." Tino leaned against a tree. He was trying not to show how exhausted he was, but the strain of hiking on empty stomachs was wearing on us all, and Tino didn't hide it well.

Lucinda was already up in his face, anger ready to boil over. "All you do is complain. If you don't like it, find your own damn way back to camp."

"Maybe I will."

"No one's leaving the group," Jaila said. "I'm not . . . We're not losing anyone out here."

"They thought this would bring us together," Jenna said quietly. "Being alone out here, forced to rely on one another. This was supposed to teach us the value of teamwork or whatever, but we're all too fucked up to work together, aren't we?"

"Speak for yourself," Lucinda said. "I'm just fine working with you." She motioned at Tino. "It's him I can do without."

"Why?" Jenna asked. "What's he done that's so bad except say what he was thinking? What gives you or anyone the right to keep him from speaking his mind?"

Lucinda opened her mouth to say something, but closed it wordlessly.

We were never going to sit around a campfire singing songs and roasting marshmallows together. When we left the Bend, we would each scatter back to wherever we'd come from and never speak to one another again. We'd slip into to our old lives and forget the others existed. The courts and our parents or guardians had sent us to the Bend hoping it would change us, but I didn't think that was possible. The things that made us strong individually were also the qualities that kept us from functioning as a unified whole.

Dipshit Doug had told us on our first day how Zeppelin Bend had been named after a knot used to tie two pieces of rope together. It was considered by some to be the ideal bend knot because it was secure and easy to tie. He'd said we were each a piece of rope, and his goal was to tie us to one another, teach us how to form a knot with the people in our lives and become stronger as a result.

But I knew a thing or two about knots, and the Zeppelin bend was also known for the ease with which it could be untied. Even if we managed to work together to find our way back to camp, we'd never stay tied to one another. We'd slip the knot as soon as we were able, and fall to loose ends. That was just reality.

And who would care? We were castoffs. We'd been told the Bend was our last chance to turn our lives around, but I doubted anyone expected we'd actually do it. Those who'd sent us here already considered us lost causes, or they wouldn't have sent us here in the first place. We'd stopped being people to them and were, instead, problems to shove off onto someone else to fix. Nothing we did mattered because, to our families, we were only what we'd done to get sent here. It's all they would ever see.

"I have to go to the bathroom," Georgia said.

"I can take you," David offered.

"Of course the perv volunteers," Lucinda said. She'd backed off from Tino, but her anger was still floating on the surface, like an oil slick. It only needed a spark to catch fire.

"I'm not—" David started. Stopped. Then said, "Forget it. Fuck all of you."

"I'll take her," Jackie said. "Maybe we'll find a McDonald's while we're out there."

Jaila looked around where we'd stopped. "This is as good a place as any to make camp. I don't think we're going any farther tonight, anyway."

Cody found Georgia a stick she could use as a makeshift crutch before Jackie led her off a distance to take care of her business, and the rest of us worked on making camp. Jenna collected kindling for a fire, Tino found rocks to circle it with, and Cody went searching for logs he could drag over so we'd have something to sit on. Everyone seemed to know what they were supposed to do, and did it without needing to be told. I went off on my own because I also needed to relieve myself, and I was hoping to find *something* to eat. But I returned empty-handed.

Sunday was sitting on a log talking to David, who was crying and shaking his head.

"That's not how it was" David was saying.

"I know, but you have to admit it sounds really messed up." Sunday was sitting close to David, but not touching him.

"That's because none of you let me finish."

"She was your sister, David," Sunday said. "Can you blame us?"

David shook his head. "But if you just hear the rest of the story, I swear you'll understand."

"Tell me, then," she said. "I'll listen if you want to finish."

"BIG BROTHER, PART 2"
by E. C. Myers

I STAYED UP that night, waiting and listening. Allie asking me to check on her made me scared; I almost would have preferred if she was lying to me instead of being just as clueless about what was going on.

When I heard the first sound, a gentle "mmmm . . ." followed by a series of gasps, I noted the time: 2:01 a.m. I hurried to Allie's room, but I hesitated for a minute outside her door as the sounds intensified. I imagined her sitting in bed and laughing at me when I burst into her room, trolling me. Maybe she'd snap a picture of me with her camera so she could send it to Ryan and Tony. I wouldn't even be pissed if I found out she was pranking me.

But that's not what I saw at all when I eased the door to her room open.

Something was hovering over Allie's bed. It was kind of faint and shimmery. See-through, so I could make out Allie's Yale pennant on the wall behind it. The thing looked vaguely human-shaped, but it was sort of leaking at the edges like a bad video signal. And each time Allie moaned, it pulsed. Or maybe, each time it pulsed, Allie moaned. She was fully clothed, and she wasn't touching herself. So that thing must have been doing that to her.

I bet you're thinking the same thing I did at first. *A ghost?*

I know what you're really thinking. *He's full of shit.*

I was frozen, peering through the door. Finally, when my brain rebooted, I did the only rational thing. Exactly what you would do in the same situation.

"What the fuck?" I said.

The thing quickly expanded and faded into nothing. *Poof!* I rushed to my sister's bed. Her room was noticeably cooler than the hallway, but she was sweating. Her eyes moved rapidly under her closed eyelids, and her lip quivered, like she was freezing, but she had gone quiet again. And I couldn't wake her.

"Allie. Wake up. Wake up!" I gently nudged her over and over again. Then I started shaking her. I was finally ready to go get my parents, call 9-1-1, when her eyes opened wide and she took a great gasping breath, like coming up for air after diving under water.

"David? What are you—?" She bolted up. "It happened again?"

I nodded. "Um. Do you remember anything? Do you . . . feel anything?"

She shook her head. "Nothing."

I cleared my throat. "Like, your, uh, breasts don't feel sensitive, or you're, um . . ." I glanced down at her. She was wearing a ratty old Gryffindor T-shirt and track shorts. I'd figured she slept in cute pajamas with cartoon owls on them like she used to, but I didn't know if she always dressed like this for bed, or at all.

"David!" She covered herself with a sheet decorated with cartoon dinosaurs.

"Sorry. But seriously. How do you feel?"

She shrugged. "I feel normal."

I pressed a hand to her forehead, the way Mom does when we're sick. She flinched away from me.

"That was not normal," I said.

"What did you see?" she asked.

"You won't believe me," I said. I told her what had happened.

"I don't believe you," she said. "That's a pretty weird story, even for you. What do we do now?"

"Well, whatever it was, maybe it won't be back again since I interrupted it."

She scrunched up her face. "Whether it comes back or not, I want to know what it is. Why me? This is . . ." Her voice became thick, like she was trying not to cry. "It's horrific, Dave. What is it doing to me? Why can't I remember?"

It happened again the next night, a Friday. This time I was ready. I grabbed my camera on my way to her room, but the thing disappeared even before the door opened, so all I caught was more audio evidence. But I also had more information: the event began at 2:01 a.m., just like the night before. And even though I no longer had the file I'd recorded the first night, the video project I was editing had been saved last at 2:07 a.m., when I had noticed the sounds.

Now convinced that something ghostlike was attacking my sister every night, I went into full-on protective older-brother mode. Allie let me bring in Ryan and Tony to help us figure it out. Our parents were at work—yes, even on a Saturday—which let us talk about the situation in Allie's room without worrying they would overhear us.

My friends didn't believe me either.

"Is this like your Sasquatch hoax?" Ryan asked.

"First of all, Sasquatch is real," I said. "I know what I saw."

"Bad luck that your camera lens was dirty." Ryan smirked. "And it was conveniently dark in those woods."

I sighed. She still thought I made up my Sasquatch sighting in another desperate attempt to get more views on YouTube, but I wouldn't fake a video. People online analyze the hell out of everything, and if they thought you were lying, you might as well change your name and move to another country. The video I shot at the national park was dark and grainy, and yeah, there was some crap on the lens that put a blurry streak through it, but I didn't make anything up.

"Tony was there. He saw it too," I said.

"Don't drag me into this old argument. We were drunk. I was seeing all sorts of things that night, but that doesn't make any of it real," Tony said.

"It looked like a bear, maybe," Allie said generously.

"Sorry, there's no way that thing in your video is a Sasquatch, Day. I'll still allow that Bigfoot *could* be real. But come on. Now you claim you saw a ghost?" Ryan gave a short, derisive laugh and threw up her hands. "Why not aliens?"

"Aside from the fact that there's no other rational explanation for what's been happening to Allie—" I said.

"Persistent genital arousal disorder." Ryan snapped her fingers. "That took me two minutes to find on Google."

"Is that the technical term for puberty?" Tony chuckled.

"It's a serious condition, Tony," Ryan said. "An invisible, debilitating disability that either gets no medical attention or the wrong kind of attention, from childish idiots like you."

Tony looked chagrined. *Uh-oh*, I thought. *What's going on there?*

"What's persistent genital . . . ?" I asked.

"Arousal disorder. PGAD. It causes unexplained, spontaneous orgasms that last for hours, days, or even weeks," Ryan said.

"Sounds awesome," Tony said.

Ryan gave him a scathing look.

"This is a little different. Allie's orgasms happen once a day, starting at 2:01 a.m. and running for about twenty minutes," I said.

Allie groaned and covered her face.

"If you want to be scientific about it, those are the facts," I said.

"Hypnotism!" Tony said.

"Not that again," I said.

Tony had been excited a few months back about web videos showing a guy hypnotizing women to have an orgasm when he gave them a keyword. Ryan eventually let Tony try it on her, but it hadn't worked. Of course.

Or had it? What if Tony had hypnotized Ryan into being interested in him? (Because talk about unexplained phenomena.) But that was a different problem for another time.

"Never mind him," Ryan said. "Lately, Tony has trouble distinguishing between fact and fantasy."

"That's funny coming from you." Tony folded his arms across his chest.

I raised an eyebrow. "*Anyway*. PGAD or hypnotism, that doesn't change what I saw with my own eyes. I'm not saying it's a ghost, but it was real and it was weird."

"Look, it's clear something's going on, and we want to help," Ryan said. "But I think you should see a doctor, Allie."

"Medical or psychological?" Allie asked.

"You aren't imagining this. If I hadn't noticed it, you wouldn't even know it was happening," I said.

Ryan gave me a look, like she was still trying to figure whether I was gaslighting all of them.

"David?" Allie asked.

"What?" I asked.

"What if this has been going on for a while? I've been so tired lately. It's been hard to focus on school, swimming—everything."

I frowned. "For how long?"

"A couple of months?"

"Succubus!" Tony said.

"What?" I turned to him. He had Google open on Allie's laptop.

"Hey, I didn't say you could use that." Allie slapped Tony's hand away from the keyboard. He grinned and kept reading.

"A succubus is a demon that has sex with men while they're sleeping. Oh, but wait, I wonder if there's . . ." He typed for a minute. "Incubus. That's the male form."

Allie paled. "Nephilim," she whispered.

"Huh?" Tony asked.

"They're in the Bible," Allie said. "They're fallen angels."

Ryan rolled her eyes. "Now we're talking about angels?"

"Not angels," Tony said. "Demons."

"Great, all we need is to perform an exorcism," I said.

"Or we call the Ghostbusters," Tony said.

"Oh, honey. They aren't real either," Ryan said.

"There's a group nearby, a paranormal investigations group that looks into reports of psychic and spiritual activities." Tony brought up the page: Ghost Sweepers.

"No," Allie, Ryan, and I said simultaneously.

"But they have cool equipment. Psychokinetic energy meters, electromagnetic monitors, infrared cameras—"

"They're just in it for the YouTube hits," I said.

"That sounds familiar," Ryan said.

"Right. And if anyone's going to get this on video, it's us. . . ." Which gave me an idea about how I could help Allie and prove that something strange was going on.

"Yeah! Let's do this!" Tony fist-bumped me.

"Whatever you're thinking, forget it," Allie said.

Tony looked at me hopefully. He wanted to make a hit viral video almost as much as I did.

"Forget it, Tony. We'll come up with something else," I said.

But I was lying. I thought that getting this phenomenon on video was a great idea, but I figured it had a better chance of working if I kept my plans to myself. Allie couldn't know I was monitoring her if I wanted to keep the conditions of the experiment as normal as possible and rule out the last little doubt that she was putting one over on me.

"Day, can we talk?" Ryan asked me.

I nodded. We stepped out into the hall.

"You're not trying something, are you?" she asked.

"'Trying something'?" I asked. "What are you accusing me of?"

"You're not using your sister for some ridiculous scheme to make a viral video?"

"Of course not," I said. "Ry, why would I do that? You know me."

She pursed her lips. "That's why I'm asking."

"Wow." That felt like a slap to the face.

"Okay, I'm sorry, but I had to be sure. Of course you wouldn't exploit your sister just to get YouTube famous."

But that's exactly what happened, even though I never intended it.

I really just wanted to get the ghost on film, to prove to the others— to prove to myself—that it was really real. When Ryan and Tony left, and Allie went to swim practice, I snuck into her room. Instead of trying to hide a small wireless camera, I decided to use the one that was already there: the webcam on Allie's computer. I always used to bug her to put tape over it, but she was too trusting. She believes the best in people, especially her big brother.

It was easy to install a remote access program on her computer so I could control the webcam and stream it to my PC for recording. But all the late nights finally caught up to me, and I made a couple of mistakes.

When my vibrating cell phone woke me up the next morning at my keyboard, I checked the recording and saw the three most devastating words of my life:

"Video upload complete."

"What? Oh shit. Oh shit." I fumbled the phone and saw it was Ryan calling. As I hastily clicked to play the video, I answered her on speakerphone.

"Day, what the fuck?" she asked. "You've gone too far! How could you do this to your own sister?"

"It was an accident! How bad is it?" I said.

"Bad." She sucked in her breath. "The worst."

Then I saw it for myself. The same video millions of people have seen. When I watched it for the first time, more than five hundred thousand people had already seen it on YouTube, and the counter was going up by the second. Thanks, Reddit. It even had a hashtag on social media already: #moaningmyrtle. I don't know who came up with that; it's awful, but it stuck until Allie had been identified. Then the really bad names started.

Why didn't I take the video down right away? There wasn't any point. It was already out there, and you know nothing disappears from the Internet; if I had deleted it, a dozen copies would have sprung up in its place, and at least I can get those removed as the owner. I thought I could control the narrative somehow. I thought deleting it would support the widespread belief that it's a hoax. Because the real kicker is the ghost didn't show up on video. Of course it didn't.

I never planned to upload that video without Allie's permission, but I was exhausted when I started recording at 1:30 a.m., I forgot to uncheck auto-upload—so when the file hit the maximum allowed size, at a little over two hours long, the software immediately posted it to my YouTube channel. If I hadn't fallen asleep, I could have stopped it.

Allie was scandalized, and it wasn't long before her school found out, and then our parents. They took action: they sent Allie to a church support group and counseling for sex addiction. Leave it to them to put the blame on her instead of an external force.

I wasn't off the hook either. Our parents accused me of

being a pervert, and the police actually investigated me for child pornography, but because you don't really see anything in the video—hell, even they're convinced it's a stunt—no charges were filed. But facts don't matter when people have already made up their minds about you.

I've never been a model son, but nothing quite matches the feeling you get when your mother won't look you in the eyes anymore and your father stops talking to you. They moved me into the basement, like they needed to put two floors of our house between me and Allie at night. And after things got worse, they sent me to Zeppelin Bend.

I wasn't doing anything but trying to help her! And maybe if I'd been in my old room, I'd have been able to do something to save her.

That's what you really want to know about, right? Where did she go? Everyone has a theory, but only I know what really happened.

Even while Allie was dealing with bullying from her classmates, she continued experiencing the visitations. She started her own YouTube channel to document what she was going through, how the bullying and sleepless nights were affecting her, since she still didn't remember anything of the actual attacks.

It's heartbreaking. You can see her wasting away in her daily videos. If you want to know what it was like, watch Allie in her own words instead of that obnoxious "Sex Files" podcast that someone posted about our family.

That night, the last night, I couldn't sleep, so I was in the kitchen grazing on leftovers when I heard footsteps above my head—from Allie's room. The clock on the microwave said it was 2:03 a.m. A minute later I heard a high-pitched sound outside. . . . No, I *felt* it, a kind of sonic vibration that set my teeth on edge and rumbled through my bones.

I rushed to the window and looked outside just in time to see a flash of light bathe the back of the house like a giant camera flash. I blinked. When my vision adjusted again, I saw something zoom off overhead, into the night sky.

It was quiet upstairs.

I bolted up to Allie's room. Her door was locked; my parents had the key. It's a lot harder to kick doors open than it looks on TV. When I entered her room, it was too late. Her window was wide open, and the room was empty. There's nothing she could have climbed down on: no trees, storm drains, or ropes made of knotted sheets. I looked out her window, and the backyard below was empty and undisturbed.

"Allie!" I called. "Allie!"

My parents ran in. Dad pulled me away from the window, and Mom screamed at me.

"What are you doing? Where's your sister?"

At first they thought I'd pushed her out the window, but there was no body. There was no sign of her. The police came, took me back to the station, questioned me. All but arrested me. I was in even more trouble than I was for secretly recording Allie, but I didn't care because she was gone. And it was my fault.

Most people think she ran away or that this is some elaborate hoax the two of us concocted together. Even my best friends finally abandoned me over it. Ryan thinks I'm lying and that I did something unimaginable to my sister. Tony cut me off for a different reason; it turns out I was right about him and Ryan being together, and he's siding with her. So there go my friends, along with my YouTube content and my dreams of making it big as a video producer. If it weren't for the video of Allie's attack, my channel would be dead. Instead, I have more subscribers than ever, though they're probably following me because they think I had something to do with her disappearance. But I know what really happened and who was responsible.

I've been calling the thing that was visiting her a ghost, but that isn't quite right. I did end up calling the Ghost Sweepers. They came to the house, examined the original video to confirm I hadn't manipulated it, and ran all their tests in her bedroom—and surprisingly, they determined that there's nothing supernatural happening in our house, and there never was. Their investigation was so boring, they didn't even bother to upload that footage on their own YouTube channel.

So if not a ghost, what was it?

Aliens.

I'm serious.

Who says that aliens have to look like E.T. or tall gray creatures? What if they can phase in and out, change their shapes, avoid being recorded on video? They could have psychokinetic powers like your typical poltergeist. What if, for all intents and purposes, these aliens look and act like ghosts? The question is: What do they want?

Insert requisite alien probe joke here.

I'm kidding, but I'm kind of not. My theory is these aliens are performing tests on humans to see how we work. Maybe they like sexual experimentation as much as we do, although they have a lot to learn about consent. Hell, they could be developing a weapon to incapacitate humanity with pleasure or using our sexual energy to power their vessels. It sounds like the plot of a campy B-grade porn video, but that doesn't mean I'm wrong.

I wish they'd taken me instead of my sister. I wish they'd come for me now. I, for one, welcome our new sex-crazed alien overlords.

It's not for the sex thing either. If they bring me to wherever they took Allie, maybe I can get her back. At home I've been sleeping in her room, recording myself every night. I've been reaching out to other people online, in case they're also being visited. It's a long shot, but I'm trying to get the aliens' attention through my YouTube videos. So far, nothing. But if I mysteriously disappear one night, you'll know what happened to me, and you can tell my story. Even if no one believes you.

In the meantime ask yourselves: Do you feel refreshed when you wake each morning? Or does it seem like you just aren't getting enough rest no matter how much sleep you get?

"Was that a fucking joke?" Lucinda asked. "Aliens? You think it was aliens who molested your sister and then kidnapped her? And you want them to do it to you?"

"You made that up," Cody said. "Right?"

David shook his head. He'd started out just telling the rest of his story to Sunday, but the others had fallen around the fire to listen as well, unable to resist despite their obvious disgust at the idea of David filming his little sister getting off and posting it for everyone on YouTube to see.

"That was your sister?" Tino said. "I've *seen* that video. There was no way that was your sister."

"It's real?" Georgia asked.

Jackie chuckled. "I'm sure you can Google it when you get home."

"I'm not—"

Cody put his hand on Georgia's back. "That's not what Jackie meant."

"Uh, yeah it was."

Jenna sat closest to the fire, as usual, holding a stick in the center of the flames, watching the end blacken and char and the tip burn until it was a bright orange ember. "If that story was fake, you've got a sick sense of humor. If it was true, you're just sick."

"My vote's for a little from column A, a little from column B," Jackie said.

"At least I didn't try to pass off an episode of *Space Howl* as my own," David said defensively.

Jaila cleared her throat, pulling the attention off David. "So we've got a problem we need to discuss."

"How none of the girls should ever be left alone with David?" Lucinda said.

Tino laughed. "You're not related so you're probably safe."

"I think we're lost," Jaila said, raising her voice to cut through the noise.

No one spoke for a full minute. Like Jaila had stolen our voices and thrown them into the fire and all we could do was watch them burn.

Tino found his first. "And who knew this was going to happen?" He looked at each of us in turn. "Oh yeah, that's right. I did."

"Why don't you shut the fuck up, Constantino," Georgia said, which caused Cody and Sunday to both stare at her. I couldn't remember ever hearing her cuss before, and it sounded harsher coming from her.

"We got turned the wrong way trying to get down the rocks earlier," Jaila went on. "And I think we've hiked too far north."

"Thanks, Georgia," Jackie said.

Cody bunched up, his expression tight and defensive. "It *wasn't* her fault!"

"Yes it was," Georgia said. "If I hadn't run off and gotten hurt, we wouldn't have had to go around the stupid boulders."

Tino pointed at Georgia. "At least someone's taking responsibility for screwing up."

"I swear to God I'm going to knock your teeth down your throat," Lucinda said.

David said, "Why don't you two go screw and get it out of your systems already."

Jenna rolled her eyes at him. "Because *they* can keep it in their pants."

Tension simmered around the campfire, and it was beautiful. All they needed was a little nudge to explode. But Jaila shushed them and said, "Look, we're hungry and tired, and we're not going to figure this out tonight. So why don't we just get some sleep, and we'll talk about it in the morning?"

No one argued, not even Tino, and we each eventually retreated to our sleeping bags, but I don't think anyone slept that night.

DAY 3

OUR THIRD MORNING in the wilderness was damp and quiet. Everyone was hungry, and everyone was angry. We were frayed and wondering if we were going to make it back to camp. Without the flare, Dipshit Doug would never know where to find us, and it began to occur to each member of our clusterfuck at different times that we could actually die out here.

I thrived on the chaos, I lived for tossing bombs and watching them explode. But even I didn't want to die of starvation or thirst or by being mauled by wild animals. Jenna had woken up screaming in the middle of the night, and I'd seen her and Georgia wander off to talk. While they were gone, I'd sworn I'd heard wolves or a bear or whatever animals prowled these mountains, so I'd pulled my sleeping bag over my head, hoping if some hungry beast wandered into our camp, it would eat one of the others and then leave.

Jaila, Jenna, and Sunday had woken up early and huddled near the fire, talking quietly and trying to figure out where we were. Tino and Lucinda joined them eventually, and it was a wonder that the meeting didn't end with anyone shouting or castrated or dead. They decided as a group that we needed to head east because even if we didn't hit camp, we'd eventually run into the main road that ran up the mountain. It seemed as good a plan as any, and there were no arguments.

Georgia's ankle was still swollen and bruised, and she couldn't put any weight on it, but she was able to hop a little using the crutches Cody had made her. She was determined not to spend the whole day being carried around in the litter, and even though carrying her would have been faster, no one was brave enough to tell her that.

"Maybe you got lucky and it's not broken after all," I overheard Cody say to Georgia after we'd started walking.

"I don't know," she said. "Maybe. But if I broke it, that wouldn't be the worst thing."

"Are you kidding?"

"Well, at least then I'd have an excuse to quit the soccer team."

"What?" Cody stared at her. "Why would you want to quit?"

Georgia stopped. "Look. I was sent here because a girl on the team accused me of sexually assaulting her."

Cody's mouth fell open. "Did you?"

"No!"

"But—"

"We kissed, that's all. And she kissed *me* first." Georgia kept her voice low. "But her parents found texts we'd sent each other, and they freaked out, and she made up this whole story."

"So does that mean you are gay?" Cody asked.

Georgia didn't answer for a while. Then she said, "I don't know. Maybe?"

"You know it's okay if you are."

"Yeah," Georgia said. "I just . . . maybe I like both. It's confusing, you know?"

Cody nodded. "I get it."

"Everything just got all messed up with that girl. She lied, she flat-out lied, and now my parents think . . ." She stopped, shook her head. "I don't know."

Sunday must have been eavesdropping because she fell in beside them and said, "My dads sent me here because of something somebody else did, too."

"What was it?" Cody asked.

"No one wants to hear it," she said.

"She's right about that!" Tino shouted from the front.

"I do," Georgia said.

Sunday's chin dipped to her chest. "Sure," she said. "Okay."

"SELF-PORTRAIT"

by Brandy Colbert

SUNDAY TAYLOR SAT next to Micah Richmond her first day at the Brinkley School, and he was the first person who was nice to her, so she trusted him right away.

She also knew right away that he was different from her friends in Chicago. At her old school, she'd hung out with the church kids because they always seemed to want her around. They invited her to birthday parties and weekend barbecues and youth group meetings teeming with sexual tension. None of it was particularly fun—she'd always felt a bit like they were all in some unspoken competition for who could be the best Christian. But they were always kind.

She'd moved to L.A. a couple of weeks ago when her father got a new job. Both he and his husband seemed to be fitting in just fine, but Sunday was terrified of Los Angeles. It was just so different from what she was used to. The city was slower, more relaxed than Chicago. Here, people who were forty looked twenty, and it wasn't all cosmetic surgery.

"Six months of winter ages you," her dad had said as they dodged moms in yoga pants and college students buying kale in the natural foods market. "Life's a lot easier when you don't have to spend half of it shoveling snow and avoiding frostbite."

They lived in the San Fernando Valley—what everyone called the Valley and what she soon realized was considered very uncool by half of Los Angeles. Sunday didn't mind it. Her school was over the hill, in West Hollywood, so she got to see plenty of the city during the week. It seemed busier there—more traffic and people. Their street in Sherman Oaks was peaceful, so quiet and manicured it felt like a storybook neighborhood.

"Sherman Oaks is cool," Micah said after asking where she lived that first day.

They had second period together too, so they ended up walking next to each other across campus. Sunday was grateful for it. The campus wasn't particularly big, but it was clear that everyone knew everyone else. They kept looking at her, and she wondered if it was because she was new or because she was with Micah. Maybe both.

"Where do you live?" she asked, taking in his profile.

He was cute enough to warrant the stares of the other students. Micah was one of the few other black kids she'd seen since she got there. He had brown skin a couple of shades darker than her own coppery complexion, a lanky build, and a dimple in his cheek. The only looks she'd received so far had been curious at most, but she was still glad to have someone else around who looked like her.

"I stay over in Beverly Hills," Micah said quickly, then: "What are you studying here?"

Brinkley was an arts-and-sciences school. Sunday had gone to private school back in Chicago, but it had a more basic curriculum. Looking at the roster of classes on the website when they were filling out her application, she'd been almost intimidated by the selection here.

"Visual arts. You live in Beverly Hills? Is it as fancy as it is on TV?"

He shrugged. "Parts of it, yeah. What type of art?"

"A little bit of everything. I mean, I want to study art history in college, so I'm taking those classes. But I'm signed up for studio art and sculpture this semester, too. Why are you being weird about living in Beverly Hills?"

"I'm not," he said. "It's just . . . people kind of judge you by where you live here, and I hate that shit."

"People do that in Chicago too." Sunday paused and then decided to change the subject. She didn't want to piss off her first and only friend or acquaintance or whatever he was. "What are you studying?"

"Guess." He led the way down the path to the building where their honors history class was located.

Sunday looked at him closely, tilting her head to the side and squinting her eyes like she saw people do when they wanted to look smart in art galleries. "Math?"

He shook his head. "Nah, I fucking hate that shit."

"Hmm . . . English?" Maybe he was an undercover literary genius.

Micah laughed. "You probably won't guess. It's dance."

"Dance? Like ballet?"

"I take classes in everything, but I want to choreograph. Contemporary. My piece last year won first place in the choreography showcase," he said with a small smile.

"That's really cool. I've never known any guys who dance." It was all sports all the time at her old school. And in the Midwest in general. If you didn't *watch* sports, people looked at you like you were absolutely un-American.

"Well, you're in L.A. now. Everybody here does everything."

They walked through the bustling hallways, and every few feet, people would wave or grin or fist-bump Micah to say hello. She wouldn't have guessed him to be popular; maybe because he was so low-key. The people in the popular crowd at her old school were all virtually interchangeable. They wore the same expensive clothes and made appointments at the same expensive hair salons, and their families went on the same extravagant vacations, sometimes together. You could spot them by the glow of superiority that practically radiated around them.

A guy in a hoodie with surfer-blond hair shuffled over just before they walked into their classroom.

"What's up, man?" Micah said easily, slapping hands with him.

"Not much, just uh . . ." He glanced over at Sunday and nodded, but didn't finish his sentence.

Ah. The universal signal that her presence wasn't wanted.

"I'm gonna go in," she said to Micah, feeling the self-consciousness that had engulfed her when she walked up the front steps that morning flooding back in full force. It had started to dissipate once Micah introduced himself in first period.

"Save me a seat?"

And just like that, the warmth in his voice convinced her that she was going to be okay.

* * *

Sunday settled easily into their new friendship. She didn't feel particularly desperate for friends; she would have happily blended into the background for a while. But Micah was nice, they had three classes together, and she'd been eating lunch at his table since he'd invited her on the first day.

She wondered if the other students thought they were dating. At her old school, people seen talking too long, too closely, or too often would be immediately questioned. But here, nobody seemed to think anything about her hanging around. And she didn't feel anything for him—not really. It was almost like they'd known each other their whole lives, but there wasn't a spark. She wasn't sure if she'd ever had a spark with anyone, but she hoped she would know when it happened.

On the first Friday at her new school, Sunday showered and got ready a bit earlier than normal. She had to make sure she caught her dad and Ben before they left for work. Well, only her father would be leaving. Ben did his graphic design projects out of the spare bedroom they'd turned into an office. But they both got up early and had coffee and breakfast together each morning, even on the weekends.

"Morning," Ben said from the stove where he was poaching an egg. "Want one?"

"No, thanks." Sunday made herself a bowl of instant oatmeal and sprinkled blueberries on top. Fruit was one of the things Los Angeles did better than Chicago. Her father had seemed positively delighted the first time he'd seen the produce all lined up in the market, practically sparkling in the bins. "Where's Dad?"

"He had to go in early." Ben's back was turned toward her, and she noticed that his ash-blond hair was starting to get a bit long. He was older than her father, but he acted younger; less serious, anyway. "What's up?"

"I'm going out with some friends after school, so I don't need a ride," she said. "I mean, if that's okay."

It was always okay in Chicago, but they knew all her friends back there. And no one was worried because she was always hanging with church kids.

She could see the skepticism in Ben's posture before he even turned around. "New friends? Why haven't you mentioned them?"

Sunday shrugged. "I don't know. I didn't really have a reason to until now, I guess. It's only been a few days."

"Are these friends actual friends or a boy?"

She swallowed a spoonful of oatmeal. "The two aren't mutually exclusive, you know."

"And you know what I mean." He carefully transferred the poached egg to a plate and moved the pot from the hot burner. Then he wiped his hands on a dish towel and turned around, leaning against the sink.

"My friend Micah invited me to hang out with him and his friends. We eat lunch and have a bunch of classes together. That's it."

"What will you guys be doing?"

Sunday shrugged. "Maybe a movie. Getting a bite to eat."

Ben nodded. "All right. Home by ten."

"I'm sixteen!"

"Eleven. And call us if you need a ride."

"Fine."

Ben's discipline and rule-setting had never been strange to her because Ben had almost always been around. Sunday's parents were teenagers when they had her, before her father began dating men and her mother realized she didn't want to be a mother. She wasn't in Sunday's life anymore, but Ben had been there since she was eight years old. Half her life.

And things would soon become even more official because Ben was going to adopt her. They'd all talked about it right before they moved. Ben had brought it up shyly, like he was afraid she'd say no. She had cried from happiness when he asked if it was okay, if she wouldn't mind him being her father, too. He'd always been so good to her; if anything, she felt like she should be asking him if *he* was sure.

"I'm glad you're settling in." He walked over to kiss the top of her head. "I just want you to be careful."

She spooned up another bite of oats. "You don't have to worry about me."

"Let's make that a promise, Sun," Ben said, stealing a blueberry from her bowl.

Micah met her at her locker after the last bell.

"Ready?"

Sunday put away the books she wouldn't need over the weekend and slammed the door shut. "Yeah, where are we going?"

"My house," he said, leading the way to the parking lot. "I told everyone to come over in, like, an hour."

"Are your parents out of town?"

"No, they're just never home and don't give a shit what I do." He shrugged. "They don't really give a shit when they're home, either."

Sunday couldn't imagine a life like that. Her dad and Ben seemed to be aware of everything she was doing at all times, even though she was never really doing anything they'd object to.

Micah slowed in front of a silver Mercedes. A black guy Sunday had never seen was leaning against the hood, arms crossed and brows furrowed. He turned his glare on Micah as they approached.

"Is this your car?" She didn't mean to sound so incredulous. After all, this was Los Angeles, and the rest of the cars in the parking lot certainly weren't shabby by comparison. But Micah had been so strange about admitting he lived in Beverly Hills, she was surprised to see he drove such an obviously luxurious car.

"About time you showed up," the guy grumbled.

Micah ignored her question and the guy's comment and sighed. "Meet my brother, Eli. E., this is Sunday."

The frown on Eli's face relaxed into an almost-smile as he looked at her. "Hey." He paused. "Your name is *Sunday*?"

It wasn't the first time she'd gotten that question this week, and it wouldn't be the last.

Sunday shrugged. "I sit next to a girl named Whisper in studio art."

He gave her a full smile this time and an almost-laugh. "Touché. You rolling with us?"

Eli didn't look so much like Micah. He was bulkier and missing a dimple, and he seemed cranky for no reason. But she instantly liked him, just as she'd instantly liked Micah.

As it turned out, Micah's definition of fancy varied vastly from hers because their house was exactly the type of home she pictured when she thought of Beverly Hills. They had to pass through a set of security gates, where the guard at the booth greeted Micah like they were best friends.

Their house wasn't the biggest on the street, but it was objectively impressive. There was a sprawling emerald-green lawn and a long circular drive and elaborate detailing on the outside that made her think the inside was probably even more gorgeous.

"This is totally Beverly Hills fancy," Sunday said accusingly as she got out of the passenger seat.

Eli climbed out behind her. "Micah likes to pretend we're poor. It's better for his image."

"Shut the fuck up, E.," Micah said, slamming his door.

Sometimes Sunday wondered what it would be like to have a sibling. Her father and Ben had considered adopting a child from the foster care system years ago, and even went so far as to discuss it with her, but they ultimately decided they were happy with one child. They always said she was such a good kid they didn't want to jinx it. Most of the time Sunday felt glad, but sometimes even sibling rivalry made her a little envious. Having a brother or sister was a connection she'd never know.

Micah left her alone with Eli while he went upstairs to drop off his backpack and the bag with all his dance gear that he lugged back and forth each day.

"Your house is great," Sunday said, gazing around the foyer. Her voice echoed back to her.

"Yeah, it's one thing our parents didn't fuck up," Eli said.

She followed him to the kitchen, which was three times the size of the one at her new house. Eli opened the door on the giant refrigerator and waved her over. "Want something to drink?"

The fridge was fully stocked. Sunday felt almost dizzy as she stared at all her options. It looked like they were throwing a full-on party later. She finally chose a can of ginger ale and stepped aside as Eli slipped a bottle of Bud Light off the shelf. He twisted off the cap and took a long swallow.

He noticed her staring and raised an eyebrow. "You want one?"

Sunday shook her head.

"You don't drink?"

"Not as, like, a statement. I just never have."

"That's cool." He took another sip, then said, "I only drink."

"What?"

Eli hopped up on the counter next to the sink, swinging his legs back and forth so the heels of his sneakers bumped against the cabinets. "I mean, I don't do anything else. Like smoke weed or take molly or whatever."

Sunday sipped her ginger ale and nodded. Eli was still watching her, and she got the feeling he wanted to say more. But then Micah walked in.

"I'm fucking starving," he said, scratching the back of his head. "You guys want to order pizza or something?"

Eli looked away.

People started trickling in about an hour later. Most of them Sunday knew from her lunch table, and she felt a little more at ease when she realized she wouldn't have to sit in a room full of complete strangers.

Eli was friendly enough with everyone, but he didn't seem to have any friends in the crowd, and she suddenly wondered how old he was. He didn't look significantly younger than his brother, but he seemed to instinctually defer to whatever Micah wanted. Then again, he'd seemed totally comfortable cracking open a beer earlier, and he hadn't stopped drinking.

They moved the pizza boxes and a bunch of drinks to the game room. Sunday's eyes widened as she took in the enormous screen where they projected TV shows and movies onto the wall like a small cinema, the various game consoles in the cabinet beneath it, and the pinball machines and shuffleboard and poker tables scattered throughout. She wondered what her dad and Ben would think about this room. Her house had plenty of space for the three of them, with big, open rooms and a huge backyard, but the lack of a fourth bedroom meant they had to combine the guest room with Ben's home office.

"Having fun?" Eli strolled up behind her just as she'd lost another game on the *Twilight Zone* pinball machine.

Sunday startled. No one had come up to her all afternoon—they waved from across the room or smiled when she squeezed past them, but that was it. Nobody besides Micah and his brother seemed remotely interested in getting to know her. And Micah had been hard to keep up with all afternoon. He kept disappearing, sometimes alone but often with one or two people.

She shrugged, unsure of how to respond. Eli seemed like the type of person who would call bullshit when someone lied to his face. And besides, Sunday wasn't exactly the best liar around. She was pretty terrible, actually.

Eli was holding two beers. He tipped the unopened one toward her. "Want one?"

"I still don't drink," she said, frowning.

"Cool, cool. Thought you might have changed your mind. It sure makes these things more tolerable." He sipped from his bottle. "Want to take a tour of the house?"

Sunday wondered if this was some grand excuse to get her alone. But Eli didn't seem like a creep. A little more serious than Micah, maybe—and certainly more surly—but not a bad guy.

"Okay," she said, and followed him out of the game room.

The Richmond home was probably the nicest house Sunday had ever been in. The art alone was enough to ease her anxiety of being at a party where she felt so out of place. Some of it was created by artists she didn't know, but she spotted an original Rothko, an Andy Warhol sketch, and a painting by Aaron Douglas that she'd never seen but instantly recognized as his.

"Your parents have incredible taste in art," she murmured, taking her time to look at it all as they wandered through the house.

Eli shrugged. "I don't know anything about art."

"I do."

They were on the second floor now, wandering the halls that she figured must hold the bedrooms.

"What's so special about it?" he asked, taking a long drink. He was on the second bottle he'd brought along, having abandoned the first one on a side table earlier, as if he knew someone would clean it up for him.

"Art?"

"Yeah. I mean, my parents bid on all this expensive shit, and then it just hangs here and they don't even look at it."

Sunday shook her head. "We go to an arts-and-sciences school. You really feel that way about it?"

"You're an artist?"

"Sort of. But I mostly want to work with it. I'm interested in the artists and the time periods and genres they worked in. And the mediums they preferred and their inspiration and—" She cut herself off, embarrassed. Those were practically the most words she'd spoken since she'd arrived. "Sorry."

Eli grinned. "I'm a math guy. Tell me more."

They were sitting on the floor of his bedroom when Micah stuck his head in.

"You okay here?" he asked Sunday, not looking at his brother.

Beside her, she could feel Eli's body tense. They weren't even touching, just sitting cross-legged on the rug in front of his bed, but she felt the change in him instantly.

"Just trying to explain to your brother why art saves lives," she said, only half joking.

Micah rolled his eyes. "Good luck with that. This one avoids culture like it's a fucking disease."

"Oh, just because I don't want to go to all your little dance performances, I'm uncultured?" Eli narrowed his eyes. "Fuck off, Micah."

Sunday had been in the middle of arguments before, but she'd never felt this level of animosity. Her father and Ben rarely disagreed in front of her, and the church kids back in Chicago didn't argue like this. Sometimes they'd raised their voices, but it never got to the point where she was worried they might start throwing punches.

Micah ignored Eli, letting him have the last word. "Gonna go on a beer run," he said, looking at Sunday. "Want to come with?"

There didn't seem to be a right answer here. If she left with Micah, Eli would clearly be pissed. But he seemed so easily angered, and she didn't really feel like being around that energy now. And she was here because Micah had invited her.

She slowly stood, avoiding Eli's eyes. "Want us to grab you anything?" she asked, but he never answered her, and after a few seconds of silence, Micah nodded toward the hallway, signaling they should go.

Sunday couldn't believe he would just leave all his friends to fend for themselves in that huge, nice house. She wasn't sure Eli could be trusted to oversee things, especially in the mood they'd left him in. The art alone was worth millions of dollars. Did Micah trust all of them, or did he just not care?

"Do you guys ever get along?" she asked, looking out the windows. It was completely dark, and the neighborhood appeared different now that the sun had gone down. The houses were cast in haloes of light that made everything look even bigger and more ornate.

"Used to." Micah sighed. "He's a couple of years younger than us. I think he sort of expected everything would be the same once he got to high school—that, you know, we'd still hang out all the time."

"What changed?"

"I don't know. He doesn't really like my friends, I guess. They don't like him much either," he added with a wry smile. "And I think the dance stuff freaks him out."

"Maybe he's jealous."

"He's not jealous. We both used to do everything—play every sport, dance, play instruments. When we got older, I dropped everything but dance. Honestly, I think he stopped taking lessons because some of the guys at school were talking shit. Like, that he was gay or whatever."

"Oh."

Sunday wasn't immune to some of the looks her father and Ben got when they were around certain people. They were different looks from when people seemed surprised or annoyed to see a black person in their presence. She could always tell when it was about her dad and Ben's relationship because the glares ignored her and included Ben, who was white.

"I don't give a shit about any of that," Micah almost spat out. "I like to dance, and I'm good at it, and fuck anyone who's bothered by it."

"Are you?"

"What?"

"Gay," she said quietly, suddenly aware of how rude a question that was. It was personal, and even though he'd been exceedingly kind and welcoming to her the past week, she didn't know if they were actual friends yet.

He looked at her from the corner of his eye. "Are you one of those people who's bothered by it?"

"No, I . . . My dad is gay. I live with him and his husband."

Soon she'd be able to say she lived with her *dads*—plural. Sunday wondered how long it would take to get used to that, but she liked the sound of it.

Micah nodded, back at ease. "That's cool. And no, I'm not. But I'm probably going to spend the rest of my life answering that question because people can't wrap their head around the fact that dancing has nothing to do with sexuality."

At the store Micah told her to stay in the car while he got the beer. "They always take my fake here, but you look young," he said. "No point in pushing my luck." He came back with three twelve-packs and a bag of chips and beef jerky.

They were quiet on the ride back to the house. Micah pulled into the drive, stopped the car, and turned to her.

"You're the first person I've seen him talking to in a long time," Micah said. "Eli. He doesn't get along with a lot of people."

"Okay." Did he want her to be nice to his brother as a favor? She appreciated how kind Micah had been since her first day at Brinkley, but she didn't owe him.

Micah didn't say anything else. Just nodded and opened his door. So Sunday did the same.

The next week, Sunday saw Eli walking toward her in the hallway after the last bell. He was loping along with his head bowed and his thumbs looped through the straps of his backpack, elbows pointed down. She wasn't sure if he was still mad at her, but she didn't want to make things any weirder.

"Hey, stranger," she said to get his attention before he passed.

Eli looked up, his face cycling through a range of emotions as he stopped and looked at Sunday: surprise, scorn, and then a resigned sort of happiness that she knew meant he was pleased to see her, even if he was doing his best not to show it. "What's up?"

"Just heading to the studio," she said, nodding toward the room across the hall.

"You have to make up an assignment?" He looked skeptically toward the door as if he thought the room might turn into a pumpkin after the last bell.

"No, some of us just go in there to work after school some-times." She paused. "Have you never been in there?"

"I don't have art until next semester," he said, and by the tone of his voice, he clearly wasn't looking forward to it.

She smiled, shaking her head. "I mean, I know it's not a chalk-board full of theorems or whatever, but you should come check it out sometime. It's peaceful. All good vibes."

He brushed a hand over his head and looked across the hall again. "Maybe some other time."

Some other time turned out to be the next day and the next day and then the day after that. Sunday went to the studio imme-diately after her last class, and within five minutes, Eli had joined her. He didn't talk much. When other people were there, he'd wander the studio, looking at the works in progress from other students—oil paintings propped up on abandoned easels, incom-plete sculptures sitting on tables, and a whole mess in the corner that Sunday explained wasn't actually debris but the components of collages.

When they were alone he sat beside her at the table, watching her work on her drawing. "You don't get bored?" he asked as he took in the deliberate, detailed strokes she made with a stick of charcoal.

"Bored?"

"You have to do so much to get it right. It looks so tedious."

"And math isn't?"

"Math is fun," he said with a grin.

Later, she walked with him to the performing arts building to wait for Micah, who was wrapping up a practice session in the dance studio. He also stayed after a few times a week, and since Micah was his ride, Sunday wondered what Eli had done to pass the time before he started hanging out with her.

Long horizontal windows ran down one wall of the studio. Sometimes the blinds were drawn across them, but today they were open, so Sunday and Eli could see right in. Micah was alone, and it looked like he was talking to himself as he worked on a routine.

He wore tear-away track pants and a white T-shirt drenched in sweat. His feet were bare. Sunday felt a little guilty watching him. She didn't mind when Eli sat in the studio with her as she worked, but Micah's choreography seemed too private. It didn't feel like the sort of work that would be appreciated if someone saw all the moving parts, but rather something that should only be viewed once it was absolutely perfect.

"Why did you stop dancing?" Sunday turned toward Eli.

His shoulders went stiff. "What do you mean?"

"Micah said you used to dance. And now you don't. Why?" She didn't exactly think he'd admit to what Micah had said, that he'd quit because he was worried about how people would view him, but she wanted to hear it from him. Maybe it would help her understand him a little more.

"Because it's stupid." Eli shrugged. "He's always bragging about winning contests or whatever, but it's a waste of time. There are, like, a million people better than him who want to be choreographers."

Sunday looked back in the room. What Micah was doing seemed to be anything but a waste of time. And if Micah knew he had an audience, he didn't let on. After a couple of minutes, he crossed the room, turned on the stereo, and unleashed the choreography that was in his head. And it was gorgeous. Not just the steps, but the way

Micah executed them. Sunday had noticed how he always seemed to be aware of the way he held his body, even when they were just walking across campus, but she never could have imagined he moved like this. It was as if his limbs turned into air, as if the music was woven into his muscles. She couldn't take her eyes off him, wondering each time how high he would leap and how gracefully he would land.

"He's a drug dealer."

Sunday was so entranced with the performance that for a moment, Eli's words didn't register. She slowly looked away from the dance studio, turning toward him.

"What?"

Eli's face and neck were ruddy, and she thought he was flushed from embarrassment, but later, she would wonder if it was from exhilaration instead.

"My brother." He lowered his voice, even though no one else was around. "He's, like, the school drug dealer."

Sunday rolled her eyes. "I'm new, not gullible."

"I'm not kidding, Sunday. He's who everyone goes to for anything they need."

"Anything?" She admittedly wasn't the most well-versed in what people were smoking or swallowing, but her mind instantly went to the antidrug posters of severe addicts with boils on their faces and track marks along their emaciated arms.

"Mostly weed. Some molly. Mushrooms. Pretty basic shit, but . . ."

Sunday's throat was dry. She was afraid to look at Micah again, worried he'd suddenly morph into a monster she wasn't aware she'd been hanging out with this whole time. How could she have been so clueless? Why hadn't he said anything to her?

She glared at Eli. "Why are you telling me this?"

He shrugged again. "Don't you think you deserve to know?"

The music inside the studio stopped. Sunday looked in, catching Micah's eye. He waved and held up a finger, signaling he wanted her to wait for him.

When he turned to grab his shoes and towel, she turned and walked out to the parking lot where Ben was waiting for her.

Micah was already sitting in first period when Sunday arrived the next day.

She said hello without looking at him, then felt him watching as she dropped her bag at her feet and slipped into her chair.

"Everything cool? You kind of ran off yesterday," he said, tapping a pencil against the side of his desk.

Sunday glanced at his hands. She felt as if they should look different now that she knew what he used them for. But they looked exactly the same, and when she got up the nerve to meet Micah's eyes, he looked exactly the same, too.

She shook her head, unable to come up with a response.

Micah leaned in close, bending at the waist so only she could hear him. "I didn't know how to tell you."

Sunday's head whipped toward him, her mouth open.

"Eli told me you know." Micah sighed. "He made it sound like it slipped out, but nothing is an accident with him. He really hates not being involved in what I'm doing."

Sunday looked at him curiously, still silent.

"Like the dance thing . . . Maybe it's because he was worried about what people would think, but honestly, he wasn't ever that good." Micah paused. "He would get so mad when the teachers praised me and didn't say anything to him. And he'd go into, like, a full-on rage at home if they corrected him in front of the class . . . which happens to *everyone* in every dance class."

Sunday frowned. She didn't want to talk about Eli. "You couldn't just say it? Like, hi, I'm Micah and I sell—"

"Knock it off," he said through gritted teeth. "Do you really have no idea how this works?"

Sunday's eyes darted around the room, but no one was paying attention to them.

"I thought you'd figure it out," he said in a softer tone a few moments later. "But then you didn't, or I thought maybe you were just cool with it and didn't want to talk about it, and . . . I wasn't trying to hide it from you."

"Why?" she whispered. "I don't get it. You don't need the money."

Mr. Moore arrived then, juggling an armful of books and a coffee.

"To be continued," Micah said, turning to face the front of the room.

After the bell they walked like normal to their second class, but Sunday felt like things between them were anything but normal.

"I'm still the same person," he said without looking at her.

Sunday considered this. She knew he was right and that she wasn't being entirely fair by judging him. It wasn't so much about the drugs. The idea of them made her nervous, and she wondered exactly how much and what had been stashed in his house when they were there. This reminded her of Emma Franklin, who was in their youth group back in Chicago. That is, until she'd gotten pregnant and stopped coming to meetings and hangouts. No one stopped inviting her, but it was understood that they couldn't just pretend like everything was the same once her belly started swelling. Sunday hadn't been particularly close with Emma, but she couldn't help feeling like she'd been betrayed by her. Emma had worn a purity ring and pretended like she was as inexperienced with guys as Sunday, and then one day she was pregnant.

It wasn't that Micah had betrayed her, but Sunday guessed she would have preferred to hear it from him instead of his brother.

"Why do you do it?" she asked again.

They stopped outside the building.

"Because . . . I don't know, Sunday," he said with a tinge of annoyance. "Because it feels good to not be the spoiled Beverly Hills kid everyone thinks I am when they hear who my parents are or see where we live. Because it's so different from what everyone else knows about me. It's not like it's going to be a career. I'll quit doing it after we graduate . . . maybe before."

She nodded. "Okay."

He cocked his head to the side as he eyed her. "We're good?"

Her father and Ben would kill her if they knew she was hanging out with the school drug dealer, but they'd never have to know if she didn't tell them. Besides, it wasn't like she wanted to be his girlfriend.

"We're good," she said. "But . . . is there anything else?"

Micah shook his head. "What about you? Are you really so . . . virtuous?"

"I'm not *virtuous*. That makes me sound like a nun."

But she knew it appeared that way, and not for the first time, Sunday wondered if that meant she was simply boring.

Ms. Bailey was in the art room when Sunday walked in after school.

She waved from her desk in the corner, then pushed her glasses up on her nose and went back to whatever she was scribbling in a notebook. Bailey was everyone's favorite because she mostly left them alone, but she knew her shit when it came to art, and she always knew what their work needed for them to take it to the next level.

Eli walked in a few minutes later, after Sunday had unpacked the materials from her portfolio and spread them out on her desk.

"Hey," he said, sitting down next to her.

"Hi." Sunday picked up the piece of charcoal but couldn't bring herself to start drawing.

"You know, it's still cool if we hang out, right?"

Sunday looked at him. "What?"

"I mean, just because you and Micah aren't friends anymore—"

She frowned. "Who said that?"

Eli's eyebrows twitched. "Well, I just thought . . . I mean, you seemed pretty upset about what I told you."

He glanced toward Bailey, but she wasn't paying their conversation any mind.

"I was . . . surprised," Sunday said with a shrug. "I'm not going to stop being his friend. It's not like he's pushing anything on me or selling to kids or something."

"Yeah, but—"

"But what?" Sunday practically snapped. She wished he would just say whatever he had to say and get it over with.

"Nothing. Sorry." He cleared his throat. "Hey, do you want to come over again sometime? There's some more art you didn't see—some stuff you might like or whatever."

Sunday wasn't feeling particularly fond of Eli at the moment, but she felt bad for him. He was younger than them and insecure, like Micah had mentioned. He was trying to smooth things over, and if it meant another chance to look at that Aaron Douglas piece, the one she hadn't been able to stop thinking about since she'd been there, then maybe it wouldn't be so bad.

She went to their house after school again on Friday, but this time it was just the three of them.

They made grilled cheese sandwiches, stuffing them with bacon and tomato. Eli heated up three cans of spicy tomato soup and they ate in front of the TV, where Micah queued up online videos of some of his favorite choreography.

Sunday expected Eli to complain about the videos or Micah's overall presence, but he seemed to be in good spirits. She'd been skeptical about coming over, but she was glad she'd decided to. Everything seemed to be normal, or at least the normal she'd been used to for the last two weeks.

Micah scooped up the dishes, carrying an armful to the kitchen. Sunday turned to Eli.

"Can I look at the Aaron Douglas painting again?" She'd been trying to be patient, but this was the reason she'd come over, after all.

"The who?"

She rolled her eyes and pulled him up from the couch by his arm. Eli happily followed her to the staircase and up to the painting.

"He was a Harlem Renaissance artist," Sunday said, leaning in closer to inspect the piece. "He was a painter and an illustrator who—"

Suddenly, Eli's face swooped in front of hers, and he was kissing her. His lips were too wet and his breath was too hot, and everything about it was wrong. Sunday put her hand on his chest, pushing him away.

"What are you doing?"

Eli blinked at her, as if this reaction wasn't something he'd ever considered.

"Eli, I . . ." She bit her lip and chewed for a moment. "I like you, but . . . not like that."

"Oh." He swallowed hard, his dark eyes focused on her shoulder.

"I'm sorry if I . . ." But she trailed off, because there was nothing to apologize for. She hadn't done anything wrong. She'd been nice to him and hung out with him after school. She hadn't flirted with him or led him to believe she liked him. "I'm sorry, but I just want to be friends."

"Sunday!" Micah shouted from downstairs. "I found another video I want to show you!"

She looked at Eli, who was standing with slumped shoulders. "Are you okay?"

"Yeah, it's—" He brushed past her, thundering down the stairs.

A few seconds later, she followed, but Eli had already disappeared. She didn't see him again that night, not even when she tried to find him to say good-bye before Micah drove her home.

Sunday had art class during fourth period, just before lunch. On Monday, like every day, Bailey greeted them at the start of class, going over what they should be working on and when it was due.

Then she left them to their own devices, strolling through the room to track their individual progress and see if they needed help.

Sunday was still working on her charcoal drawing. Bailey had asked her to start with the bowl of plastic fruit sitting on the table up front. It was a pretty basic assignment, but she knew Bailey wanted to see what she could do in her room, and Sunday planned to give it to her farmer's market–loving father when she was done.

Sunday was moving a little slower that day, still groggy from the weekend. She couldn't get Eli and the kiss out of her mind, though. She hadn't seen him since he'd run away from her at his house, but she hoped they could go back to normal. She hadn't told Micah. She'd bet money that Eli was too embarrassed to have said anything, either.

"How's the charcoal going, Sunday?" Bailey was at her elbow, holding a paper cup of coffee from the faculty lounge.

"Pretty good, I think?" Sunday unzipped her portfolio, rooting around for her sketchbook among the loose papers and class handouts.

She pulled out the book. There was something squeezed between the pages, leaving a gap in the middle. Sunday flipped it open, thinking one of her pencils or gum erasers had gotten wedged inside.

She didn't understand what she was seeing at first. It was a plastic sandwich bag, the kind that zipped closed along the top. That much was clear. But as for what was inside . . .

"What's this?" Bailey frowned, setting her coffee cup on the corner of the table. She picked up the bag between her index finger and thumb, only looking at the contents for a few seconds before she sighed deeply. "Is this yours?"

"I don't . . . I mean, this is my book and my bag, but I don't know what that is."

"Pack up your things and come with me, Sunday," Bailey said, her voice harboring what had to be every ounce of disappointment in the world.

The room was completely silent. Everyone was watching, eyes wide and mouths open. Others were already on their phones, texting furiously.

Magic mushrooms. They looked like regular old mushrooms, with stems and caps, but these were the sort that made a person hallucinate. That's what the head of school said when Bailey dropped the bag on her desk.

"Sunday, the Brinkley School has a zero-tolerance policy," Ms. Ashforth said. She didn't seem livid, like Sunday had feared, but she was unsmiling, and one of her eyebrows appeared to be permanently furrowed. As if Sunday didn't already know how serious this was. Zero tolerance meant expulsion.

"They're not I've never done a drug in my life," she said in a voice so soft she wasn't sure they could hear her. "I've never even seen any."

Ashforth exchanged a look with Bailey. "Okay," she said slowly. "Then tell us where you got them or whose they are, and we'll go from there."

"I didn't get them from anyone. They just showed up in my bag, I swear."

Bailey sighed. "This will be so much easier for everyone if you tell us the truth, Sunday."

"I *am* telling the truth," she said, though she knew they didn't believe her and probably never would.

"Do you have any idea who could have put this in your bag,

then?" Ashforth again. "If it wasn't you, we need to know where else to look. Otherwise, we'll have to call your parents to come down here to talk about next steps."

She didn't even want to think about how angry her father and Ben would be. They trusted her, but more than that, she knew how much her father expected from her. She couldn't remember a time when he hadn't explicitly stated how differently people viewed them because of their skin color—how she had to work twice as hard at everything she did, simply because she was black. There was a huge list of activities that Sunday had always known were not an option, no matter how forgiving other parents might be: getting pregnant, drinking and doing drugs—even bringing home a grade lower than a C (which, to be honest, he was pretty peeved at anything below an A). Getting caught with drugs—hers or someone else's—was certainly at the top of that list.

Sunday knew without a doubt where the shrooms had come from. She wasn't positive who had placed them in her bag, but in that moment, she felt Eli's hot breath on her skin, his unwelcome lips pressing against hers. . . .

"Sunday?" Bailey prompted her. She got the feeling Bailey wanted her to be cleared from this just as much as Sunday did.

But she couldn't speak. Even as she thought of Eli's spitefulness, the way he'd tried to get her to stop liking Micah by revealing his secret, she knew she couldn't tell. If she ratted him out, he'd tell on Micah, and Micah didn't deserve that. He'd been doing his thing long before she got there—she couldn't make everything come crashing down for him in just two weeks. He didn't deserve it.

And she thought of Emma Franklin, the pregnant girl back in

Chicago. The youth pastors, parents, and even their friends had tried to get Emma to reveal who the father of her baby was. But Emma never told. Sunday didn't know if she was protecting someone in the youth group or maybe an older guy she was never supposed to be seeing, but Emma kept her mouth shut, and even after she virtually disappeared, the secret never got out. Sunday had always respected that, even if other people called Emma cowardly and immature.

Sunday wasn't sure what her father would do; she'd never been kicked out of anything. Or been in any trouble, really. What if this meant she couldn't get into any other private schools in the city? Or that she couldn't study art in a place where people respected it? They'd searched long and hard for Brinkley, and there'd been a huge celebration when she was accepted. They had been so proud, her father and Ben. She didn't want to think about how they'd look at her now. She didn't want to think about the fact that they might not believe the mushrooms weren't hers.

But most of all, she didn't want to listen to that little voice at the back of her head. The one that said maybe it wasn't her father at all who would be the most upset—that maybe this would disappoint Ben so much that he'd no longer want to adopt her. What if he decided she was too much trouble, that he didn't want to be the official dad of someone stupid enough to get caught with drugs? She knew he wouldn't announce something like that, but she also knew it would be much worse if they just became silent about the topic— swept it under the rug until they thought she'd forgotten about it and was too embarrassed to bring it up herself.

She wanted Eli to pay for what he'd done, but was it worth ruining Micah's life too?

The second hand on the clock in Ashforth's office ticked and ticked, counting down to the worst decision Sunday had ever had to make.

"Call my dad," she finally said, her voice quiet.

Bailey closed her eyes and exhaled. Ashforth shook her head as she reached for the phone.

Sunday's lips trembled but—with the last amount of dignity she could muster—she kept her mouth closed and held her head high.

Jackie was laughing. "If that doesn't win for best story, it should definitely win an award for best bullshit."

"It wasn't bullshit," Sunday said. "It's true."

Lucinda was smiling. "So you had two hot guys after you that you blew off, and one planted drugs on you as revenge?" She shook her head. "Sounds less like a problem and more like a party."

"For real," Tino said. "Maybe when we're out of this, I could visit you in L.A. and—"

"You really think we're going to speak to one another after this?" Sunday asked. "I mean, get real. My dads wouldn't let me within a mile of any of most of you." She glanced at Georgia. "No offense or anything."

"I get it," Jenna said. "My parents are the same."

"That's because parents are assholes." Lucinda's smile had faded. "It's true, right? They'd look at Jenna and see a pyro, David a perv, Sunday a drug dealer, Cody a—" She stopped, tilted her head. "Well, I think your story was bullshit, so I don't know what they'd see when they looked at you, but it probably wouldn't be good."

"We're all fuckups, right?" Jackie said.

"I'm not a pyromaniac," Jenna said defiantly.

Jackie shrugged. "I got arrested for stealing a movie prop from a sci-fi con. We're *all* fuckups."

"Exactly," Lucinda said. "Except we're not. We've been out here two whole days, and we're still alive. Maybe we won't make it back to camp today, but we will make it back. Our parents see us as these problems to solve, delinquents to deal with. But we're more than that. David clearly cares about his sister—"

"Maybe a little too much," Tino added.

"Shut up," David said.

"And Sunday's always helping out when she can, and Cody's protective and Jaila's the smartest person I've ever met."

"None of that makes a difference, though," Jenna said. "Not if all people see is what we've done rather than who we are."

Lucinda smiled; grinned, really. "But that's the thing. What we've done *is* who we are. Even if we don't want to admit it."

"What'd you do, then?" Tino asked. "And don't give us some old-time movie version of it, either."

"That's easy," Lucinda said. "Mine is a story of pure injustice. And it's totally true."

"A VIOLATION OF RULE 16"

by Suzanne Young

THE LIGHTS IN the hallway between English class and the principal's office flicker above me. They've been in need of replacing for at least three months, and I once asked Mrs. Greer, my English teacher, why it hasn't been done yet. She told me some excuse about how the fixtures were outdated and the bulbs were special order. I feel like that sums up my entire school district—out-of-date and waiting for replacement.

I pull open the office door and walk into the lobby, warm air blowing over my pale skin. The woman behind the desk frowns when she sees me, but it's not because she doesn't like me. In fact, Mrs. Patron is one of the coolest adults at this school. She has a superstraight bob and a killer collection of silk scarves. And like me, she thinks this rule is bullshit. She nods for me to go in.

I pause at the entrance of Mr. Jones's office and then knock on the open door. He looks up from his desk and immediately sighs when he realizes it's me. His agitated reaction stings a bit, but I go to sit down when he waves me in.

Mr. Jones is in his fifties, black with a shaved head and a crisp gray suit. He keeps his beard neatly trimmed; his desk is immaculate. I often joke that he seems like someone who uses a ton of hand sanitizer. And to support my theory, his office always smells a bit like rubbing alcohol.

"Ms. Banks," he says in his deep voice. "Lucinda."

"You know this is bullshit," I say, and he closes his eyes.

Mr. Jones has been my principal for my entire career here at Heritage High—he's exceedingly patient, even when I'm not the most tactful.

"If you could please watch your language," he says, and motions for me to start over. I take a steadying breath, trying to temper down my annoyance, and smile politely.

"Well," I say, my voice strained. "Mrs. Montgomery marked my card and sent me to you. Violation of rule sixteen." I cross my heel over my thigh so he can see the black leggings. I also tug on the hem of my T-shirt, which is long enough to cover my ass.

Mr. Jones tightens his jaw, but doesn't say anything at first. He opens his desk drawer, takes out a pen, and outstretches his hand for my card so he can initial that I was here.

He writes on the card, and then lifts his eyes to mine before handing it back. "This is the fourth time this month," he says.

"To be fair," I reply. "I dispute every instance. Two weeks ago I was in here for a bra strap. It's bad enough that I have to wear a bra at all, but then . . . as if that layer plus a layer of clothing isn't enough barrier between boys and my breasts, they can't bear to see a quarter-inch strap that is nowhere near my boob?"

Mr. Jones shakes his head, looking down at his desk. He's heard my arguments before, but I don't let up.

"Then last week," I continue, "I was here for a bare shoulder. Okay, I wore a strapless bra so there would be no straps. I wore a tank top *underneath* a tank top so there'd be no skin showing under my armpit. But even that wasn't enough. Because boys can see one inch of my shoulder blade?" I ask. "This is Phoenix; it was a hundred and twelve outside. At what point do the rules address male behavior? At what point are they responsible for their damn selves?"

"I'm sorry," he says. "But four marks equal in-school suspension for the rest of the day."

I swear, my blood turns to lava, and I feel my entire face heat up, my cheeks burning.

"I don't get to go back to class? Let me ask you, Mr. Jones," I say, slamming both feet down on his carpeted floor. "How many boys have you brought in here this month? If they're so distracted by the mere outline of my calves, then I'm sorry—they're the ones with the problem."

"It's the rule," Mr. Jones says. "Rule sixteen, and you know it."

"Like I said, it's bullshit."

"Don't make it two days, Lucinda."

"Did you ever think that Mrs. Montgomery is the problem?" I ask. "I mean, besides our poor boys who can't control themselves, apparently. No, Mrs. Montgomery *looks* for a reason to send me out. She's obsessed with the dress code—why? Why does she get off on it?"

"Nobody's . . . getting off," Mr. Jones says. "She's following the rules."

"The rules?" I repeat. "Why doesn't someone send Miss Heely down, then? Her pants are so tight you can see when she has a wedgie. Or how about Mr. Rentry? He smells awful, and I personally find that distracting. But no," I say, standing, "it's only the teenage girls who get sent down here. Ridiculed. Controlled. And if you can't see that—"

"Lucinda," Mr. Jones says, his temperament cold now that I've criticized his staff. "That's two days. Head there now."

Two days of in-school suspension? I should have probably stopped arguing, but I guess part of me didn't expect him to go through with it. I think I might cry. Instead, I stand straighter.

"I'm disappointed in you," I tell my principal, my voice shaking. And then I turn around and walk out.

I used to be an A student. Seriously—straight As in every subject, excelling in math. But this year the new governing board added Rule 16 to our handbook. We don't have uniforms; this is a public charter school. We've been nationally recognized for our excellence in academics. We won a grant for our outstanding work with girls in STEM. Hell, we were progressive.

The new governing board is made up of four old-ass men and one mother of six. I only know this because my own mother goes to the meetings and comes home fuming mad.

"They're trying to erase science!" she yelled one night, slamming her purse on the kitchen table. My mother's a nurse, and she's fiercely protective of her research hospital.

My father told her to calm down; they couldn't actually erase science. But every meeting his attempts to console her worry became less and less convincing.

I've heard them talking after I've gone to my room, and something my mother said stuck with me. "They're doing this because the girls are outshining the boys," she murmured. "I swear they're trying to take us back to the fifties."

I expected to hear my father immediately refute her claim, but instead, in a quiet voice, he said, "I think you're right."

So meaning to or not, my parents have fed my feeling of injustice. The girls here are excelling, and that scares the people in charge. They're trying to control us. They're putting the responsibility of male learning on us. They refuse to confront the actual problems.

And sure, I've read the dress code. But like I told Mr. Jones, it's bullshit. And I won't follow it.

The in-school suspension room is a small, block-walled room with no windows. It's off the cafeteria, so we can hear the students during lunch hour, laughing and having fun while we sit in silence. That's part of the psychological punishment: we're not allowed to work on anything. We can't read, write, or do our homework. We have to sit there.

In my opinion the school shouldn't get paid a fucking dime from the government when a student goes into that miserable room. They're not providing an education—in fact, they're withholding it. Why should they get paid for that?

I walk in, and Shelly—a staff member—glances up to see me. She shifts her lips to the side in an expression of concern and holds out her hand for my behavior card. She's tiny, known for wearing sneakers with everything. Even dresses. Like now, she's wearing a blue-checked dress with a pair of Converse.

I stop at her desk in the front of the room while she checks over my card. I causally glance around to see who's here to share hell with me.

The view is underwhelming at first. Michael Bellagio—a rich kid with an affinity for getting high in the parking lot before school—and Doug Wilkerson—a guy from my English class. Doug was sent out yesterday for calling Mrs. Montgomery a bitch when she wouldn't accept his tardy pass.

And there's Cece Garcia, who I pretty much grew up with. Her mother is from Mexico, and Mrs. Garcia babysat me when we first moved into our neighborhood. Cece nods a hello at me, and I roll my eyes to let her know just how shitty I think our situation is.

"Here you go," Shelly says, handing back my card. I look down at it, disgusted by the red box filled in next to today's date. Like I'm so awful that I don't deserve to be in class.

I'll admit, it hurts my feelings. This year—my senior year—I have become a solid C student thanks to missing out on class time.

"Sit where you want, Lucinda," Shelly says. She picks up her copy of *The Awakening*, pulls her leg underneath her, and leans back in her chair to read silently.

I sit next to Cece. Her heavily lined eyes slide over to me, and I pinch the fabric of my leggings and let them snap back. She snorts a laugh.

"I didn't turn in my homework assignment," she whispers. "Never mind I got a hundred on the last quiz."

"In-school for homework?" I ask.

She smiles. "In-school for pointing out that Randall didn't do his homework either, but he got excused because he had a game. Last I checked, basketball wasn't a required course."

"Yeah, not yet," I say, sinking down in my seat.

I hate this place. I long for my freshman year, when we organized pep rallies and dances, guys and girls together, as if we were the same species. Something the administration clearly doesn't consider to be the case now that my boobs have gotten bigger.

There's movement from the door, and I look up and see Jameson Merrick walk in. He has brown hair, blue eyes, and seriously wrinkled cargo shorts. We've been hanging out for the past six months; nothing confirmed. He's cool, though.

I kind of love him.

Jameson winks at me and goes to Shelly, who seems surprised to see him.

"Jameson," she says. "What are you doing here?"

He shrugs, pulling one of those boyish smiles that everyone likes. "Got in trouble," he says innocently. "I set the bunnies free in agriculture class. Didn't know they could hop so damn fast."

I actually laugh out loud and then quickly cover my mouth when Shelly gives me a stern look. She checks Jameson's card, her expression somewhere between disappointment and amusement. She eventually sighs, marks it in pen, and tells him to have a seat.

Jameson comes to sit directly in front of me, nodding a hello to Cece. I can smell his shampoo and see the ends of his hair are still damp from showering. He turns, glancing back at me.

"Are you in here because of me?" I ask quietly.

"I wasn't going to let you serve time alone. I tried to call you this morning. Brian Sokolowski texted me to say Montgomery was waiting for you in the hall before class. She got a vendetta or what? When did you piss in her houseplants?"

I laugh, and we all immediately lower our heads so Shelly won't separate us. When it's clear, I lean in, and so do Cece and Jameson.

"See?" I tell them. "I knew she was being unfair. But Mr. Jones won't listen to me. Why is Mrs. Montgomery obsessed with how I dress?"

"I heard her husband was behind the school board vote," Cece says. "He campaigned for one of those old dudes. Part of the same cult, maybe?"

"Or they could be from an alternate universe where all the men are terrible," Jameson adds.

"That's an alternate universe?" I ask, and then grin when he looks over at me.

"You're so funny, Lucinda," he whispers, narrowing his eyes play-fully. "I wonder if that's why Mrs. Montgomery doesn't like you. Just too damn funny."

Truth is, I don't know why Mrs. Montgomery hates me, singles me out. I've never done anything to her; I just dress how I want. Be an individual. I'm not even rude to her face—and believe me, that takes a significant effort. Yet she acts like I'm openly defiant. But it's her bad attitude that makes me have to prove a point. I can't . . . fold. Let her win when *she's* wrong.

"Listen," I say to Cece and Jameson. "We have to destroy Rule sixteen. It is legitimately preventing my education. Who knows? I could have been valedictorian."

Jameson smiles at this and murmurs something like "You still can be," when another person walks in the door. I'm surprised to see it's Mr. Jones.

He smiles politely at Shelly, who quickly closes her book and stands. Mr. Jones looks around until he finds me. "Lucinda," he says, waving me forward.

My cheeks immediately heat up, and I'm concerned what this

means. I shouldn't have said "bullshit" in front of him. I toughen up, though—straight back, tight jaw, and get up from my desk.

As I pass by Jameson, he reaches out to touch my hand, just a gentle reminder that he's with me.

I've known Jameson Merrick since middle school, and I hope it's not shallow to say I didn't really think of him in a romantic way until he got superhot. He was *always* my friend, though. I still think about the first time I realized I liked him. We'd been out at a party, and after a drink—just one—he came back to my house to watch some YouTube videos. We sat in my basement, laughing. Cringing at people making fools of themselves. And at one point . . . I just looked over at him and thought he was so damn cute.

And when he turned to me, I think maybe he thought the same thing about me. I'm not ashamed to admit that I asked him if he wanted to hook up. He gave me a resounding yes, and leaned in and kissed me. We've pretty much been together ever since. Neither of us were virgins, although I'm the only one whose past has ever been brought up in the locker room. Jameson punched a dude for calling me a slut, which was nice of him. I would have happily done the punching myself if Dickhead McBryant had said it to my face. But he hadn't.

Just like the school, he judged me. Locker-room talk and unfair dress codes—symptoms of the same problem. Both spearheaded by assholes.

Jameson and I don't talk about our relationship. We don't brag about it. We're just . . . together. And, yeah, I kind of love him. And he kind of loves me, too.

* * *

"So what's this about?" I ask Mr. Jones as we turn down the arts-and-sciences hallway on the second floor. There's a flurry of movement; several students from the agriculture department running around, frazzled and concerned. One of the girls protectively holds a fluffy white bunny. I press my lips together to keep from laughing.

"I've been thinking about what you said—missing class time," Mr. Jones says. "Mrs. Montgomery has come up with a solution."

I furrow my brow, not willing to trust the suggestion of my persecutor. Mr. Jones motions to the small room at the end of the hall—the room they use for the fashion design elective.

"What are we doing in here?" I ask. We walk inside the room, and I immediately see Mrs. Montgomery, her arms crossed over her chest, a smug smile on her face. I have a visceral reaction, and my fists clench.

"Lucinda," she says. I don't respond and turn to Mr. Jones.

"This isn't my class. I want my classwork."

Mr. Jones gives me a look, like he wishes I were someone else entirely, and nods to my teacher. "This is what Mrs. Montgomery has suggested as an alternative," he says.

Confused, I look at her just as she pulls a shirt off the screen printer. It's gray, and across the chest in black are the words "Violation of Rule 16." Next to the printer is a pair of oversize sweatpants with the words on them as well.

I stare at the clothes. I stare so long my eyes start to water, but I refuse to blink. "You have got to be kidding me," I say in a low voice. "Have either of you ever read *The Scarlet Letter*? Why not just put a big *A* on my chest?"

Mrs. Montgomery's smile fades, and Mr. Jones adjusts the button on his suit jacket.

"Now, Lucinda," he says. "This is the compromise. Sending you home isn't the answer. And perhaps in-school suspension isn't the answer either. But you don't get rewarded for violating the rules."

I turn to him fiercely, shocked he'd believe this nonsense. But his expression makes me think he's reciting Mrs. Montgomery's explanation. I look at her.

"You want to shame me," I say. "That's why you're doing this."

"Shame, Lucinda," she says patronizingly, "is a way of learning from bad behaviors. If you willfully disregard the rules, there must be a punishment."

"You're psychotic," I growl.

"Hey, hey," Mr. Jones says, stepping in front of me. "Let's not . . . Let's all just take a moment. What Mrs. Montgomery is suggesting is a tactic other schools use as well. You'll cover your current outfit with the provided school clothing. End of the day, you drop them back off. It's not difficult. And you get to stay in class."

"I'm going to sue you," I say to both of them. Although for what, I don't know. And how, I couldn't say. But this feels so egregious, so goddamn dismaying, that it's all I can do to not burst into tears and run out into the hallway.

"The school makes the rules, Lucinda," Mrs. Montgomery says. "Either follow them or don't, but you have to learn that violating the rules has consequences."

Her blue eyes trail over me, and it's like I can see her hatred. Resentment. No one has ever looked at me the way she does right now—like I'm beneath her. Like I'm the problem of an entire generation. Who knows—maybe she had some repressive, fucked-up childhood. Or maybe her husband is the force behind this. Whatever reason, Mrs. Montgomery is using me to prove her moral superiority. And I won't be a symbol for her misguided leadership.

"No," I say simply, and turn to Mr. Jones. "Yeah, no. I won't wear that."

"Then I'm sorry, Lucinda," he says, sounding like he means that. "You're suspended indefinitely pending a board review."

My mouth falls open. And I'll be honest—in that moment I want to burn the entire place to the ground.

"Is that how you ended up here?" Georgia asked, interrupting Lucinda. "You burned down your high school?"

"No," Lucinda responded. And then in a lower voice, added, "Not the entire high school."

"I'd like to go back to in-school suspension until my mother can pick me up," I say, my voice shaky. If they think I'm going to put on a uniform that's intended to shame me, embarrass me— Well, I'd rather stand here naked.

Mrs. Montgomery looks over at Mr. Jones, clearly annoyed. But Mr. Jones ignores her and motions for me to wait in the hallway. I don't say a word to my teacher and walk out the door.

I rest against the light blue wall, wrapping my arms around myself. In the quiet of the hallway, this uncomfortable feeling slides over me. It takes me a moment to process it, and I realize that I feel violated. The way Mrs. Montgomery wants to hold me up for ridicule, like putting me on a pillory for people to throw food at.

Inviting people to hurl insults at me. Inviting them to mock me.

Tears well up in my eyes, and for a second I wish I wasn't a girl. Constantly judged and objectified. I'm fucking sick of it. I just wish . . .

I sniffle and look down at the shiny white floor. It wouldn't matter what I wish. My crime is being female in a place that values male education over mine. And I hate them. I hate them all for making me regret even one second of being who I am. I hate the way they've made me feel outnumbered and helpless.

There's a tickle on my cheek as a tear slides down, and I wipe it roughly with my palm. I clear my throat, hearing the soft murmur of conversation float out from the room. My sorrow passes, and I'm instead filled with rage. The injustice of it all physically hurts me. Bakes me from the inside. Tears me open.

I don't wait for Mr. Jones. My phone is in my backpack in the in-school suspension room, and I need to call my parents. I need them to know what the school plans to do. They'll fight for me.

With a quick look at the open door, I back away until I jog down the hallway, heading to the cafeteria and the in-school suspension room.

Cece is at her desk, her elbow on the top, her chin in her palm. She straightens as I walk in, probably noticing that I'm upset. She reaches across the aisle and slaps Jameson's shoulder to get his attention. When he turns to her, she nods at me.

I go over to Shelly's desk, and she seems curious about what went down with me and Mr. Jones, but she doesn't ask. "I'm going home," I tell her.

"They're sending you home?" Cece yells from her desk.

"Yeah," I respond. "Indefinitely."

I turn to Shelly and ask her if I can collect my things. She agrees, and I see a bit of sympathy in her eyes. Does she know that I've been humiliated? Can she see it on my face?

I get to my desk, and Jameson is staring at me wide-eyed, his normally cool demeanor faltering.

"He fucking suspended you?" he whispers fiercely.

"I guess," I say, and Jameson leans back in his seat, his brow furrowed. "Does it still count if I took off before Mr. Jones could call home?" I ask.

"Uh, yes," Jameson says. "That's still suspending."

"Well, damn." I smile at him, even though I'm furious. Hurt. But now I have the chance to make this right. Okay, maybe not *right*. But I have the chance to get revenge.

"I'll call you later," I tell Jameson, and bend down to pick up my backpack. I glance at Cece. "Try to sneak out," I tell her. "I need your help with something near the art room."

"On it," Cece says with a smile.

I loop my backpack over my shoulder, and head down the aisle. I need to get out of here before Mr. Jones comes looking for me.

I take the back stairs, waiting near the door to the second floor until the bell rings. I walk into the corridor just as students begin to flood the hall, and I slip into the stream of them, trying not to draw attention to myself.

When I get to the art room, I check to make sure Mr. Jones and Mrs. Montgomery are gone. Then I go inside and close the door behind me. There aren't any classes in here in the mornings, since the art teacher who helps with the fashion design elective does half days at another campus.

My gaze falls on the screen-printed sweatshirt, still waiting on the table, and I feel sick all over again. It couldn't be a mistake the way she had the words placed so boldly over the breasts, the word "Violation" darker than the others.

And fuck her because it worked—she shamed me. Even though I'm not wrong, I feel embarrassed. My nose burns as tears gather again, but there is a rattle on the door, and I quickly duck down. Cece pops her head in the window, and I go over to let her in.

She checks me over, but doesn't mention that I'm about to cry. Instead, she looks fierce. She waves a pass she got from the office, one that excuses her from in-school while she meets with her counselor. Fortunately, the branches of high school government don't interact so they'll never know if she doesn't show.

"So what's this about?" Cece asks. "Why did they suspend you?"

I pick up the sweatshirt and hold it up. Cece's eyes widen.

"That for you?" she asks. "You're not wearing that."

"It's for all of us," I say. "You know, if we dare to show our shoulders, bra straps, outlines of our legs, and whatever body part they outlaw next year. Maybe ankles? But instead of talking to Lance Duncan and his leering eyes and grope-y fingers, they pull me into the office. They suspend me." The tears well up again, but this time they're from anger. "And I'm sick of it," I say.

"Then what are we going to do about it?" Cece asks.

I shake my head, unsure. "What can we do?" I ask. "What rights do we even have?"

Cece bites one of her long fingernails, thinking it over. "We should walk out," she says. "All the girls should walk out."

"That sort of goes toward them denying our education, though,"

I say, slumping onto the table. "We need something bigger. I want to . . ." I pause because even I realize the violence in the words. "I want to ruin them," I say in a quiet voice.

I look up at Cece, and she seems surprised but not entirely opposed.

"What do you suggest?" she asks.

I glance around the room, see balls of newspaper coated in polyurethane, the beginnings of some art project. I see more paper and glue next to it. I look at Cece.

"Want to help me build a girl?" I ask.

She snorts a laugh. "Only if I get to do her makeup." And she comes over to the table, and we get to work.

When Cece and I finish with the project, it's close to lunchtime—which is perfect. We stuffed the clothes with the coated newspaper, like a Halloween scarecrow, making sure to fill out the female form. Over the chest of the sweatshirt, we changed the words. It now reads "Rule 16: A Violation of Our Dignity."

Now I just need to get to the cafeteria and put it on display.

"I think we should call her Barbara," Cece says, gazing down at the stuffed clothing. I look over at her, crinkling my nose.

"What the fuck?"

She shrugs. "It's what I called my first Barbie," she says. "She had, like, three houses, a Jeep, and she got to wear whatever she wanted. Barbara was fierce."

"Oh my God, I love you," I say with a laugh, but then notice the time. "You should get back to the in-school room before Shelly gets worried," I say.

"It's fine," Cece replies. "I'll tell her I had a lot of shit to talk through." She leans in to give me a quick hug good-bye. "Just hurry up and get out of there," she adds. "They can't prove it was you if they don't see you." She smiles reassuringly even though she knows I'm busted already. My indefinite suspension may never be lifted.

And I'm not sorry. I won't be used as an excuse for bad male behavior again. I won't be used by Mrs. Montgomery to explain her fanatical view about my role in society.

I'm worth more than that.

"Be careful," Cece warns, and then grabs her pass off the table and leaves.

I see a lighter on the teacher's desk, and I shove it into my pocket. I check the time on the wall clock and realize I only have a few minutes before lunch starts. I gather up our creation—Barbara—trying to balance both halves of the body and make sure the hallway is clear before sneaking down the back stairs.

The cafeteria is empty, although there's a flurry of movement in the food line where the cooks are getting everything set out. I look cautiously at the in-school room, but the door is closed. No one sees me.

I set the body parts on the floor, grab a chair, and drag it to the center of the room. It's in full view of the entire place, and I set Barbara on the chair, sitting her up like she's a person. The words are visible, and as I take a step back to admire my work, I'm struck again with the feeling of humiliation.

It's shocking now that I see it. They wanted this to be me. They thought I deserved this because I wore leggings and a long shirt. This is what they would have done if they could have.

I know part of me is being irrational; that's the thing—I *know it*. But I can't stop the impulses. They've broken me—Mrs. Montgomery, the school board, all of them. And now I want to break them.

The bell rings, startling me. I quickly move behind a pole, not completely hidden from view but not obviously connected with Barbara. I watch as students walk in, some with crumpled brown paper bags. All of them stop to look, to read the sweat suit.

The guys laugh, mostly—their brows pull together with confusion. But it's the faces of the other girls, the way they read the words with alarm and then anger. They see the original intention of the suit. And when that anger passes, they nod their heads in agreement. Rule 16 is a violation. And we all feel it.

A crowd has formed around Barbara, and for a moment, I feel vindicated, even if they don't know it was me. I even start to smile. The bell rings, but no one is eating lunch. The door to the in-school suspension room opens, and Shelly and the students come out to see what's going on.

My heart starts to beat faster. There's a booming voice, and we all look over to see Mr. Jones marching over from the entrance, asking what's going on.

He comes to a stop in front of Barbara. There are a few laughs, and some of the students get out of his way and go to sit down. I watch my principal read the words, seeing when he realizes it doesn't say what he thought it would.

Mr. Jones spins around, searching, until he finally finds me standing next to the pole. Out of the corner of my eye, I see Mrs. Montgomery and another teacher enter the cafeteria.

I step out from my hiding spot, and stand next to my project. In my pocket my fingers touch the lighter that I grabbed from the art room.

"What is this?" Mrs. Montgomery yells shrilly. "This is destruction of school property." She points to Barbara and then looks to Mr. Jones for backup.

I'm sure he will, but I don't wait to be proven right. I'm well past that.

I glance across the room and find Jameson standing with Cece, watching it all unfold. He's clearly worried, but then, as if saying the point is bigger than me and maybe I should see this through. I smile at him and take out the lighter.

And I don't know what I'm going to do next, but I look at Mrs. Montgomery and . . . maybe part of me is hoping she'll make this right. She'll admit she was wrong. Instead, she glances from me to the lighter.

"You have no respect for yourself," she says, her eyes narrowed. "At least have respect for your classmates."

With a flash of anger followed by an eerie calm, I look directly at her. "That's the thing, Mrs. Montgomery," I say. "I'm doing this for all of us."

I flick the lighter and hold the flame to the newspaper.

To be honest, I expected a slow burn that could have easily been stomped out. A scorch or two on the floor that would serve as a reminder of the time I burned Barbara and her violation suit. But that's not what happened.

The polyurethane-soaked paper inside the suit goes up in a whoosh—the flames at least six feet high. The material of the sweat suit melts away like wet cotton candy, and it is a raging inferno of Barbara.

I drop the lighter and fall back a step, the heat singing the hair on my arms. The fire alarm sounds, and the students run from the cafeteria. I notice Jameson running toward the fire—toward me—just as the overhead sprinklers all burst and begin to rain down throughout the school.

Smoke, screaming, and a rush for the door. It is complete mayhem.

Mr. Jones does his best to get students toward the exit, but Mrs. Montgomery is gone. Figures she wouldn't help. The water is freezing cold, but it feels nice on my arm, where I'm sure I've been burned by the flames.

Jameson calls my name, but before I respond, Mr. Jones grabs me by the shoulders.

"The police are on their way, Ms. Banks," he says through clenched teeth. The sheer terror on his face is almost enough to make me feel sorry for what I've done. But in the end my principal didn't have my back. I'm more disappointed than anything. So, no. I'm not sorry. And I tell him so.

And as he roughly leads me through the raining water toward the exit door—sirens already sounding in the distance—I pass by Jameson.

He watches me with shiny eyes, and just as I pass, Jameson whispers, "You're my fucking hero, Lucinda Banks."

"So that's how you ended up here?" Jenna asked.

"Yep. Arrested and charged. My mom had a lawyer-friend who negotiated a compromise: this place."

"And did they change the dress code after that?"

"Nope," Lucinda said, the injustice still burning. "Now they all wear uniforms."

"How come you didn't burn the Bend down over these nasty-ass uniforms?" Jackie asked.

"Because we all have to wear them and not just the girls," Sunday said. "That was the point of the story, right?"

We'd gone back to carrying Georgia when the crutches had begun to hurt her arms and shoulders, but we'd made good progress. Jaila and Jenna seemed to think we were on the right track and might actually make it back to camp by nightfall. I wasn't as confident, but I also didn't give a shit. I had everything I needed right there in those woods.

"I don't know," Georgia said. "You didn't have to set the dummy on fire."

Lucinda opened her mouth to speak, but Tino cut her off. "I get it," he said. "If you don't show them how far you're willing to go, they'll never take you seriously." He was the last person anyone had expected to defend Lucinda, but there it was. "I mean, look at all of us, stuck in this shit hole camp for whatever. Doug and our parents and our teachers—they think we're probably nothing but a bunch of animals, but we showed them who we really are. We showed them that they can't ignore us."

Jaila stopped to take a drink from her canteen. We'd had the chance to refill an hour back, but the day was getting hotter, and I hoped I wouldn't run out. "I don't see how being sent to prison camp is anything other than being shipped out of sight and out of mind."

"And," Sunday added, "I'm not sure anything we did is worth being proud of."

"You didn't turn in that boy when you could have," Tino said. "And I bet the next school Lucinda goes to won't try to stick her in a uniform."

Cody stood beside Georgia, grinning. "Mike probably won't ever mess with me again."

"See?" Tino said. "It's about respect."

"But you earn respect." Jaila was looking in the direction we were supposed to be walking, and I wasn't sure she'd meant to say anything out loud. But then she turned to Tino. "It's like you said: we're not animals."

Tino nodded. "That's right. We're people, and this is us letting everyone know we won't be ignored."

"That's why *I* did it," Jenna said. Her voice was louder than normal, like she was finally done whispering.

Sunday nudged Jenna with her shoulder and offered her a comforting smile. "Tell us," she said. "Tell us the rest."

"THE CHAOS EFFECT"
by Marieke Nijkamp

I'M NOT A PYROMANIAC, I already told you. But according to the Minnesota criminal statutes, the car fire is arson in the second degree. Who knew Grandpa's car was that valuable? Who knew he even had anything of value left? It makes me wonder if Dad had it fixed up for him; it's exactly the type of thing he would do.

It hardly matters. In the end everything burns. And every morning I scatter the ashes on my way to school.

I don't remember the first night. I blocked it from my memory, and I'm perfectly happy to never access it again. I remember too many nights since. The creak of the door opening. The light from the hallway falling into the room—one long yellow bar of light that edges all the way from the door's threshold across the floor scattered with clothes—and the books from school across the comforter, lying haphazardly over the bed—to the wall just behind me. The footsteps.

The touches.

The smell and caress of his sour breath.

The impossibility of escape.

He always smiles in the morning.

Paper does not burn as well as matches. It smolders and curls and almost immediately turns to ashes, until there's nothing left of the drawings I made, the equations I solved, the formulas that help me make sense of the world. I don't understand them anymore, anyway.

I do remember the first night when I let myself go numb. I couldn't move. I couldn't stop him. I could only pretend it wasn't happening, pretend I didn't feel his hands on me, his skin against my skin, his grunts in my ear.

I tried to scrub his touch off once. I took a scalding hot shower. I emptied an entire bottle of shower gel. I scrubbed until my legs were raw and my fingers bled.

It didn't help. Not even for a day. I hurt all over and still smelled of bergamot and orange blossom when he came a few nights later. So I decided there and then—I could pretend to go numb. I could pretend not to feel. I could pretend not to feel for long enough that I would start to believe it.

Until I forgot what it meant to feel altogether.

Adam gave me a T-shirt for my fifteenth birthday a couple of months ago. It's an olive-green top with "F(X) = |X|" printed on the front. The back simply says "AVOID NEGATIVITY." He found it in a thrift shop, and he was *so* proud of it. It was the first time he bought me a present all on his own. He wrapped it himself.

The shirt has languished in my wardrobe ever since. I told him I was keeping it for a special occasion. And I did.

It burns surprisingly well.

The worst times are when we're all alone through the night. On days when Dad's work sends him to offices in other states and he takes Mom along for a quick getaway. When Adam is at T. J.'s because the large house spooks him in the dark.

When it's just us and there's no one to sneak around for, no need to worry that anyone might walk in.

Those are the nights that last forever.

Hair does not burn well either. It melts and sizzles and smells. It burns a little easier when you cut it off, but it's not nearly as satisfying. The strands of hair are nothing but lifeless extensions of me.

When I come downstairs with my hair cut ragged, Dad is already on his way to work. Adam grins broadly, Mom sighs her displeasure, and Grandpa smiles. I try to shift away from it and focus on Adam's happiness instead.

He gives me a double thumbs-up. "Wicked, sis."

I reach up and run my hand across my scalp. It feels different, though I'm not sure if "wicked" is the word I'd go for. It's prickly. Lighter.

I glance at my reflection in the window. *Green. Mine.*

"You look like a troll. A really cool one," Adam continues glee-fully. "Doesn't she, Grandpa?"

"She looks like a creature of legend, that's for sure." Grandpa thumps Adam's shoulder. They're good friends, the two of them, and I have no idea how that ever happened. "But I wouldn't go for troll. Wood nymph, perhaps. Or a mermaid."

"A *nymph*? An Ent, maybe."

"Oh no, she's far more elegant than—"

I don't *want* him to think me elegant.

They continue to talk about me, as if I'm not there, until Mom snaps, "Would you be quiet, the two of you?"

I pour myself a mug of coffee and sit down at the kitchen table, as far away from Grandpa as I possibly can, and brace myself for Mom's reaction. She continues making breakfast, punctuated by long-suffering sighs, but once we all have bacon and toast, she rounds on me.

"I know you're going through a . . . *phase*"—she spits out the word as if it tastes disgusting—"and we've made allowances for your anger and for your stories. But the school has informed me your grades are falling. And this is simply unacceptable. Whatever will Reverend Winters say?"

Perhaps he'll notice me, I want to tell her. Instead, I stuff a strip of bacon into my mouth and chew with abandon.

Adam snickers. Grandpa raises his mug in salute.

"Between this and your grades, it seems your dad and I will have to have a conversation when he's home," Mom says.

"Sure." I shrug, but it only seems to infuriate her more.

* * *

I successfully avoid Zoe for almost two weeks, with only the most perfunctory of greetings when our paths cross in class, but I can't avoid her forever. And right on cue, as if my green hair's a beacon, when I walk to my locker, she comes bounding down the hallway. She screeches to a stop when she sees me, her sneakers skidding on the linoleum.

"Jenna Georg Cantor. You dyed your hair green."

I hesitate. "Way to state the obvious, Z."

"It's different." She walks around me, observing me, and even though I know it's Z., my skin crawls. "It's different, but it suits you. Did your mom go through the roof when she saw it?"

"Pretty much," I say. I can't smile yet. I keep my voice level. But I hope this means she's forgiven me.

Her hand sneaks into mine, and she pulls me to a quiet corner. "Are you okay? Like, really okay?"

"No." I flinch. I wish I could take it back the moment I say it. "I don't think so, but I'm trying to be."

Z. doesn't look convinced. She always has such an easy smile. She isn't pretty by traditional standards—her light brown hair is always tousled, her nose is crooked from that time she broke it during volleyball, and she's broad and muscular. But when she smiles she is radiant, and I miss that smile.

"I'm sorry?" I try.

"Don't be silly." She wraps me in a one-armed hug. It's slightly awkward, but it also feels a little safe. She squeezes. "We all have our ugly moments. We all have our secrets."

I draw in a breath and wait for her to say more, wait for her to tell me she knows *my* secret. Her words sound like the perfect lead-up, and outside of my own family, Zoe is the one who knows me best. She must have noticed *something*.

But she hasn't. No one has. She doesn't say anything more than "Don't you dare disappear on me like that again."

And I want to be relieved. I *am* relieved. But somewhere, deep down, I would much rather she guessed it. I'd rather she knows and breaks the dam that keeps my words inside, barred by a hundred throwaway comments.

If hope is the thing with feathers, as Mrs. Lee taught us, then secrets are things with talons. They're light at first, almost unnoticeable. They're comfortable and easy to hold. But over time they grow heavier and develop sharp edges. Words become harder to share, and secrets cling to you and claw at you until they've dug themselves so deep, you'd have to tear yourself apart to get rid of them.

Until you do they'll strike out at everyone who gets too close.

I spend the whole school day with Zoe, and it feels like old times except when it doesn't. She makes jokes about things that happened in the days before, and I don't have a reference for them. She comments on hanging out with Kamal who, it turns out, is a theater kid. She shows me the flyer for a musical the theater club is putting on at the end of the year—*The Addams Family*—and notes for the role she wants to learn to be a part of it.

"I didn't know you were into theater," I say.

She slowly eats the whipped cream off her mocha, savoring each bite. "I didn't know either, but it sounds fun."

"I'm sure both your coaches will be thrilled by another

curriculum." As always, Zoe's schedule exhausts me just thinking about it.

"Spoilsport." She rolls her eyes. "Volleyball season will end soon, and so will our swim meets. The rest of the year will just be swim club and endless free time. I can fit it in."

She hums and then sings, "*Let your darkest secrets give you away.*"

I take a bite from my brownie. It tastes bland, though I'm quite sure that's me and not the Coffee House. Our entire class comes here, frequently, because the coffee is good and the sweets are better. And Zoe . . . Zoe would be a regular if she didn't schedule her days to the fullest. "You're impossible."

She spoons up some whipped cream and unceremoniously presses the spoon against my nose. I bat at her, and she laughs without abandon. I love her and I hate her at the same time.

When we've reached the bottom of our mugs and have scraped up all our crumbs, Zoe leaves me for a bit to go to the bathroom. I try to gather all her scattered belongings to put them back into her backpack.

I fold the flyer carefully, and then I stare at the papers for Zoe's new theater project. They're three notebook pages filled with finely scribbled notes and comments, in Zoe's hand and another. Kamal's, maybe? Zoe wants to play Alice, but beyond the name, I can't find much about the character. The Addams Family, on the other hand, are outlined in quite some detail. Kamal calls them "objectively dysfunctional but supportive and macabrely happy."

My fingers curl into a fist, crunching the paper. I breathe hard.

I should *fold* the notes and put them with the flyer.

I *should* fold the notes and put them with the flyer.

I cannot let my anger get the best of me, but it burns, too. A deep and steady burn that, when it flares, eviscerates everything in its path.

And the people around me are laughing and talking like the world is still the same as it was three months ago, as if nothing at all has changed.

I crumple the notes further and stuff them into the pocket of my jeans.

Once Zoe is on her way back to volleyball practice, I dig my lighter out of my coat and let the fire lick up the notes. I'm sorry, Z.

I scatter the ashes on my way home.

When I'm home, Dad sits on the couch. He stares at me, and I drop my backpack on the floor. He doesn't comment on it. It's such a flashback to our conversation this summer, and I'm sure something must have happened.

For a brief, irrational, *awful* moment, I want him to tell me it's Grandpa. It doesn't have to be something bad; maybe the bank decided not to take his house. Maybe Aunt Beate has decided she can take him in after all. Maybe. Maybe. Maybe. I just want him gone.

"Dad?"

He runs his hand through his hair, and it sticks up a little. He's still wearing his tie and his jacket. "Jenna, your mom called me, and she believes we should talk."

My stomach drops, but when he indicates I should sit on the couch, I do. In the farthest corner. He looks nothing like Grandpa, and it may be a small mercy, but I'm forever grateful of it.

"Your behavior this last couple of months has been unlike what we've come to expect from you, Jenna. I know Grandpa's presence has required all of us to adapt, but I thought you and he got along. He's been trying, and this . . ." He gestures at me, at my hair. "Your acting up only makes things worse."

I open my mouth and close it again. The words stick in my mouth. They claw at me.

The first time I tried to tell Dad. I told him Grandpa scared me.

He told me I just needed to get used to him.

The second time I tried to tell Mom. I told her Grandpa touched me.

She was too busy with preparations for her PTA meeting. It wasn't her fault. It was far easier to tell her when she wasn't paying attention to me.

I just wish she had been.

"Work is sending me to Chicago after the weekend. An impromptu meeting at HQ. Mom is coming along. It'll only be for a day or two, but I expect you to take that time to sort out whatever is bothering you about this arrangement. We expect you to pull your weight at home. We expect you to raise your grades. And we want to know how you plan to do it by the time we get back. Talk it through with Grandpa if you want. He'll be here, and he volunteered to help." Dad reaches out to take my hand, and I let him. I don't know what else to do. "We don't care about the green hair—which is to say, Mom will get used to it. You're fifteen—you're supposed to experiment and we want to give you that freedom. But we have to be able to trust you to be responsible, okay?"

Silence falls heavily between us. Then I do what I'm supposed to do. I nod. I'm a good girl who listens to her parents. Even when they don't listen to me.

"Yes, Dad."

I get up from the couch and start walking.

I start walking, and I don't stop.

If you keep feeding the fire, it will grow and wait to devour you. You don't realize it until it's too late.

I don't know where to go. I could go back to the empty office building, but afternoon leads into dusk, and dusk leads into late night, and too many people will be there. I can wander the streets, but as my parents have taught me time and again, it isn't safe for a girl to be out on her own at night. But then again, when home isn't safe either, does it really matter?

Without consciously making the decision, my feet take me in the direction of the office building. I felt comfortable there. Perhaps I can squat there. Or disappear. Perhaps I can light the whole thing ablaze and dance with the flames.

I walk to the very edge of our neighborhood. The office building is haphazardly planted between it and the business park another mile or so down the road. Perhaps that's why renting the floor space never caught on. Or perhaps they always meant to build it as a teen playground of sorts.

I sneak around the fence, but at night the building is nothing like the one I know. There are lights inside, and faded music drifts down from the roof. A few yards away from me, someone laughs. I step back.

A beer bottle smashes against the concrete walls.

Then the yellow beam of a flashlight suddenly shines in my direction. I raise my arms against the sudden brightness.

"Who d'we have 'ere?" someone slurs.

A guy steps into the light. He's blond. Black-rimmed glasses. Maybe a few years older than me. He clings to a beer bottle, and it looks like it's all he can do not to stagger.

The light beam moves, and another guy steps closer too.

I freeze. I push my hands deeper into my pockets, and my heart picks up the pace.

"What are you doing here, little girl?" the first says.

The second guffaws. "Are you going for the Big Bad Wolf aesthetic, dude?"

"She looks lost," Bottle defends himself.

"Am not," I mutter, but probably too quiet for anyone to hear. Still, the words matter to me. And the guys are too wrapped up in their fairy tale.

"Oh Grandmother, what a big mouth you have."

"All the better to eat you with."

The beam shakes as the second person laughs. The two reach out and bump fists because they're drunk and gross and teen boys through and through.

Bottle steps a little closer again. "Come here, little girl, I'll show you something big."

I want to move. I don't move. I can't move. And I hate myself for it. What am I if I can't even protect myself from this?

But deep in my pocket my fingers curl around my lighter. I play with the spark wheel, and for a moment I think I could accidentally set myself on fire. And while I can push lit matches against my arm to remind myself to feel, I can't do that. I will burn down the world before I burn with it. I can blaze this path too.

I turn around and start walking. One step before the other. Slow at first. Faster.

"It's just a game, little girl," one of the guys jeers. His feet crush glass, and a moment later, another bottle smashes against the outside of the building.

I keep walking. I don't look back.

It's just a game. It's *not* just a game.

It's the first time I've ever been able to walk away, and if it's also the last, it will still have meant everything. But even fractals start at a random point. Perhaps, eventually, patterns will emerge.

The butterfly effect is one of the principles of chaos. Fractals are too: they're never-ending patterns, repetitive, and infinitely detailed. They're the most gorgeous designs.

That seems contradictory, doesn't it? Chaotic designs? But at the heart of chaos theory is this: there are patterns everywhere, even when they seem complex and entirely random. That's why the method for creating new fractals was originally called "the chaos game." Fractals will become patterns. And under the right conditions, chaos will start to form order.

Perhaps if I create enough chaos, order will come again.

I walk until I'm back home, until I sag down against a tree in our front yard. I light the lighter in the cup of my hand. Let is extinguish. Light it again.

The flame is a comforting ball of warmth in the darkness. I could stare at it forever. But it isn't enough. The papers, the clothes. The hundred small things I burned. It isn't enough to create chaos, and it won't stop Mom and Dad from leaving me alone again with him.

I want patterns. I want flames to reach to the skies. I want him to feel fractured too.

I'm not a pyromaniac. I told you I can control my impulses quite well. But I won't be the only one hurting anymore.

The interior of a car burns easily. I break a window and spread gasoline across the seats. It stinks, but I know it'll burn. I've grabbed the newspaper from the door pocket next to the driver's seat and turn that into a torch.

With one of the windows open for oxygen, and the dark of night around me, I wait until the paper smolders.

Then I toss it in.

The gasoline flares. The flame spreads like wildfire, and within moments it absorbs everything. It's loud. Violent. I wonder how long it'll take for Grandpa or my parents to wake up.

I walk across the street. Sitting down on the sidewalk, I rest my elbows on my knees and watch.

This is calculation. This is chaos. This is freedom.

The lights from the Bend shone down below us. We'd spotted them a while back and had limped toward them like a beacon calling us home. The sun had long set, but the others were determined to make it back before midnight, and there was no power in the world that could stop them. Georgia had decided she was going to walk the last mile on her own, and I kind of admired that about her.

Jenna let Georgia lean on her as we trudged through the wilderness. "We don't live that far apart," Georgia said. "Maybe we could, I don't know, see each other or whatever."

"Maybe," Jenna said.

There hadn't been much to say when she'd finished her story. I think most of us had guessed what was going on, but hearing her tell it was different. No one should have to go through what she went through, and I kind of wished she'd burned her grandfather's car with him still in it. But then she would have been in prison instead of with us, and I don't think she deserved to spend her life in a cage.

"I wish I could have met someone like you at camp," Georgia went on. "Not like that, I mean. I'm not—"

"Gay," Jenna finished. "I know; you already said so."

Georgia shook her head. "Maybe I am. I don't know. I just meant that I like knowing you."

Jenna didn't say anything for a minute. Then "Yeah. I like knowing you, too."

I fell back to walk near Lucinda and Tino. She hadn't threatened to punch or castrate him once since she'd told her story and he'd defended her.

"You still with that Jameson guy?" Tino asked.

"Why? Because you think *you* have a shot?"

Tino shrugged. "Maybe."

"You don't."

"Can't blame me for trying."

Lucinda rolled her eyes. "Like hell I can't."

I moved between the groups, ignored and unseen. I listened to Jaila and Sunday laughing as Jackie told her the whole story of how she'd got caught stealing from a science-fiction convention. And I heard Jaila tell about how she she'd wound up in the Bend because her best friend Ursula's older brother, Mauro, who Jaila had been in love with had been found murdered and how her father wouldn't let her go back to Xalitla Guerrero for the funeral, so she'd run away from home multiple times. She made it all the way to the border crossing on money she'd earned busking before she was caught.

Sunday swore the story she'd told us really had been true, so she talked about her dads instead. It sounded like she had a nice family, and I kind of envied that.

"My sister really did disappear," David said to Cody as they walked. "And I do think it was aliens that took her."

Cody didn't say a whole lot, but there was a strength in his walk that made me think he was channeling those old movie star actresses he loved so much.

"I put nails under Mike's tires," he said. "But I think my parents really sent me here because they thought it would make me into a 'real man.'"

Tino had stopped to readjust his pack, and started walking with them. "Being a man isn't about how you walk or talk. It's about being you, right? So you swish and glide and do whatever the hell you want. And if people don't like it, they can fuck right off."

"Thanks?"

"I'm serious," Tino said. "My stepdad was always acting macho and talking shit. He thought *he* was a man. At least he did until I shoved his sorry ass down the stairs."

"I'm guessing that's why you're here," David said.

"Sometimes there's only one way to show people you won't be ignored."

I thought they were done talking and was about to slip away to eavesdrop elsewhere when Cody said, "But if there was another way, you wouldn't have done it, right?"

Tino cocked his head to the side. "I'm not saying I'm sorry about what I did, but yeah. If I could have made him stop some other way, I would have."

"Because we're not animals." David took a puff from his inhaler and coughed, and the three boys walked on.

Jaila started singing in a language I didn't know as we walked the last quarter mile. A slow, earnest song in a voice that carried the scent of summer and shook the leaves. I'm not sure she was even singing for us or cared that we heard. She just sang, and it was beautiful.

Doug and the other counselors were waiting for us when we finally reached the Bend. Tino carried Georgia to the infirmary while Doug tried to chastise Jaila for not using her flare. But Jackie cut that right off and lit into him about not making sure to give us a flare that actually fucking worked. Eventually, we all went our separate ways to shower and eat and sleep in something resembling a bed.

I wasn't tired though. I lay on a picnic table and stared at the stars. People spend a lot of time thinking about the planets that might orbit all those stars, but they ignore the worlds inside themselves. We're all worlds; we'd spent the last three days on nine other planets, orbiting each other. I don't know how much of what any of them said was the truth, but it doesn't matter because the truth doesn't exist in our words but in the spaces between them. You could spend a lifetime exploring the vastness between a person's words and still never really know them. That's the only thing that's really true as far as I can tell.

But I do think Tino was right. Our parents and teachers and all the other adults in our lives might have seen us as animals, as feral youth determined to destroy our lives and the lives of those around us, but we weren't. We were people, and we would not be ignored anymore.

I didn't hear Cody come up behind me until he sat on the table near my legs.

"Hungry?" he said.

"Not really." I sat up and scooted beside him.

"How come *you* never told a story?"

"Judge doesn't have to."

Cody elbowed me in the ribs. "So you're not even going to tell me why you got sent here?"

"Aren't we all here for the same reason?"

"No," Cody said. But then he bit his lip. "Okay, maybe. I don't know."

"You're cute when you smile."

At the compliment Cody lit up like a neon sign. He smiled again, but it was a little self-conscious. Still cute all the same. "You think so?"

"You should try hooking up with guys your own age."

"Maybe I will."

Cody and I lay on the table beside each other for a while, and we watched the stars . When it got late, he said he was going to bed. Before he left he said, "Hey, so you never told us who won the contest."

"No," I said. "I guess I didn't."

"And?"

"And I'll tell you later."

After Cody's footsteps faded, I reached into my pocket, pulled out a crumpled hundred-dollar bill, and held it in front of my face.

I said I was going to tell the truth, and I did. We were a cluster-fuck, but we'd survived. I didn't have any romantic notions that we were going to remain friends after what we'd been through. I didn't believe for a second that Lucinda and Tino were going to call each other when they got home and start a long-distance relationship. I didn't imagine Jaila and Jackie were going to meet up at a science-fiction convention and hound the cast of *Space Howl* for autographs together or that Jenna was going to fly to L.A. and have coffee with Sunday. We might have tied ourselves to each other for the three days we spent in the woods, but those knots had already started to loosen now that we'd returned.

That's not the important bit, though. It didn't matter whether we'd stay bound to one another, only that we'd learned to tie the knot at all and had gained the strength to show the world that *we are not animals*. We are not the feral youth they believe us to be. We are people. We are real. And we will not be ignored.

Or something like that. You're going to believe what you want, anyway. I'm just here to tell the truth. Maybe.

I smiled at the hundred-dollar bill in my hand, folded it, and tucked it back into my pocket.

ABOUT THE AUTHORS

Shaun David Hutchinson

Shaun David Hutchinson is the author of numerous books for young adults, including *The Five Stages of Andrew Brawley*, which won the Florida Book Awards' gold medal in the Young Adult category and was named to the ALA's 2015 Rainbow Book List; the anthology *Violent Ends*, which received a starred review from *VOYA*; and *We Are the Ants*, which received five starred reviews and was named a best book of January 2016 by Amazon.com, Kobo.com, *Publishers Weekly*, and iBooks. He lives in South Florida with his adorably chubby dog, and he enjoys *Doctor Who*, comic books, and yelling at the TV. Visit him at ShaunDavidHutchinson.com.

"The Butterfly Effect" and "The Chaos Effect"
by Marieke Nijkamp

Marieke Nijkamp is the #1 *New York Times* bestselling author of *This Is Where It Ends*, which follows four teens during the fifty-four minutes of a school shooting. Marieke was born and raised in the Netherlands. A lifelong student of stories, language, and ideas, she is more or less proficient in about a dozen languages and holds degrees in philosophy, history, and medieval studies. She is a storyteller, dreamer, globe-trotter, and geek.

Marieke's second young adult novel, *Before I Let Go*, will be out in January 2018. Visit her online at mariekenijkamp.com and follow her on Twitter at @mariekeyn.

"A Ruthless Dame" by Tim Floreen

Tim Floreen writes young adult fiction. The New York Public Library named his first novel, *Willful Machines*, one of the Best Teen Books 2015, and in a starred review, *Kirkus Reviews* called it "gothic, gadget-y, and gay," which is an accurate assessment. *Booklist* called his second novel, *Tattoo Atlas*, "incisive, startling, and intense." Tim lives in San Francisco with his partner, their two cat-obsessed daughters, and their two very patient cats. To find out more about Tim and his secret obsession with Wonder Woman, visit him online at timfloreen.com.

"Look Down" by Robin Talley

Robin Talley is the *New York Times* bestselling author of four novels for teen readers starring LGBTQ characters: *Our Own Private Universe*, *As I Descended*, *What We Left Behind*, and *Lies We Tell Ourselves*. Robin has also contributed short stories to the young adult anthologies *A Tyranny of Petticoats* and *All Out*. Robin lives in Washington, DC, with her wife, their daughter, and an antisocial cat. You can find her at robintalley.com.

**"Big Brother, Part 1" and "Big Brother, Part 2"
by E. C. Myers**
E(ugene). C. Myers is the author of four young adult novels and
dozens of short stories. His first novel *Fair Coin*, received the
2012 Andre Norton Award for Young Adult Science Fiction and
Fantasy, and YALSA selected *The Silence of Six* as one of its "Top
Ten Quick Picks for Reluctant Young Adult Readers" in 2016. He
was assembled in the United States from Korean and German parts
and raised by a single mother and a public library in Yonkers, New
York. Visit ecmyers.net and follow him on Twitter at @ecmyers.

"The Subjunctive" by Alaya Dawn Johnson
Alaya Dawn Johnson is the author of six novels for adults and young
adults. Her novel *The Summer Prince* was longlisted for the National
Book Award for Young People's Literature. Her most recent, *Love
Is the Drug*, won the Andre Norton Award. Her short stories have
appeared in many magazines and anthologies, including *The Best
American Science Fiction and Fantasy 2015*, *Zombies vs. Unicorns*,
and *Welcome to Bordertown*. In addition to the Norton, she has won
the Nebula and Cybils Awards and been nominated for the Indies
Choice Book Award and Locus Award. She lives in Mexico City,
where she is getting her master's in Mesoamerican studies.

"A Cautionary Tale" by Stephanie Kuehn
Stephanie Kuehn is the author of four novels for young adults. In
2014, *Charm & Strange* won the American Library Association's
William C. Morris YA Debut Award, and her three subsequent
books, *Complicit*, *Delicate Monsters*, and *The Smaller Evil* have

cemented her reputation as one of YA literature's most unique and daring voices. She lives in Northern California and is a postdoctoral fellow in clinical psychology.

"Jackie's Story" by Justina Ireland

Justina Ireland enjoys dark chocolate, dark humor, and is not too proud to admit that she's still afraid of the dark. She lives with her husband, kid, and dog in Pennsylvania. She is the author of *Vengeance Bound* and *Promise of Shadows*. Visit her at justinaireland.com.

"Self-Portrait" by Brandy Colbert

Brandy Colbert is the author of the young adult novels *Pointe* and *Little & Lion*, as well as short stories and personal essays published in various anthologies. She lives and writes in Los Angeles. Visit her at brandycolbert.com.

"A Violation of Rule 16" by Suzanne Young

Suzanne Young is the *New York Times* bestselling author of the Program series. Originally from Utica, New York, Suzanne moved to Arizona to pursue her dream of not freezing to death. She is a novelist and an English teacher, but not always in that order. Suzanne is the author of several young adult novels, including the Program series and *All in Pieces*.

Keep reading for a look at another multiauthored novel from Shaun David Hutchinson and sixteen other acclaimed authors!

VIOLENT ENDS

Susanna Byrd turned nine that Thursday morning at 7:17 a.m. She kept her eyes on the digital clock on the stove, the spoon of Cream of Wheat with a swirl of clover honey halfway to her mouth, and when it flickered from :16 to :17, she grinned and chomped that spoonful.

Miss Susie had a steamboat.
The steamboat had a bell.

No gifts at breakfast—that'd been the rule forever. But there were three cards under her bowl of Cream of Wheat when she came to the table, and there was her mother, standing behind her chair, smiling.

"Did Dad leave already?"

Mom frowned and nodded, her head cocked at a sympathetic angle. "And Byron, too."

Susanna's big brother—the high schooler. He was never around and Susanna didn't care, anyway.

She'd saved the cards till 7:17, of course, and then she pushed aside her barely eaten bowl of Cream of Wheat with a swirl of clover honey. The top card was from Byron. Susanna tore the envelope (and a little of the card in the process) and scanned his scrawled note that might as well have said, "You suck and I hope you die," even if it actually said, "Happy birthday, Sis. Love, Byron."

The next card on the stack was from her grandmother in New York, Susanna's only living grandparent. That one had a check in it. Susanna adored checks. She pulled it out—it was a pink one—and folded it once and then once again and shoved it into her back pocket.

"Do you want me to bring that to the bank for you today?" Mom asked.

Susanna shook her head. "I wanna go with you. Wait for me to get home."

The bottom card was from Mom and Dad, with a message from each inside, their handwriting as different as a hammer and a nail.

After breakfast—Susanna ate every last speck of Cream of Wheat with a swirl of clover honey—her mother tied three silver ribbons into her hair, which was the color of buckwheat honey, and she said, "Happy birthday, Susanna. I hope you have a perfect day."

It was three blocks south and three blocks east to the bus stop. Susanna would rather walk diagonally, but the streets weren't made that way. Sometimes she fantasized about soaring like a crow straight from the top of her house to the bus stop, over the other houses and fenced-in yards and other kids. Sometimes she imagined tunneling way down deep, under the basements and sewers and electric cables.

Sometimes she just slipped out the front door and waved to her mom and set her eyes on the road ahead till the door closed behind her. Then she skirted the homes and pranced across the grass and cut across backyards and front yards and went diagonally anyway.

> *Miss Susie went to Heaven*
> *And the steamboat went to Hell—*

"I like the ribbons in your hair." Susanna stopped at the words and let her backpack drop down her arm so the strap settled into her hand. She found Ella standing there, right smack in the middle of a backyard that rightfully shouldn't have held either of the girls. Ella Stone was the tallest in her grade—but only eight for another six weeks. That gave Susanna seniority.

Ella had hair the color of starflower honey. So rare and desirable.

"Why do you have ribbons in your hair?"

"It's my birthday," Susanna said. She didn't add, "I'm nine." She hoped Ella would ask.

Ella didn't.

"Are you going to school today?" Susanna asked.

Ella coughed twice into her elbow—the Dracula; that's what Susanna's teachers called it since preschool—and then shook her head. The waves of starflower-honey hair—such a prettier and gentler honey than Susanna's honey hair—caught the morning sunlight and made Susanna shiver.

"Not ever? You're skipping school?"

Ella coughed like Dracula again. "I'm going to the doctor. I have pneumonia, Mom says."

Susanna took a step backward and lifted her bag onto her shoulder again. "Bye."

-O! operator
Please give me number nine

Susanna crossed Cassowary Lane. She didn't look both ways. In fact, she closed her eyes as she crossed diagonally through its intersection with Heron Lane, and she listened. She listened and she listened hard, and she didn't hear a thing. She knew it was safe. The whole time she knew it was safe, but she wasn't sure she was alive till she felt the grass beneath her feet on the far corner. Then she opened her eyes, and above her a crow croaked and cawed. Susanna had to squint to find it against the sun, still low over the houses of Birdland. It landed at the very top of a fir tree in the nearest backyard.

"I'm nine," she said to the crow in a quiet, private voice. "Today's my birthday."

The crow heard her—she was sure of that. It cocked its head just like Mom.

Crows recognize faces. She saw that on PBS, and PBS only tells the truth. Dad told her that. Susanna couldn't tell one crow from another, but at least all the crows in Birdland would know her.

She was still looking at the black bird—it shined under the cloudless blue sky, and if its feathers were black (and they were), then its eyes were blacker still, deeper than onyx, deeper than the peak of the night sky if stars didn't exist—when there came a *crack*, another *crack*, and the bird seemed to puff into its own feathers, feathers that fluttered too slowly and fell out of view. The bird was gone.

Susanna dropped her eyes and found three boys. They stood in the backyard two over from that fir tree, and the middle boy—he stood in the center, and was taller than the shorter boy and shorter than the taller boy—held a little rifle. Susanna hurried to the fence and stood there, glaring at them through the chain-link.

"What do *you* want?" said one—the shortest one. His hair was sandy—barberry honey—and close cut, and his eyes were the color of celery and set far apart. His ears stuck out quite a bit, and the whole package made his face—especially once he grinned, revealing his braces—look like the front view of a family car. He was thirteen, she guessed, because he looked particularly mean, and Susanna set her mind again never to kiss a boy, never to marry one, and never to have babies.

The boy with the gun brought it down from his shoulder and held it by the butt, letting the nozzle bounce along the grass as he walked to the fence. "We shot that bird," he said. "Are you going to cry about it?"

Susanna shook her head. "Why'd you shoot it?"

"We're allowed," the middle boy said. His hair was shaggy and thick, and Susanna imagined putting her fingers in it. She thought they might get stuck. His eyes were like hot chocolate with a single black mini marshmallow in the middle. There's no such thing as black marshmallows, though. "It's October. We're allowed to shoot crows this whole month."

Susanna didn't know if this was true. It didn't seem to make sense that it would be okay to kill a bird in October. Why October? Would it be okay to kill the same bird in November if you shot at it in October and missed? If you went hunting for crows on Halloween, did you have to stop at midnight?

Still, the boy didn't answer her question, and Susanna didn't push it. She turned her back on the fence and hitched up her bag and kept on toward the bus stop.

And if you disconnect me
I'll chop off your behind—

The next street—through two more yards—was Egret Lane, and Susanna stopped again. She was early anyway. Ten more minutes till the bus would get there, and it usually sat for five at the corner since it was the last pickup before the school. She stopped this time because she found another boy.

He was twelve, and he sat in a front yard, wearing his St. Luke's school uniform and reading a superhero comic book. Susanna didn't care for superheroes. Byron did, or he used to. Susanna had no idea what he cared for nowadays, but his disposition in favor of superheroes had turned her off from them forever. Forever and ever, amen.

His hair was no honey color. It was shiny and black and wet or greasy, like the crow that got shot. His eyes were red at the edges and his nose was peppered with freckles. She didn't have to get close to know those things because he was Kirby Matheson and he lived in that house. The house with a pine tree in the front yard whose lower branches reached wide and close to the ground and made a little hideout beneath them. He said to her when he saw her staring, "What do you want?"

"Nothing," Susanna said, but she walked across his yard and stooped under the low-hanging pine branches and sat down with him on the bed of brown needles and dirt and sparse grass.

"So get out of here."

Susanna didn't, though. She brought her bag around and put it on her lap and said, "It's my birthday today. I'm nine."

"Good for you." He breathed in through his nose and let it out through pursed lips. "Happy birthday."

"Thank you. Where's Carah?" That was Kirby's eleven-year-old sister. She and Kirby were usually outside together in the morning.

"She has a doctor appointment."

"Is she sick?" Susanna thought about Ella and her pneumonia.

"I don't know."

The Mathesons still felt new in Birdland to Susanna because she could remember when they moved in. She couldn't remember when anyone else in the neighborhood moved in—at least anyone with kids.

"You shouldn't wear shiny ribbons in your hair and then sit under a tree."

"Why shouldn't I?" Susanna reached up and found the end of each ribbon with her fingertips. They were all still there, all still in place.

"You'll attract crows. They like shiny things."

"That's magpies," Susanna said. "And it's a myth, anyway."

"Like you know anything," said Kirby. "You're nine."

Susanna let him sulk a minute and decided to poke at him. She asked, "Were you crying?" It made her feel older for that instant, but also a bit worse. It hurt her heart.

"Get out of here, okay?" Kirby said.

Susanna didn't. She picked up a pinecone—a dry and brown and open one—and ran her fingers along its teeth. She doubted those flaps of stiff plant matter were really called teeth, but she liked the notion of pine trees dropping hundreds of thousands of brown, sticky teeth. "Did you hear the gunshots?" she asked him, but she didn't take her eyes off the pinecone.

"Yes." He grabbed his own pinecone now—Susanna caught him with the corner of her eye—and started pulling the teeth off. "They shot a crow."

"Did you see it?"

He shook his head. "They do it all the time."

"Are they in your grade?"

"Yeah. I don't like those guys, though."

Susanna watched the bus stop—she could just make it out through the branches and down the block. Kids gathered, most of them with chins down, kicking at curbs, swinging around the stop sign at the corner by one hand, with feet together against the base of the sign like dancers without partners. "They're mean, right?" Susanna said. "They seem mean to me."

"I guess," Kirby said.

Susanna spoke over him. "You look like a crow to me," she said. "Because you have shiny black hair and black eyes."

"I have brown eyes."

"They look black."

"Because it's dark under here."

Susanna leaned forward and squinted at him. "They look black to me."

"They're not."

Susanna tossed her pinecone and pressed her sappy forefinger against her sappy thumb, hard enough and long enough so they stuck for a moment when she pulled them apart, and the skin of both fingers stretched a bit as she did. "You look like a crow."

"Why are you even here? Go wait for the bus like a normal person."

Susanna stuck and unstuck her fingers four more times and then grabbed a handful of needles and stood up. She let the needles rain down on his slacks.

"What are you doing?" he snapped, brushing the needles away more violently than necessary. "Get out of here!"

This time, Susanna did.

—*the 'frigerator*
There was a piece of glass

"Hi, Susanna," said Henrietta Waters at the bus stop. "Happy birthday."

"Thanks," Susanna said, because it was polite and decent to say thanks, but she still thought about Kirby Matheson under his tree and wondered if he'd get up and climb out from under that pine tree to wait for the bus to St. Luke's, which should be rumbling up Egret Lane any moment now. The boys—the three boys with the rifle— cut across Kirby's lawn as she watched from the stop sign with one hand on the smooth green stop-sign pole. They didn't have the rifle anymore. They didn't see Kirby, either.

"I like your ribbons," Henrietta said, and Susanna thanked her again. She held on to the pole and let herself swing around it, all the way around—once, twice, three times.

"Did you get any good presents?"

"Not till I get home," Susanna said, and quickly corrected herself. "Not till my dad gets home from work. But I'm getting a scooter. I think."

"Ooh, I have a scooter."

Susanna knew that and she didn't care, and at that instant she hoped for anything *but* a scooter. She didn't like Henrietta Waters, whose hair was nothing like honey as much as Kirby's hair was nothing like honey, but instead of crow black it was too-bright yellow, like a dandelion head. Dandelion *honey* was a pretty color, but this wasn't it. This was sickening.

A silver sedan slid around the corner from Cardinal and slowed as it passed the bus stop. "There goes Ella Stone," said Henrietta as she gave Susanna a little shove in the arm, meant to get her attention, but rougher.

It was Ella Stone. She sat in the backseat next to the window and looked at her classmates on the curb, coughing into her elbow as they passed.

"She's dying, you know," Henrietta said. "My mom told me."

"No, she's not." But Susanna believed her. She even wanted to believe her.

The bus coughed and rumbled up Cardinal Lane and turned wide and rude onto Egret to stop with a hiss for the riders. Susanna watched the pine tree across the street, catching glimpses of it between heads as she moved up the dark, green aisle of the bus. She sat down toward the middle, as usual, next to Andrea Birch, second grader and renowned tattletale. Susanna stretched her neck and looked out the window, and she saw Kirby Matheson, out from his conifer hiding place, and plodding to his bus stop, his shoulders high and his eyelids low, dragging his bag behind him like the dregs of his morning.

Miss Susie sat upon it
And broke her little—

It was a school day like any other for Susanna, inasmuch as a day is like any other when the whole of Mr. Welkin's third-grade class sings "Happy Birthday" to you and you walk up and down the room passing out erasers with cartoony drawings of frogs and penguins and hippos and unicorns.

"These are dumb."

Susanna stood next to the Bald Eagle table—they were all named for animals native to the state—and looked down at Simon Loam and his blackberry-honey hair that made her hungry.

"They're not dumb."

Simon said it again. "Because those three"—he gestured at the erasers still in her bag—"are real, but this"—he held up his eraser, a unicorn—"is fake-believe."

"It's *make*-believe," Susanna said. "And if you don't like it, put it back."

"I didn't say I don't like it." He shoved the favor onto the back of his crayon. "I just said it's dumb."

Ask me no more questions
I'll tell you no more lies.

Henrietta Waters wasn't on the bus home. Neither were two of the boys who shoot birds. One of them was—the tallest one. Susanna didn't know his name.

None of this was odd. Plenty of kids stayed after school or went home with other kids for playdates in the afternoon. Susanna pulled her book from her bag and flipped through the pages till a chapter title caught her eye—the place where she'd left off or close to it. She didn't use bookmarks. The sight of a bookmark sticking out from the pages of a book depressed her.

Susanna didn't walk diagonal from the bus stop to her house. Crossing yards in the afternoon meant dogs off their leashes and parents in kitchens looking out back windows and seeing children not their own traipsing through. They didn't like that. In the morning they were drowsy and pleased to have their children out of the house, but by late afternoon, with dinner to make, they were grumpy and run-down. So Susanna stuck to the streets, walking with one foot on the grass and the other on the pavement.

When she was half a block from her house, she spotted the black coupe in the driveway beside Mom's van, and she smiled with her mouth open wide and ran, letting her backpack bounce up and down without a care in the world about how she must have looked to everyone peeking out their front-room windows and the rest of the kids from the bus somewhere behind her.

"Dad!" she shouted as she pushed in through the front door. "You're home early!"

He stood back from the door, clear across their modest entryway, and crouched with his arms wide. "Here's the birthday girl."

She ran to him and smirked at his *humph* as she collided with his body. She closed her eyes as his arms fell around her.

The boys are in the bathroom
Zipping up their—

Dinner was fish sticks and sweet potato fries with as much ketchup as she could fit on her plate, in spite of Byron's wailing and moaning on the subject, and in spite of Mom's head shaking and tongue clucking with every last fart-sounding squirt. Dessert was medovnik—a Czech honey cake of paper-thin layers that took Mom three days to make. Susanna could have melted with every forkful. She could have collapsed to a puddle of honey goo and slid to the dining room floor.

The gifts came at the end, when the dishes were cleared and the table was wiped down and Dad had carried Susanna like a queen from her seat at the table to the very middle of the deep pillows of the living room couch. Byron's was first: a hardcover copy of *Anne of Green Gables*, her favorite book, which she only had in paperback.

"Thank you," she said after a squeal for the book. It had to have been Mom's idea, because the gift was much too thoughtful for Byron alone.

Mom and Dad each got her a gift of their own choosing in addition to the big gift that leaned against the coffee table in its awkward wrapping, about as clearly a scooter as a scooter could be. First, though, from Mom, was a helmet in golden yellow with a smiling bee on each side, and from Dad, an electric rainbow to shine in her room.

She thanked them both and then grabbed the big present. Byron rolled his eyes, but Mom and Dad laughed as she tore off the paper and there it sat: her scooter, all put together, shiny metal without a speck of color, just like she asked for.

"Do I have to wear the helmet *every time*?" she said, knowing full well the answer.

"You still have a little light," Dad said as he dropped the helmet down on her head and fiddled with the straps.

"Be back in fifteen minutes," Mom added.

Dad clicked the clasp under her chin.

"Fifteen minutes," she said, and she dragged the thing behind her toward the front door.

Flies are in the meadow
Bees are in the park.

Birdland was blessed with gentle slopes and curves and streets almost entirely devoid of traffic. Cars that passed—when they did, which was rare—rolled slowly, the drivers smiling and waving, their faces as familiar as the fronts of their homes.

Susanna rode her scooter like she'd done it a thousand times before, but she hadn't. She'd ridden Ella Stone's three times, only for a few moments each time because Ella wasn't fond of sharing. Susanna wondered briefly who would get Ella's scooter when she died, if she really was dying.

Evening crept in, and the sun was low over the park at the bottom of Cassowary Lane. From the top of the hill, Susanna could see ten or more kids in the park, standing in little clusters or running across the ball field or climbing on the monkey bars. She pushed off lightly and let gravity pull her to the park. If Henrietta was there, she'd show off her birthday scooter. If not, all the better.

"O! Susanna!" sang a boy's voice as she got close to the park. "O! Don't you cry for me!"

Miss Susie and her boyfriend
Are kissing in the—

She tried to find the voice and the pair of laughs that followed, but the light was dim and she was moving faster now. She hit the curb and tumbled from the scooter onto the grass. She heard the three boys' collective teeth-suck and, when she sat up and made it clear she wasn't seriously hurt, their laughter again.

"Shut up," she said as she stood. She went to her scooter, which lay in the gutter, and dragged it up onto the grass and into the park, where the clusters of kids had all stopped, had all froze to watch her recuperate from her crash.

"Yeah, guys," said the middle boy, the gun boy, the boy with thick hair and eyes like black marshmallows. "Shut up. She probably broke her scooter."

"I didn't." She turned her back on them and pushed it farther along, deeper into the park, where she hoped she might find Ella if she was still alive, or Henrietta if she'd forgiven her for her mean thoughts about her. They were her friends, after all. She could sit with them or stand with them or climb with them and then the gun boys would leave her alone.

She reached the sand of the playground and the scooter's wheels became useless, so she let it fall and sat on the rim of the playground, her helmet in her lap, watching the kids on the monkey bars, all younger than her, and all boys. She felt the gun boys behind her before they spoke. They seemed to heat the air around her.

"She's still crying about the crow you shot."

Susanna wasn't crying.

"She's a baby."

"Babies can't ride scooters."

"She can't ride a scooter. She crashed, remember?"

Susanna sniffed and wished she hadn't. "Go away," she said, and she lifted her chin in time to see Kirby Matheson on the far side of the playground walking slowly, and stopping to watch her and the gun boys.

"No, no," said the middle boy as he crouched beside her. "Because we can't just let a baby be alone with a scooter. It's a safety issue."

He took it by the handles out of the sand and before she could grab for him—the other gun boys held her wrists anyway—he was off on a joyride.

"Give it back!" she shouted, but he kicked and kicked, and he circled around the playground in a wide loop, even passing right by Kirby Matheson.

He said something then, that boy who looked like a crow, but Susanna didn't hear what. She only heard the laughter of the tall gun boy and the short gun boy and she only felt their hands on her arms. She did hear the middle boy—the boy who'd stolen her scooter—snap back at Kirby, "Shut up, Matheson. Don't be such a baby."

Then he rode that scooter at top speed toward her, shouting to his friends, "Hold her there. Hold her right there."

They did—they stretched her out by the arms as the boy sped toward them, and now Susanna cried. She cried because she couldn't break free. She cried because her wrists hurt. She cried because this was her birthday. She cried because the gun boy was going to kill her.

"Oh my God," whispered the boy on her left wrist, scared.

"He's going to do it," said the boy on her right, afraid.

And like that, they let go, and Susanna dove onto the sand, and the middle gun boy zipped by, shouting at his friends, "What the hell?"

SHAUN DAVID HUTCHINSON

"A writer to watch." —*Booklist*

★ "Bitterly funny, with a ray of hope amid bleakness."
—*Kirkus Reviews*, starred review, on *We Are the Ants*

★ "Hutchinson artfully blends the realistic and the surreal. . . .
An entirely original take on apocalyptic fiction."
—*School Library Journal*, starred review,
on *The Apocalypse of Elena Mendoza*